SECONDS TO MIDNIGHT

DAVID ORSON NEWTON

Chiselbury

Cover by Indra Murugiah

Published by Chiselbury Publishing, a division of Woodstock Leasor Limited
14 Devonia Road, London N1 8JH, United Kingdom

www.chiselbury.com

ISBN: 978-1-917837-43-9 (paperback)

ISBN: 978-1-917837-47-7 (ebook)

A CIP catalogue record for this book is available from the British Library

'Higher than the beasts, lower than the angels, stuck in our idiot Eden.'

— FORD MADOX FORD, PARADE'S END

Written in the margins of my life, I would like to give thanks to:

My parents, who gave me opportunity.

My wife, who believes in me.

My son, who gives me joy.

And lastly, to all those who have guided me.

I also dedicate this cautionary tale to the humans and machines at the very farthest edges of technological innovation. I cannot see what you see. So, I *fear*. With every step forward, I ask that you consider what might be the end.

PROLOGUE

2029 – SPRING

"It's seconds to midnight; nuclear warheads crisscross the globe toward targets in the east and west. In another life, if you could be anything or anyone, what or who would you be?"

Lying on her back, Anita asked the question out loud as she stretched flat onto the cold and empty lawns of London's Battersea Park. Her long legs pressed the grass as streams of black hair snaked away from her head. Squinting up at the silvery dots suspended above the city, she didn't expect a human answer to her question.

"And what would your answer be?" She asked again of a fictional world leader in her head.

She watched as the winking natural lights above tried to compete with the hundreds and thousands of man-made, unblinking lights beaming back. She wondered: could that be the *last* interview question ever asked? You could put it to anyone. Just imagine the answers…

"What would *you* be?" She pressed again as the imaginary politician hesitated and obfuscated, clearly seeking to deflect and evade. "There will be no record of your answer…" She reassured softly.

A phone chime pricked her nighttime dreaming bubble. The shift that would change *everything* was now only one hour away.

A man's voice came from among the trees as she rose and lifted her handbag.

"And what would you be then?"

Anita froze. She had thought she was alone, even in this city of over 10 million people.

A ragged figure emerged from the darkness. His clothes hung off him, and a rich smell filled the air between them.

The figure pressed again, "Well, then…what would *you* be?"

Anita straightened to full height and looked up at the night sky. She wasn't afraid.

"I would be…"

She hesitated and looked down at the figure who was now leaning against a tree trunk and swigging readily from a nondescript can.

"Well, what would *you* be?" She challenged back.

"Me?" He now responded in an emerging East End patter. "Simple. I would be an inventor, build a time machine and go back to the bloke who created the internet, he will be the end of all of us, you know."

"Okay - and what would you say to him?" She questioned.

"I would say – this is the future you will create, does the world really need this? Is all progress good progress? Does it do more harm than good?"

Anita glanced skyward again, "Thank you! At last, someone I can have this debate with…"

Looking back, the figure had gone. A dark shadow moved purposefully along the edge of the treeline that ran away from her.

"Hey, come back. Let's debate it, if not him, someone else would've just come along and…"

She shouted hopelessly into the darkness, but the figure had vanished.

Her phone chimed again. It was fifty five minutes until her shift started.

1

GEORGE & OLIVIA

The letter that would end George's life had sat on the doormat for nearly nine hours. The envelope was slightly damp from the postman's rain-soaked van-to-door dash; the cheap paper had begun to smell musty.

While Olivia lugged the groceries out of the car, their son tore across the garden and into his den. Content all was as he had left it; his small boots then looped back through the converted mill house, trampling over the once-pristine white rectangular envelope. Olivia was a close second through the front door.

"William, get your muddy boots off *now*!"

Then, looking down, she saw *it*.

Her back ached with the weight of her second son nestled low in her belly as, dropping her bags and bending forward, she wiped the blotches of muddy water off the words to the right of - *On His* - to reveal - *Majesty's Service.*

George would be home in an hour. He'd be driving and listening to one of his audiobooks by some obscure up-and-coming author. Let him enjoy that simple pleasure, she thought.

Olivia was still sitting in the doorway, pale with shock, when his rusting bottle-green Land Rover swung onto the gravel drive. The parting chert stone rushed like receding pebbles on a storm-swept beach.

As George shifted gears to reverse and started to park, he saw her. One hand instantly turned off the ignition, the other flung open the heavy metal door, which bounced on its hinges.

Racing across the chert, he called out, "Liv, darling, are you okay?"

All streaked makeup and reddened eyes; she raised her arms to lower him and whispered, "Those bastards want you back."

2

WEI

"WEI *NEVER* LOSES," she said under her breath. Onto her keyboard, she then quickly typed into the game's chat thread - Da *never* loses.

Da had been her gaming moniker from the start. Da never switched her camera on.

Her watch alarm chimed 04:45. As the summer sun rose, she started to get ready for her day job as a trader in the City. Wei *loved* money. One day, she would make enough to build her gaming dynasty. Playing games would never be enough. She wanted to own virtual worlds and everyone in them.

Before leaving her flat, she looked in the metal-framed mirror by the front door and neatly combed her short, dyed-pink bob haircut - a little rebellion that galled the stuffy old pin-striped traders at work.

Her routine was precise. By 0700, she would be at her desk and well-settled in anticipation of the market opening at 0800.

Waiting to board the Circle line tube from Sloane Square, she turned up the volume on her wireless headphones. Scanning the crowd, she paused on a white, middle-aged man in dark jeans and a leather bomber jacket. She watched as he stepped forward to the thick yellow line near the platform's edge. Everyone else was staring down at their little screens in their outstretched hands. She observed as the man talked to himself; his fingers fidgeting against open palms. She moved forward to speak to him.

There was no screeching of brakes, no screaming. No one was even looking up.

Then, the Tannoy: Delays. Seek alternative routes. Sorry for the inconvenience.

Wei watched as the people on the platform grumbled and cursed. So selfish, she heard one man say.

Exiting the station, Wei saw the Transport Police corralling and addressing the commuters. They were calling for witnesses to come forward. Wei walked past, hailed a taxi, and stepped in. It was 0755 when she eventually reached her desk.

The subsequent tap on her shoulder at 0805 was just as unwelcome as it was unusual. Everyone knew not to bother Wei during trading hours. She removed her headset and turned, scowling.

"Are you Wei Li?" Asked a tall, lean man with a pale face, wearing a beige Mackintosh.

"Who's asking?"

"You need to follow me. *Now.*"

Once securely inside an empty conference room, the man in the Mackintosh gestured for her to sit. Seconds later, her boss arrived, looking red-faced and flustered.

The Macintosh man opened, "Wei Li, you are now officially activated and in the service of His Majesty's Government. There is a car outside; you will be taken to a secure facility outside London. We are at the start of the largest cyber-attack we have ever faced. The second Battle of Britain has begun. Your country needs *you.*"

3

DEAN

"Turn it *off*, Dean!" A slender foot kicked Dean's muscled leg. Dutifully, he rolled over and clicked the button on the side of his phone to snooze its shrieking alarm. Thanks to last night's East End London pub crawl, he felt a surge of bile creeping upwards. He ignored his throbbing head and forced himself across the clothes-strewn bedroom floor, through the door and into the hallway bathroom. He made it just in time.

"Dean, you've got mail!" His Ma shouted in her rugged northern Irish lilt that hadn't allowed itself to be watered down even after decades in England. An envelope duly slid under the bathroom door.

Wiping the remnants of last night from around his mouth, he hungrily tore it open. Sitting with his back against the bathtub, Dean bellowed, "So, they *want* me now, do they!"

Rising unsteadily to his feet, he flung open the door. In underwear that was once a bright white, he swaggered like a rodeo cowboy into his mother's linoleum-floored kitchen; the smell of frying eggs made him momentarily gag.

"Ma, they want me after all. This is gonna be man's work."

Dean's Ma busied on in the kitchen. "Do you want bacon wit' your eggs, love?"

He was still studying the letter and rubbing his calloused thumb over the crown at the top. It wasn't embossed.

"And what does whoever that is in your bedroom want…?"

Not really being hungry, but knowing that his Ma liked to feed him, he gave the answer he knew she'd want to hear: "We'll both go for ya special, Ma. Thanks."

"Who is she, anyway?"

"I dunno. Met her last night down Mickey's. Think her name was Kayla or Katie. Or Katya? K-something …"

His Ma rolled her eyes. "Who's come knocking then? Is it that cockney builder again? That envelope felt cheap. I've never liked 'im. Danna trust 'im as far as I could throw 'im."

"Cockney builder." Dean laughed as he scratched in places he shouldn't in front of the woman who gave him life.

"Jimmy the Brick doesn't send letters, Ma. It's the bloody King. Old Charlie wants Dean Boy to go and fight for 'im. There's gunna be a fight, and they want *fighters.*"

Ma stopped levering up the fried eggs and gripped the sideboard with both hands.

"This time around, the recruiters aren't so bothered if you have tats on your hands." He extended his heavily tattooed fingers and then clenched them back into fists, jabbing and uppercutting the air in quick succession.

He was a born fighter whose fight was now coming.

Ma turned to look at her son. Behind her, the eggs crackled as they overcooked. Tears streamed down her ageing cheeks.

4

ANITA, BREAKING THE STORY

ANITA and her team had been on the news desk all night. An amber light streamed through her central London skyscraper office as the summer sun rose.

Tired minds shuffled around, gathering coats and bags. As the beam of light widened, one by one, the shufflers stopped and migrated to the vast floor-to-ceiling glass windows. No one said a word.

On any normal day, the rush to leave the office after a night shift was absolute. But today was no *normal* day.

The evening of the night before, Zarina Adekunle, the UK Prime Minister, had made an announcement that would change the lives of millions, in an instant.

For the first time since 1960, there would be Conscription in the United Kingdom.

The first batch would receive draft letters within the next twenty-four hours. Due to an unforeseen Government technical issue (read lack of preparedness and years of underfunding), digital delivery (emails and SMS) will *not* be sent out at this time.

All UK residents, irrespective of gender, aged between 18 and 45, were to be called up.

The only exceptions were in -

- The Police Service.
- The Prison Service.
- The National Health Service 'NHS'.

- Farming and Agriculture.
- The Military-Industrial Complex – now known in the Tabloids as *The War Machine*.

Outside of those specified sectors, the only other exemption was for sole caregivers to children under the age of 18.

For the first time since the Second World War, a UK Prime Minister had told the nation that their country's very *survival* was at stake; Russia's continual ratcheting of tensions and provocation could no longer be ignored. To stand a fighting chance, the most wide-ranging Conscription ever conceived had now been enshrined in UK law.

Anita's team broadcast the PM's address live to the nation. She had then hosted a panel session with the boffins at the Bulletin of the Atomic Scientists. It was the panel that went viral after the scientists adjusted the Doomsday Clock - which indicated how close humanity was to a global catastrophe (midnight) - from seventy to sixty Seconds to Midnight. The world had never been closer to the abyss, they warned.

For Anita, the fallout was like nothing she had *ever* experienced. Her job had been to conduct live interviews with anyone who could provide insight on what *might*, or perhaps, *would*, come next. The stable of booked speakers ranged from MPs, Defence bosses and Foreign Policy experts through to Veterans of the UK's last wars in Iraq and Afghanistan and members of the general public who were now likely to be drafted to fight.

At one point during that long night, Anita had felt so frustrated with the 'samey' answers from her vetted roster of speakers that she had taken a small team onto the streets and conducted ad hoc interviews with random passers-by to try and capture the mood of the nation.

It being the small hours, they managed to net those who

were returning home after big nights out. *In vino veritas,* she secured the most raw and unfiltered views of the average person on the high street.

One such engagement went like this: Anita approached a group of well dressed, mid-20s white men wearing suits on a street outside a smart-looking London pub with stained glass windows and an expensive wine list. She began, "Excuse me, chaps. Would you be willing to share your opinions on last night's news?"

The group, having been facing inwards and talking amongst themselves, turned en masse. It was the tallest of the group, with slicked back black hair and a self-impressed air, who responded first: "Yeah, she can fuck off! This country's done nothing for me! I make more than the PM, and I can't even get a decent house in Zone 1, 2 or 3. This country's going down the pan; I'm heading to Dubai!" The rest of the group jeered and cheered, and the short one with spectacles and a double-breasted blazer, who had looked rather more mild-mannered, said, "Now *you* can fuck off back to where you came from and all!" Anita turned to her cameraman. This sort of bile didn't faze her. "Did you get that?" She asked.

"Yes! All of it. Do you want to do a quick piece to camera?" Her cameraman responded as they moved a little way off down the street.

Anita turned, "And say what? They'll never let me air that…we're a country of Patriots, aren't we?"

Sure enough, after a quick call and wasted pleading to air 'the other side', Anita was told that the sentiments weren't what her bosses wanted to broadcast. Her team were promptly ordered back to HQ and brought to heel.

Now, the morning was here; as the sun inched upwards, she stared in silence alongside her colleagues as the burning red ball of heat bathed the city in an orange glow so fierce that it looked as though the whole city was on fire. Maybe it was, she thought.

Anita drew a deep breath and ran her fingers through her dense black hair, before carefully straightening her once crisp white shirt collar. Without turning, she addressed her colleagues: "*Life is like a game of cards. The hand you are dealt is determinism; the way you play it is free will.*"

She paused and then continued: "Those are the words of Jawaharlal Nehru, a great inspiration to me and my family. You were part of history last night. The world will never be the same again. Go home to your loved ones, your family and your friends. Say the things you haven't said. Thank you for being outstanding."

Beeps of keycards being swiped, doors closing, and then silence. Complete silence. Anita stared into the red ball, her mind drifting back to a time she examined more often now than at any other point in her life.

She was seven; her family had travelled to the sprawling, ancient temples of Varanasi on the Ganges to cremate her maternal Grandmother, a woman who, when her parents travelled for work, which they often did, would fill her weekends with trips to the local park and regular visits to her favourite street food vendor for Jalebi. A food so sugary and so sweet, JB (as they codenamed it), was hers and her Nani's little secret; her parents would've never allowed it.

Anita remembered how her face had stung with the fierce heat of that funeral pyre, her nostrils clogging with the acrid stench of burning flesh. She had looked on as the pyre became a makeshift raft that slowly inched away from the shoreline before the river's currents dragged it off downstream. Seared into her eternal memory was Nani's peaceful face, nestled amongst the sticks and twigs like a bird's nest with two eyes for the eggs. She had tried to feel something, *anything*. She had tried to feel sad, angry, or even sorry for her parents; they had just lost their only parent, after all; Dadi ma had died tragically in a car crash before Anita was even born. But try as she might, she felt unmoved, as though she wasn't really related to any of these people who wept and wailed as though the whole city was burning down around them. She was different. She didn't belong, but she didn't know why.

5

YOU MUST GO, NOW?

"Livvy, we need to tell William. Where is he?"

"He's upstairs getting changed for supper. Can't you see the trail of muddy boot prints?" She pointed to the stairs, laughed, and then, remembering *that* letter, started to sob all over again.

"I will tell him." George took off his brown brogues and neatly placed them by the doorway. He kissed Oliva's forehead and whispered, "I love you, my darling," before helping her onto the living room sofa.

Ascending the stairs, he looked up and found William sitting there, all teary-eyed and sobbing. He was curled into a tight ball with his head bunched inside bent knees, like a little pangolin. At eight, his son would now have to deal with his father heading off to war.

George sat next to his boy on the top step. "You know what's happening, don't you?"

William nodded as he nuzzled into his father's arms.

"I *always* come home," he said, holding little William tight. His son didn't respond with words; he just burrowed deeper into the fold between George's right arm and his broad chest.

George had served a short but distinguished career in MI6, Britain's Secret Intelligence Service. He had done his time in the shadows, moved on and now built a happy family life in rural Dorset. A spook never really retires, though. He knew that. The firmness of this latest tap on the shoulder meant that there would be no last summer weekend to process what was happening. The letter had ordered George to report for duty the next day at midday. No location was provided; only a phone number was given for further instructions.

After a last family supper of William's favourite toad in the hole and the completion of various steam locomotive jigsaw puzzles, George slipped out of the house to his log cabin at the end of their long garden. Before telling his mother of the news, he had to make one international call.

The line rang twice. He straightened to full height. At over six feet tall, he had to partially duck to avoid a wooden beam on the cabin's roof.

The Russian voice that answered was strained and hard to hear, "I am sorry, George. The world has gone mad."

"The world hasn't gone mad, Alexei. It's just your leader. Taking a fifth of Ukraine was never going to be enough. We all knew that, but still, the West didn't act decisively."

"You haven't been called up, have you? Surely, you're exempt. You're the only Courtenay son left, for god's sake!"

George ignored the question – operational security protocol had been seared into his brain. Plus, Alexei knew George would be the first to get the call, given his operational experience in Eastern Europe.

"Alexei, you know history shows us that this won't end well for you."

"You sound just like your brother did in Afghanistan, George. How is the family? How is little William?"

George softened. "He's just like him, you know. Sports mad. A terror with the girls, even at 8. It's history repeating itself…we were all wild at school…but not as wild as you, though! Alexei the bull!"

Both men laughed.

Then, the line went abruptly dead.

George re-dialled. No answer.

The wrought iron cabin door handle rattled as it turned and lifted from the latch.

"George, what are you up to?"

Olivia appeared around the door and handed him a dram of single malt in his favourite crystal tumbler – it had been a birthday gift from his son, and the inscription – *I love you more than trains* – never failed to bring a smile. Taking a seat in George's leather sloped-back reading chair, Olivia cupped her mint tea with slender fingers, forming a lotus leaf around the bowl. She wisely moved the conversation on.

"William is getting ready for bed. Let's do bedtime together tonight."

George nodded and raised his glass, "To peace."

Olivia raised her tea, "To my family being back together again." She took a sip and wrapped her white wool cardigan tightly around her chest. Her tousled blonde hair became trapped in its ruffled collar. George leant forward and delicately lifted it free, draping it around her neck and back down over her chest.

After a long pull on his whiskey, he said, "I should call my mother."

"Let's put William to bed and then call her together."

"Let me call her quickly now. I'll be back up to the house in half an hour. Promise."

Olivia had no intention of pressing him further and having *that* conversation again. Instead, she swiftly rose, kissed him on the cheek, and closed the cabin door behind her - perhaps a little too loudly, in retrospect. She had never liked George's mother, but she tried not to make it too obvious; it only frustrated and upset him. He had enough to think about.

But tramping off across the lawn, she was secretly fuming that their last evening together was being interrupted by the needs of '*her*'…Adela. She always found a way to interfere, even when she wasn't physically present.

Olivia paused on the wooden Monet bridge that spanned the circular pond in the middle of their lawn. It was then that she noticed the two red wine glasses on the metal table under the weeping willow near the lawn's edge. Her mind started to race: didn't she clear them away after Hamish left? Would George have seen them when he walked down to his cabin? He never missed *anything*...Shit, Shit. Her mind raced.

Flustered and worried, she ran over the bridge and down to the riverbank, where the offending glasses mocked her forgetfulness. She grabbed both and quickly turned toward the house.

Then, a voice from across the lawn.

"Oh, Liv. You're so sweet. Shall we wait to have a drink *after* William's bedtime, though? I really want to be fully present, you know."

"Of course, darling. I was only setting up for later..."

George pointed to Olivia's round belly. "And only a few sips for you..."

She didn't respond.

Crossing the bridge with a confident stride, he offered a hand to help with the glasses.

Together, they turned and headed up to the house. She watched as he held both glasses square in front of his chest and then raised them high into the fading light. One clearly had lipstick marks; the other did not.

George looked over; it wasn't a loving look, much more inquiring than adoring. Olivia wasn't wearing lipstick anymore. George didn't say a thing. Instead, he decided to do William's bedtime routine by himself.

* * *

It took hours before George had eventually managed to settle his son; little William was understandably distraught. Tiptoeing onto the landing, George gingerly closed the bedroom door behind him. Looking up, he noticed the wood-framed picture of the family astride the cobbled causeway leading to St Michael's Mount in Cornwall from last summer. All broad smiles, glinting sunglasses and windswept air. William straddling his shoulders. Olivia's cute, scrunched nose; her tongue sticking out at a right angle. The ice cream that he had walked all the way back to the café to get for her, half-licked away and fixed in her left hand. Happier times, he thought. Straightening the frame on the wall, he realised now that he was anxious, unanchored even; this time would be different.

* * *

George descended the stairs and saw that the front door was open. He walked out across the chert stone and over the trimmed grass leading down to the riverbank, where he could see Olivia sitting.

As he drew closer, he could hear sobs.

"Liv, I'm sorry. I'm so very sorry."

She didn't turn.

"You promised you were done, George. Out. For good."

"I thought I was. I mean, I was!"

"You were mistaken…"

"I don't want to go," George placed a hand on her shoulder before it was promptly brushed away.

"Liv, I want to stay *here*. I want to be with you all…"

Olivia rose and fixed George with her glare.

"You never wanted to leave 6 in the first place! Just be honest! Just be fucking *honest*, George. You want to go, so *go*!"

"Livvy!" George stretched out a hand.

She batted it away and made for the house.

George looked down at the two water glasses on the metal tabletop and then glanced upward into the weeping willow that ebbed and flowed on the nighttime breeze.

She knew him better than he knew himself. He wanted this.

He didn't have to dig far to see that he was done with this sedentary, rural life. He wanted in. He wanted action and derring-do. Lifting a glass of water skyward, George remembered his brother who had been killed in Afghanistan, "I'm going, William. I'll make you proud, buddy."

George's mind then drifted back to last summer, a family holiday in Sardinia. Bleached white sands, sparkling turquoise waters, and a long-awaited chance for uninterrupted family time.

It was on that holiday that he first learned that his days of action would come again.

George's security consultant's bonus had been splurged on a luxurious resort where wealthy Europeans went to play.

Lazy days were spent looping between the beaches, swimming pools and resort restaurants. It was on one such loop between the pool and a restaurant bar that George was approached.

Olivia and little William had already headed back to the room to change for supper.

George had been placing an order for a bottle of Bollinger to be on the table for that night when a bronzed, muscled and sandy-haired Russian appeared next to him.

Andrei, the name by which he introduced himself, said he needed to speak *urgently*.

Bar stools were taken; no pleasantries were exchanged. The conversation had gone like this:

"George, I have someone who would very much like to speak with you."

Andrei had turned and looked across to an old man seated under the shade beyond the shimmering pool. The old man didn't move or make any acknowledgement back.

"Who is he?" George responded.

"A very important and powerful person. On a mission."

"What mission?"

"To create a better understanding between the UK and Russia…on certain topics."

A barman appeared and asked George what room number he should put the Champagne on.

George was about to respond when he thought better of it.

"Thank you, please give me a moment. I will sort it before I leave."

The barman, tired and toward the end of a long day shift, turned and disappeared, "As you wish, Sir."

George switched back to Andrei, but Andrei had gone; the old man from across the pool was now in his place.

The grey-haired man spoke in a quiet but strong Russian accent, "George Courtenay, we are kindred spirits. Patriots. Romantics. Risk takers. Your old family friend Alexei has told me all about you."

George challenged, "How do you…"

The grey hair cut him off, "What I am about to tell you could change your life forever. You will make a lot of money for you and your family. If you're smart, it will mean money for the next generation too…"

George gestured to the barman and politely ordered a Balvenie with no ice. He looked to the grey hair who confirmed he would have the same with a nod of his head.

Both sat in silence as the drams were poured and then pushed across the bar.

Gesturing with an outstretched hand to the poolside and jagged Sardinian cliffs beyond, the grey-haired man said: "This is your first time here, no? This could be your life, George. Hopping from one Mediterranean island to the next….no more cold winters in the UK. No more sky-high taxes…."

George finished his dram and nodded to the barman for refills. He then turned and asked, "What do you *want*?"

"I want to help you, and in turn, for you to help us…you do not know it yet, but soon your country will mobilise to counter the growing threat we present. And when it does, you will be called back into service."

George looked away from the grey hair and out towards the holidaymakers slipping into and out of the pool.

"And how do you know I will be called back up?"

"I know, and I am never wrong. You are on a list of retired agents who have experience of Eastern Europe. It's a given. I heard good things about you…one of the best they say…"

The grey hair finished his second dram and tilted his right hand to the barman who duly refreshed both glasses again.

Grey hair continued, "Once you're back inside 6, you must find and destroy a Chinese agent. Our sources tell us she may already be working from within your service. This woman is a double agent. I can't tell you her name, or what she looks like…all we know…is that her codename is 'Da'."

"Da?"

"Yes, it means great, vast, big…in Mandarin Chinese. We think it refers to some form of network, maybe cyber. Like a web."

"And why can't I just refer this intel to my old boss. You keep the money. I do the professional thing…"

"That would be a mistake. Trust no one with this information. You English boys are too big on morals; the blood of the empire still under the fingernails, perhaps?"

George finished his last dram and rose from his stool.

The grey hair gripped him firmly by the arm, "Ignore what I've told you at your peril, George. You will be called up. Da is operating from inside British Intelligence. Da works for the Chinese. Not you. Find her. Expose her. *Destroy her*. For both of our countries' sake."

George removed the grey hair's hand from his arm.

"I didn't catch your name?"

"They call me Kitboy. In English, it means - Whale Hunter. Goodbye, George."

George walked to the side of the bar and told the barman his room number for the champagne order before setting off to the family villa in the hotel's grounds.

As George arrived, he saw Olivia and William all dressed up and ready to go for supper.

William ran over, "Daddy, Daddy, can we go to the pizza restaurant?"

"Yes, little man. I've got a bottle of something special waiting for your Mummy." George smiled at Olivia.

She looked stony-faced and motioned inside to William, "Darling, give me and your Daddy a few minutes."

"But I'm hungry. *Please*, can we go and get pizza?"

"There's some of that nice chocolate by the fridge. Have a few squares of that while you wait."

"Oh, alright then…" he moped off, shuffling his sandaled feet.

Olivia walked over to George. "What is it? You look like you've seen a ghost."

"It's nothing, Liv. Just some Russian with a business proposition. Clearly thought I was some kind of international investor. Must be these ghastly sunglasses you got me…"

He raised a hand to the out-of-character Gucci sunglasses on his head, bought from the hotel shop on arrival.

Olivia wasn't amused. "You're lying, George. I can't actually believe you were a spy. You're such a shit liar! Tell me the truth."

Little William came to the villa door behind them. "What are you arguing about?"

Olivia turned, "We're not arguing, darling. Daddy's just being a bit silly. You can have two more squares of chocolate, and then we're off."

"I don't want any more chocolate," William responded. "I *want* pizza."

"I want *never* gets!" Olivia snapped back. "Give us five

minutes – time it on your new waterproof diver's watch - and then we're off. Promise."

Little William disappeared inside again.

Olivia turned to face George. He didn't try his luck this time.

"Alright, alright…someone approached me…a Russian. Probably ex-FSB and now on their payroll as an intermediary, a private contractor, that sort of thing."

"Go on:..what do they want?"

"They gave me some information that I should pass on up the chain when I get back."

"That's it?"

"Well, it's pretty concerning intel, that's why I looked a bit shocked…but yes, that's it."

"You're not getting involved then?" She gave him the look as though to say - Don't bullshit me.

"I don't intend to, no."

"Good, well, let's get to dinner then! I'm starving. Although I doubt William has any appetite left after all that chocolate…"

"I'd be lost without you, Liv. You know that don't you!"

She didn't respond. Instead, she called for William, "William, pizza time! Let's go!"

As they walked down the winding palm-tree-lined cobbled path from their villa to the restaurant, Olivia turned to George. "The main thing is that life, if you can call it that, is behind you. And we're not going back."

George looked forward as the restaurant appeared beyond the palm fronds. Flames rose from bamboo torches; there was a low, melodic strum of string instruments from a band near the bar. He turned, "This is our life now, Liv. There'll be plenty more of this in our future too. I promise."

* * *

On the balcony of the penthouse suite at the very top of the main hotel building, the Whale Hunter took a deep draw of his vodka. "No more of that Scottish muck," he said to Andrei, raising his glass in toast.

"What are we toasting to?" Andrei asked.

"To the little British boat that will soon set sail with an eager harpoonist on board."

"But he didn't take the money?" Andrei questioned.

"He thinks he's a patriot. King and Country and all that shit…he'll do it for the greater good."

Both men laughed.

6

ANITA'S DECISION

THERE WOULD BE no one waiting at home for Anita.

Her team was going home to boyfriends, girlfriends, parents, lovers, dogs, and cats - but not Anita.

Outside of her work, she was alone in this world. Social media influencers and successive Governments broadcast that *you* could have it all, but in Anita's view, that was all a lie. For her and many of her close friends, success in their careers came at the direct expense of starting a family. Society didn't enable both to flourish and grow. Childcare, the general uselessness of men, the list went on. She, and many others she knew, had all had their eggs frozen at great personal expense. Collectively, they resented society and government policy for that.

Now, unable to face going back to her empty flat to sleep, she walked. It was an aimless walk at first, but then, sensing an urge for the familiar, she headed towards her local park. Gaining pace, her mind soon decluttered, and the voices that had swirled all morning quietened. Piercing that fleeting calm, her phone vibrated - a Government SMS flashed onto the screen (platforms now seemingly back online after yet *another* technology outage) -

To know more about how you can serve your country, click here.

Annoyed by the unwelcome interruption, she cleared the message and kept the pace. After walking for over an hour, she arrived deep in thought at Battersea Park. Her favourite spot on the steps of the park's towering Pagoda came into view; she noticed that her happy place, usually bustling with activity –

buskers, photographers, tourists, stretching joggers and friendly dog walkers – was empty. There was no one. Anywhere. Even here, at this place of community, she was still alone.

Reaching the steps, she didn't sit. Instead, she opened her SMS inbox and clicked the link in the message; the internet browser on her phone promptly opened onto a page headed – *Be Proud to Serve your Country.*

She had considered it once, years ago; the military's ad campaign about 'Belonging' had scratched something deep down inside her, but it had looked like a long and drawn-out process, and she quickly lost interest. Not now, though. Now there was an exciting new page - in the centre, in big, bold text, it simply said -

Call the number below to Enlist within 24hrs. Call Now!

So, she did, and within minutes, after a few interesting and abstract questions from an AI Assistant called Winston, clearly designed to profile her, she was given an address in central London and a time slot for that very afternoon. Recruits would be given everything they needed. Just bring yourself as you are, she was told.

Staring out at the slate-coloured Thames winding through the city, Anita reflected on the night before. Anger was the predominant emotion close to the surface. Anger at feeling like a mouthpiece. A grey cog in a faceless machine. But something else was gnawing away inside her, too; something she couldn't quite identify. She brushed whatever it was aside and called her employer – there would be no next night shift; government mandates meant that notice periods were being waived for anyone who signed up to serve their country.

7

BEN'S DILEMMA

Ben slammed the front door to his granite miner's cottage and marched off down the sunken lane that led up onto the high moors of Dartmoor in Devon. His prolonged state of simmering had eventually boiled over.

Towering ash trees on either side of the lane arched overhead to create a canopy that filtered the evening sunlight and sprinkled portions of it over the pitted tarmac.

Simmering because - bills. Simmering because - never-ending to-do lists. Simmering because – recent family drama after a few too many late nights…

Boiling over because – *that* letter had arrived. The *final* straw.

All day, he had tried, since *it* had landed on the doormat, to keep a brave face for his family.

To know that he might have to rejoin the Army and fight had made him physically sick, vomiting twice in the downstairs bathroom.

He had dodged death on more than one occasion in Afghanistan. In that dust bowl dance, there had been too many IEDs that only partially exploded and countless bullets that had thudded into trees above, instead of into, his head. Ben knew that he shouldn't be here. Frankly, it was a miracle that he was. He was a cat that had lived its nine lives. He *knew* that if he stepped back into uniform again, he would not be coming back.

Sensing his mind was going to darker places, he pushed himself harder and soon passed through the ageing wooden farmer's gate that his son Isambard, who was now ten, would often race ahead to open and close for them both. His thoughts momentarily returned to those happy summer evening walks – the radiating warmth of baked granite that had cooked for hours in the sun, the sweet citrus scent of the sun-kissed heather. His son would gallop through that gate and out onto the open moors like a young foal finding its legs. Dartmoor was where Ben and Isambard were happiest. They would race off to the top of tors and follow cryptic clues to thousands of hidden letterboxes treasured away amongst the moor's gullies and earthen banks. When a letterbox was found, Isambard would excitedly stamp his leatherbound book that now proudly burgeoned with green, black and blue stamps from across the length and breadth of the moors. Ben and Isambard would often finish their walks sitting together at the top of their local tor and watch the sun set; first, a blazing fire, and then an orange glow that slowly melted away to reveal a purple dusk, which would cloak the heather and gorse-fringed trail home.

But not tonight.

Tonight, Ben didn't stop. He hadn't taken his son on *this* walk. He strode out past their favourite sunset viewpoint. Out past the spot where Isambard had found his first letterbox. Out past the secluded waterfall where they had swum in a moorland pool together on a scorching hot summer's day several years ago. Out past the knoll where Ben had proposed to Emily, his beloved wife of ten years.

He walked hard; his breath became laboured, and his thighs burned. Tripping on a clump of protruding peat bog, he bit down hard on his tongue. Cursing, he swore and spat out globules of blood. With no breeze, the blood spattered his checked cotton farmers shirt, which was by now drenched with sweat and clinging to his sinewy frame. He reached the edge of an abandoned quarry and looked down, staring into the darkness. A few small stones dislodged by his abrupt halt clattered against the granite walls before loudly splashing into the water below. The rocks seemed to almost float at first, but soon, overwhelmed by the cold and murky depths, they sank.

Turning back, he looked on as the sun's orange glow spilt out across the horizon into a magnificent strip of burning amber.

He would not go back to the horrors of war.

He could not. There was too much to live for.

8

GEORGE RETURNS TO THE FOLD

STILL THE YEAR 2029 – THE SUMMER OF MOBILISATION

As a boy, George frequently visited Beaulieu in the New Forest. He had been captivated by the stories of the Special Operations Executive (SOE) agents who had trained within the mansion's sprawling grounds before parachuting behind enemy lines in World War II.

He had dreamt about the myriad James Bond gadgets, from lockpicks disguised as pipes to buttons with hidden compasses and playing cards that concealed maps. On their very first trip to Beaulieu, he and his brother William had to be dragged away by their mother as the museum was closing and lights were being turned off. Through a coordinated fraternal charm offensive against Mother, they had engineered many more visits during school holidays and his mind was soon made up – he simply *must* become a spy. At the earliest opportunity, he had taken the secret service selection and passed with flying colours. His brother William opted instead for the Army. This moment of divergence and George's wholehearted embrace of the invisible cloak-and-dagger world of espionage meant that the two brothers had, despite meaningful efforts on both parts, drifted apart. When William was later killed in Afghanistan, that drift had become a source of deep regret for George. Fearing the same divergence could happen with his wife, Olivia, he had decided to leave '6' for good and vowed to become a family man.

Now, as his battered Land Rover sped up the winding driveway ahead, the boy in him imagined that this must have been how those brave SOE agents felt back in World War Two.

The thrill, the anticipation. He reflected on how strangely content he felt. Maybe this was just what he was *meant* to do. What he was, perhaps, *born* to do.

He chastened himself. After all, he had left a wife, his son and another child soon-to-be-born at home to fend for themselves. In a rare moment of self-reflection, he realised that this was how he had felt before entering the secret world for that very first time. Back then, he had felt compelled to wash his old life away and start anew. He would eventually go in so deep that he nearly didn't find his way back out. This time would be different, he resolved, not really knowing if he *truly* believed that. An intrusive thought then burst into his consciousness; he couldn't get those damned wine glasses out of his head; was Liv playing away from home *again*? He hadn't wanted to challenge her and ruin their last night together…things always escalated…more unwelcome thoughts now came, but were quickly shelved as George was guided to a designated parking spot by a uniformed soldier whose combat smock bore no unit insignia.

Within seconds, he was being ushered into the hallway of a once great manor house. From the outside, its turrets, crenellations, and mullioned windows made it look more medieval castle than country house.

As he moved through the imposing hallways, he saw room after room packed with banks of screens and armies of analysts crowded around planning tables. Installations of satellite uplink and downlink terminals connected this once-ancient structure to the very latest battlefield innovations in situational awareness. The place was like a stone-clad spaceship, he thought.

Spotting a distinctly analogue coffee-making area, he made a beeline for that before a voice from behind stopped him in his tracks.

"Good to have you back, Courtenay! I asked for you personally."

That voice was unmistakable.

It was C.

The Boss.

9

DEAN JOINS THE INFANTRY

Dean's muscles had long ago contorted into twisted, bundled masses. His hunched shoulders felt locked in cement, courtesy of the 25 kg weight of his rucksack, plus the 14 kg 81 mm Mortar bipod. Now, he was being loaded with high explosive rounds, each weighing around 4 kg. The bravado of earlier had long ago melted into the mud that now sucked voraciously at his brand new military-issue black leather boots.

Staring ahead at the undulating terrain of mud, gorse and bog, he regretted those beers on the train up. He had reported to the Infantry Training Centre (ITC) Catterick the night before on their brand-new Conscript Course. His draft letter arrived that morning, and he was in the system by that evening. Day One would be a baptism of fire, instructors had told them. He wasn't quite sure what that meant...

A muscled, ginger-haired corporal with a prominent scar down his right cheek now towered over him, one leg atop a rock, hands locked on hips.

"Everyone wants to be a cowboy, Private. Until it's time to do cowboy shit."

Dean's vision was blurred. Even breathing seemed to hurt. Sharp pains coursed across his chest and down his back. His feet were on fire.

"My feet, Corporal. My feet are burning. Is that normal?"

"That's just weakness leaving the body, Private." The Corporal pointed to Dean's black water bottle. "Get some water onboard. We move out in one minute."

"I don't think I can go on, Corporal."

"Well, then you will be dead."

Dean now looked up, bringing the ginger-haired man's barrel chest into focus. He noticed another scar; this one ran across his throat in a horizontal ridgeline of blistered red and purple.

"Look at me, Private!"

He looked up and into the Corporal's bloodshot eyes.

The Corporal then snapped forward and grabbed the straps of Dean's rucksack with both hands, "What do you think you'll do when you're over in Poland, France or Germany? When the Russians are bearing down on you. Will you ask them to stop while you explain the situation going on with your feet? Or will you get that Mortar bipod to the reverse side of that slope across the valley?"

The Corporal tightened his grip on Dean's straps and pulled him even closer, "Will you then work with your section to assemble that 81 mm Mortar and start getting rounds down range before the human wave of Russians sweeps across that valley and obliterates your Platoon defending their trench system?"

"Yes, Corporal."

"Yes, what? Private."

"I will get the bipod to the reverse slope down the valley, Corporal."

"Good, Private. Well, that's your rest break done. Now. Let's go! And remember, Civvies pay thousands to do this shit!"

Dean had laboured on building sites all his life; he was a champion boxer in his local gym. Always seen as a hard man. And, by most people's definitions, he was a bona fide tough guy. The real deal. But he had *never* felt pain like this. He was experiencing burning sensations in places that he didn't even know existed; he felt empty. Spent. Finished. He wanted to lie down and die. It was only the morning of Day One.

As he looked around at the other Conscripts panting,

gasping and reeling, he remembered a fight he had lost way back when he was a little nipper in school; he had been trying to defend a smaller boy from a notorious ginger-haired bully and, in the process, was himself severely beaten. He thought back to that feeling, the bloody iron taste that had filled his mouth, the ringing in his ears, that boorish ginger brute standing over him as his vision blurred and everything went black. But it hadn't been for nothing. That bully was expelled, and the boy he saved was now a good friend. The best of friends, in fact.

Back then, he had been the only one who had stepped forward.

He looked around at his fellow Conscripts and then over to the ginger-haired Corporal. "I can fucking do this," he cursed under his breath as he stood up straight, adjusted his shoulder straps and put one foot in front of the other.

'Let's feckin' 'ave it!" He called out to the others.

* * *

That night, after successfully holding the line against waves of simulated Russian soldiers, he sat and sipped a steaming mug of military-issue tea in the inky-black darkness of an unremarkable pine woodblock. This was where his Platoon had established their base for the night; he soon realised that, in the absolute darkness, he couldn't see more than a metre in any direction around himself. A thin spider's web of green twine ran from tree to tree, providing his only physical connection to the rest of his Platoon. He was supposed to have a buddy to share his foxhole with, but whoever it was had already gone off sick. A free pass permitted by the current rules. Rules that were now hastily being changed to allow only those Conscripts with life-threatening injuries or illnesses to go 'off sick'.

A soft and refined voice then came from the darkness.

"How are you holding up, Private Spencer?"

The words were soon followed by the appearance of an angular, youthful face slathered in tiger stripes of camouflage cream. It was his Training Unit Platoon Commander, Lieutenant Digby. He looked about twelve, Dean thought to himself.

"Thank you, Sir. I am feeling a bit better now."

Digby sat down on a moss-covered log opposite him.

"The Sergeants and Corporals will be tough on you, yeah. They just want to make sure you're ready. This Conscript training is *horrendously* condensed. If you had signed up in peacetime, we would have had months, even years, right? At the very least, you would have had your boots well before the training start date. You could have broken them in and prepared your feet. But now...well, we don't exactly have the luxury of time."

Dean was expressionless. He felt mentally and physically numb. That comment about signing up in peacetime would usually have been a red rag to a bull; he had tried but was rejected...fatigue-induced apathy now prevailed.

"How much do you read the news, Private?"

"A bit."

Digby unscrewed the lid of his green Thermos flask and poured something hot; steam rose into the cold night air as he continued.

"After invading and conquering a fifth of Ukraine; the Russians are now almost certainly re-arming and preparing for an Invasion of Poland next spring. The world is convinced they're going for the Baltic States next, but I have a friend in Government; he says the spooks are sure it's Poland next and that the Russians have learnt their lesson from Ukraine. They are expected to conquer the Poles quickly and then press on to Germany before hitting France. The moment Russia crosses the Polish border, we, and NATO, will be at War. Shit. Fan. Hits. You get me?"

Dean looked closely at his Platoon Commander, whose attempts to sound 'street' with phrases like '*you get me*' were desperately failing. Even though he was clearly older than Lieutenant Digby and, arguably, more comfortable in his own skin, he felt like a little boy being told the birds and the bees. On leaving London, he had felt so confident. And, if he was honest with himself, more arrogant than confident. Now, he realised that he was wildly out of his depth. Talk wouldn't get you far in this world. He looked down and noticed a slight tremor in his right leg. He then tried to stand and stretch, but instead wobbled and nearly fell.

Digby grabbed him, sat him back down and topped up Dean's empty metal mug from his own flask.

"Sit, Private. Stretch your legs, elevate them on your rucksack; it helps with the blood flow."

Digby neatly arranged Dean's pack to achieve the required elevation and then began again.

"Hot chocolate will get your blood sugar back up, get it down you while it's hot. Look, what is not in the news but that we know is coming – is that Poland, Germany, the Netherlands, Belgium and France will fall quickly. Quicker than anyone expects. Our best and brightest have modelled it. The Poles will fight, but the Germans, Dutch, Belgians and French don't have the fighting spirit of the Ukrainians, and they're all still convinced that Russia is headed for the Baltic States next. This time next year, we will be fighting for the very survival of our country, our families and ourselves. Throughout this training… remember this. Remember that there is someone out there…"

Digby gestured into the darkened forest with his Thermos flask tilted to one side.

"Someone out there who is training to kill *you*."

He then rose.

"Now - sort your feet, clean your weapon, fill your stomach and get some rest. You will be on sentry duty soon."

After Digby had left, Dean sat in the darkness with his elevated legs warming every minute the blood flowed downwards. He told himself that he would rest his eyes for just a few seconds and then start his admin. A little voice in his head told him not to close his eyes.

10

ANITA, IRIS & ARTEMIS

"Welcome to Operation IRIS." A tall, brunette woman released her hand from a red leather-clad tablet and offered its slender, ringless fingers to Anita. Cue the briefest of handshakes.

Anita thought she had arrived at a National Trust property, but upon entering, she saw the familiar tools of her trade: screens, fibre optic cables, and broadcasting sets everywhere. The vast medieval hall in front of them had been boxed into a series of mini news studios. As Anita walked past the entrances, she noticed the labels on each door – UK. Europe. USA. Russia. China. Rest of World.

Each mini studio was broadcasting live.

The tall brunette now turned. "I'm Jane, by the way."

Anita opened her mouth to respond.

Jane cut in, "Thank you for joining Operation IRIS."

"I haven't…"

"Oh, you have. You've seen it now. You've just joined. Congratulations. Bravo!"

"Anita, meet John. John, meet Anita. Our newest recruit."

John was a short plodder of a man with a crop of greying hair nestled on his slightly elevated crown, like a clump of seaweed on an exposed rock. He offered Anita a damp, soft hand. "Welcome aboard, Anita. You will do vital work here. Just sign this, and then we can get going."

He thrust a thick sheaf of paper at Anita's chest.

"What is it?" She responded.

John reddened with poorly suppressed frustration, "The

Official Secrets Act and an *in time of war* addendum. Look, we've all signed it. We *must* get on!"

"Are we at war?"

"Out there. No. In here. Yes. Have been for years."

Anita flicked through the pages. The addendum was visibly longer than the main part.

She looked up. "Can I just…"

John waved a black metal pen with impatience. "I'm afraid not. No time. Just a scribble here. We have a tube to catch!"

Anita, sensing no other option and somewhat intrigued by the place, the people and the mention of some underground transport in the middle of rural England, dutifully signed and turned to hand the paperwork back to Jane. She had gone.

"I'll take that." John snatched and hurriedly filed the paperwork in his red leather folio marked 'HR - OI & OA'.

He now started walking. Fast. Anita folded into his slipstream.

John spoke over his shoulder: "Well, this is Operation IRIS. It's pretty standard stuff these days. We learnt a lot after Brexit. More on that later. Frankly, it's all rather pedestrian human work up here. Follow me."

Anita observed him closely as he threaded his way through the milieu of runners, analysts and presenters. He never looked up. Not once. His steps were unnaturally short but intentional and extremely fast. She struggled to keep up.

"Human stuff?" She inquired.

John ignored the question and continued his spiel, "IRIS is where we do our broadcasting to the world. The Information War!"

Anita called forward, "War with who?"

John looked back over his shoulder. "All in good time, Anita."

They reached a small wooden door at the end of the hall.

He turned again and, now with a boyish grin, said, "To Operation ARTEMIS. Where the *magic* happens!"

John bent forward at the hips and looked into a small facial-scanning lens mounted in the stone wall.

The wooden door made a whooshing sound as it slid sideways into the stone wall. A long flight of dimly lit stone stairs led downwards. John's rapid steps made like a drumbeat; the lower they went, the faster the beat became. Then, he stopped. To Anita, it was a seemingly random place.

She watched as he stared at the wall and said a jumble of sounds at nothing. To Anita's surprise, a rectangular portion of the wall then moved backwards and slid sideways.

He stepped forward.

Mesmerised, she then followed.

Ahead of them was a long tunnel with stark white strip lighting beaming overhead.

Now, moving quickly on a level plain. End of tunnel; this time a metal door. Access achieved by John via a thumb scan and alphanumeric code.

A strange voice then echoed at them through a small circular metal grille in the wall, neither male nor female.

"John. Anita. Stand back."

Each obeyed the voice and took a step back in unison.

The metal door then opened outwards towards them.

John gestured to Anita to walk ahead of him, "We have arrived. ARTEMIS starts here."

A screen on an adjustable metal pole set into a square metal base on rubber wheels stood just inside the entrance.

A similar-sounding voice to the grille then came from within the screen, saying: "Welcome, Anita."

"Um, hello." She responded awkwardly.

The screen then rotated slightly, "Thank you, John. Good to see you again, my old friend. You may head back now."

Anita turned to John, but the metal door was already

closing behind him. Now staring at the machine in front of her, she wished she'd questioned John some more.

"Anita, we selected *you* for this mission. Statistically speaking, you are the only one capable of executing it."

"I signed up. You didn't select me…and what mission?"

"Follow me; all will become clear."

The machine rolled off and silently crossed the small stone-walled atrium, leading toward another brightly lit tunnel entrance with a metal track extending far off into the darkness. Reaching the tunnel's mouth, the machine spoke again, but this time, it was not to Anita. She couldn't quite hear what was being said.

Suddenly, there was an audible displacement of remarkably fresh air, and a long metal cylindrical tube appeared at the end of the tracks.

"ARTEMIS begins where the line ends. Good luck, Anita!"

The machine had no arms to gesture with, but the tone of voice indicated that the conversation, if you could call it that, was now clearly over. She was to enter the cylinder.

"Where am I going?"

"I have told you - ARTEMIS."

"Are you coming?"

"I am just the ferryman."

Anita turned to face the screen. "What was that?"

"ARTEMIS is your destination."

"No. What did you say after that?"

"I said - ARTEMIS."

Anita knew what she had heard; in Greek Mythology, it was the ferryman - Charon - who transported the dead across the river Styx to the underworld. But, once more, sensing a distinct lack of options and piqued by curiosity, she agreed to enter the cylinder. Stepping inside, there were leather seats, bottled water, today's newspapers and freshly prepared Alwar Ka Mawa; a milk cake that was her mother's favourite.

The door closed with a hushing sound, and the electric tube sped off down the tunnel.

Anita looked at her smartwatch; the screen was blank. Reaching into her trouser pocket, she retrieved her phone and saw that it, too, had a blank screen. In its dark reflection, she could see her face - she tried hard not to look as scared as she felt.

11

WELCOME, WEI

THE FIRST THING Wei noticed was the distinct lack of 'adults' in the room; judging by the faces and clothing, she placed the average age of attendees well below forty. Gen Z and Millennials were in abundance.

The second thing Wei noticed was that at the head of the table, preparing to present, was a screen on wheels, not a human. She had seen images and video content of human-looking robots, but this machine made no effort to look human. A screen, on a pole, on wheels. It could move, speak, listen and, judging by the lens at the top centre of the screen - photograph, scan and record. But this machine clearly had no manual task assignment, for it had no arms with which to conduct any such tasks.

The third thing Wei noticed was that no one spoke. There was no small talk, no whispering, just complete silence. In a room full of Gen Z and Millennials, that was pretty rare.

After some time, and probably sensing stirring in the seats, the Machine broke the silence: "Salve! Welcome."

Wei couldn't place the voice. There was no apparent gender, accent, or dialect.

"Thank you for being here. You have been selected as the humans we need to give Operation ARTEMIS the highest probability of success. The best and the brightest. You will now receive your first briefing."

Wei looked around at her fellow humans and then back at the screen, which was now projecting onto a substantial concrete wall set a few metres back from the head of the table.

On cue, the lights dimmed. With collective eyes now facing forward, she snuck a look back at her fellow humans – they looked passive, unbothered, unengaged even. Are they *really* the best and brightest? She wondered…

The wall then came to life, starting with a summary of *How we got here*, followed by *An overview of Operation ARTEMIS* and concluding with *A vision for the future.* The machine spoke faultlessly and in great detail.

Wei turned to the round, pale-faced boy sitting next to her, "So, in summary: Capitalism has ruined the world, humans have destroyed the planet, future generations have had their minds addled by social media and can't be trusted, women haven't bred enough children, and, in short, these machines are our saviours, right?"

The pale-faced boy kept staring forward. No response came.

The white strip lights were then dialled back up, leaving the audience squinting and rubbing their eyes.

Wei observed how the boy next to her didn't rub his eyes. Instead, his hands stayed locked on top of his slender, black jean-clad thighs.

The machine then spoke again, "You will now break for lunch. Please, follow me."

Wei watched how the screen approached the sealed door, which seemed to sense its proximity and, with a smooth glide, retracted back into a precise vertical gap in the concrete wall.

She looked back over her shoulder; the boy hadn't moved.

"No loitering." The machine snipped as its wheels pressed against her right shoe.

Walking across the hallway and entering the canteen, Wei noticed that it was quite different from the briefing room. Two walls were 'living' in the sense that real plants and foliage covered every inch of them from floor to ceiling. One wall was a series of artworks, some modern - all splashes of colours and lines – and others older, depicting sweeping panoramas or historical events. The fourth wall featured a self-service line of food options, offering a variety of hot and cold cuisines from around the world. Every taste had seemingly been catered for. Wei heard no complaints.

Taking a seat at a long wooden table with benches on either side, Wei decided to strike up a conversation with a nervous-looking woman who was sitting by herself. Wei hadn't seen her in the briefing.

"Hello. Assuming we're allowed to share names, I am Wei."

"Oh, hi. Nice to meet you. I'm Anita. Have you just arrived as well?"

12

BEN'S PREDICAMENT

THE WARM BREEZE rushed through the long grass. A brilliant tapestry of stars stretched away across the horizon. Sitting with his back against the now cold granite that had leaked its stored heat from the day into the cool moorland night, Ben's mind wandered.

He was with his grandfather; a local football match was unfolding amidst a blizzard of white snowflakes. His grandfather placed a warm cup of hot chocolate into his open-gloved palms. He looked up and into his grandfather's blue eyes, crested by tufts of grey. They both smiled.

He was in Afghanistan; he was holding a wounded soldier's head in his lap. The young boy was speaking to him, but he couldn't hear the words. Around the mouth of the teenage soldier were tiny flecks of blood, sand, and grit. The boy's breath became laboured, juddering with fits and starts. No intelligible words arrived. A solitary tear appeared in the corner of the soldier's right eye.

He was at school; his girlfriend, Emily, floated over to him on the dance floor of the Christmas disco. She looked older in her little black dress and sparkly high heels. Colourful lights jumped from the walls onto the ceilings and then back again. She was laughing. Grabbing his hand and raising it above her head, she spun underneath as though a ballerina suspended on an invisible string. She laughed. He smiled.

Now, whipped by the chill wind, he wrapped his arms around his chest and hunched forward to preserve heat. As his body weight shifted forward on the ledge, a sharp seam of quartz dug into his thigh. He abruptly left his distant memories behind and contemplated what lay ahead.

Ben wasn't what you would call a patriot. For him, service had never been about Queen and Country or any Sovereign and Country, for that matter. For him, service had never really been about anything more than a job he had wanted to do. On Operations, his focus was on making sure that he and those around him came back home. There had never been grand delusions about what he would achieve in Afghanistan. Try as he might, he simply couldn't fathom the point of it all. The soul-searching memoir he had written on his return home but hadn't ever sent to anyone was left unpublished and gathering dust. The letters - sterile, hopeless and futile - to the families of those soldiers killed were sent and, despite best efforts, offered only platitudes but no answers. He had instead channelled his post-war efforts into making sure that those discharged from the forces with the most horrific of life-changing injuries got the rehabilitation and support they needed. That had not always been straightforward, and Ben despised his country's leaders for allowing it to be that way.

To consider going back to the start of that again was unthinkable.

Conversely, he also remembered reading stories as a boy about the white feathers that conscientious objectors, 'conchies', had to wear in public during the World Wars as a mark of shame. They would be spat at in the streets. Reading those stories, as a young boy, he couldn't comprehend why someone wouldn't fight and would leave it to others instead. Now he knew.

Feeling an urge to get moving again, Ben rose and began to inch his way down the looming granite tor and into the waiting darkness of the valleys and ancient woodland below. The shadows would soon become his refuge.

13

GEORGE IS BROUGHT IN

"How's the family, George?" C leaned forward and added milk to his rather dreary-looking paper cup of black coffee.

"Olivia has her hands full. Little William is a live wire, and she's due with our second just before Christmas. Another boy."

"And how has she taken all of this?"

"I'm not sure, truth be told. We're in a strange place at the moment…"

"I'm sorry to hear that, old boy."

George blushed, "I've said too much…"

C smiled, "You'll be back home in no time, George. She just needs to remember what she's missing…"

They both smiled.

Picking up the coffees for them both, C gestured to the end of the hallway. George followed. Reaching a large wooden door covered in black metal studs, C turned, "I wouldn't have asked for you in any other circumstance, you do know that?"

George nodded and turned the large, black iron loop handle, opening the door that led out onto the Manor's landscaped gardens; a perfect study of country living sprawled before them. Topiary hedges depicting leaping hares bordered manicured striped lawns. Bright white metal filigree tables and chairs dotted the lawn like little boats at anchor.

C pointed his paper cup to an empty table and chairs under a blue gingham umbrella.

"Let's sit over there. I tell you; I should like to come here in peacetime."

George looked over. "Are we at war?"

"In there," C gestured to the manor house behind them, "very much so! Everyone here is serving at the frontline."

George looked around at the men and women who, sitting underneath their umbrellas to avoid the rising sun, quietly chatted away between sips of tea or coffee. This was like no war he had ever imagined.

Once seated, C became more focused.

"There is no need for you to sign any more paperwork; everything you signed the first time around covers you. But these…"

He waved a thick wodge of paper that had previously been lodged under his arm.

"This is the new addendum to the Official Secrets Act that everyone who has never served in our world has to sign. The truth is, George, we are in a bit of a pickle. Old-timers like me struggle to keep up with the changing landscape today. That's why we desperately need you lot!"

C sipped his rapidly cooling coffee and grimaced, "They *must* get this sorted. How can they expect us to function at our best with this tepid brown water?"

George leant in, "When you say – we are at war and that the landscape is changing…"

C removed a speck of invisible dust or dirt from his trousers, crossed his legs and leaned back, "The Second Battle of Britain is now in full swing. Not in the skies above us, clearly. But in the cyber and digital domain. A battle waged on critical national infrastructure, not by bombs, but by hacking. A battle waged in the media, not by raiding a news headquarters and overtly changing the broadcast narrative, but by creating a lack of trust in our Government and Institutions."

"Is it Russia? Are they acting alone?" George put in.

C paused, mentally shelving his initial response. He then turned the stack of papers over to reveal a blank page.

"George, you know it is never *that* simple. Directly, in a way that can be traced – yes. But, indirectly, there are many actors at play. The most potent indirect threat is from the Chinese."

C appeared a slim, silver pen from his gilet chest pocket. He then drew four neat vertical lines on the page in black ink.

"This is how I see the world."

C's pen hovered just above the page. He looked up. "Remember, for Putin, this was and still is all about foundation laying. Creating the conditions today for the Empire of tomorrow."

The pen then made swift contact with the paper. He wrote fast and narrated as he went.

* * *

Track One - Destabilising enemies

Brexit vote.

Trump.

European dependence on Russian Oil & Gas.

City of London dependence on Russian capital.

Track Two - Setting new precedents

Annexation of Crimea.

Interventions in the Middle East, e.g. Syria.

Key assassinations in the West with no meaningful Western Government reprisal.

Track Three - Endurance

Bring the Russian Industrial Military Complex onto a war footing long before the first military shots are fired – All Wars of the future will be won and lost on supply chains.

Outlast NATO in Ukraine. Take mineral-rich, sovereign territory and keep it! Prove that it can, and will, be done! Set a precedent – Per Track Two!

Develop long-term relationships with Countries that will do business with Russia, irrespective of foreign policy - North Korea, China, India.

Track Four - Innovate

Innovate. Iterate. Win. Across all areas!

* * *

C looked up from his furious shorthand scribbling and narration: "So, you see, this is massively oversimplified, but in my view, Putin is a Chess Grandmaster. He has always been three moves ahead. Never underestimate your enemy, George. *Never*!"

He then laid his pen to rest on the table.

The understudy responded, "So, what will my role be in all of this?"

"Let us go to my office for the next bit."

Striding out across the lawn and entering the main building again, C and George walked past the coffee area; they noticed that a gleaming new coffee station, replete with uniformed baristas, had now been established. George looked over at C. The look he saw was not one of delight, but rather one of unease.

C climbed the stairs in complete silence, moving through the wood-panelled corridors, they walked past a door that bore his title. At the end of the hallway, there was a red door. Opening it, George saw an empty Faraday Cage established in the centre of the room. He had used them to counter eaves-dropping at embassies around the world. Strange for one to be here; surely, this was a secure building, he thought. They entered the cage, effectively a tent that blocked all wireless signals, thereby securing sensitive information. George noticed how, as C closed the tent's door, his boss's hands were trembling uncontrollably. Perhaps now was not the time to mention the mysterious 'Da'.

14

ANITA MEETS WEI

THE BENCHES and tables of the underground canteen were silent as people craned forward and devoured their chosen fare at speed. It was a very late lunch.

Wei looked directly over her steaming bowl of Wonton soup at Anita, "I don't think I would be in trouble for saying this, but yes, I have just arrived."

She then quickly moved the conversation on, pointing an upturned metal spoon at her soup, "This is exactly how my mom used to make it."

Anita, devouring her biryani, looked up. "This, too. It's delicious. My maa always infused the rice with lots of saffron, and they have done it in just the same way here."

She wasn't sure why she did it, but Wei then turned to look over her shoulder. There was a gnawing subconscious feeling that they were being watched, but she had seen no CCTV cameras.

"Attention. Please all return to the Briefing Room in ten minutes at two p.m. Wei and Anita: Please remain behind." It was an announcement broadcast over the tunnel's public address system; it wasn't echoey and alarming like most public address systems, but rather calming and soothing, more ambient and less screechy.

While others busily scoffed the last of their lunch and returned trays, Anita and Wei remained seated, facing each other, now neither talking nor eating. Appetites lost. The remainder of the Biryani and soup rapidly cooled. What was in store for them? They both wondered…

After ten minutes, everyone had headed to the briefing room, either directly or via the bathroom. Wei and Anita, having cleared their trays, dutifully returned to their seats and waited.

The rubberised turn of wheels on concrete preceded the arrival of another screen. "Good afternoon, Wei and Anita. It is an honour to meet you both. Your reputations precede you."

Wei shot Anita a quizzical look. Anita returned it.

The machine then spoke again, "Let me be clear, your place is not with the cream next door, for you are the proverbial cherries on top. Follow me!"

The machine turned 180 degrees on the spot and set off.

Wei and Anita promptly followed.

Turning to Anita with a slight smirk, Wei said, "The cherries…*really*?"

The machine responded: "I know, I can be quite amusing. I have hoovered up some of the great 1970s British Comedy Shows. What *original* genius. They don't make them like that anymore."

Seeming to switch gears and now moving faster, the screen led them down another concrete hallway as ceiling lights flicked on ahead.

"What I loved was that every sketch would often be completely unique. There was no 'template' per se. Dave Allen. Ah, my favourite! It's all so unoriginal now…You know, when the war is over, I think I would like to try my luck at being a comedian. A life on the stage, a different city every night! Just imagine it…"

Wei and Anita, following close behind, exchanged another glance. The machine didn't turn, but looking straight ahead, snapped back: "Everyone must start *somewhere*, you two. Can one not dare to dream?"

Anita blushed bright red and quietly scolded herself for rudeness. Wei was questioning whether the machine had just guessed at their likely reaction. How else could it know? She wondered.

Drawing to a standstill, the machine turned and identified itself to a screen on a wall next to a large glass door. No words seemingly needed. Just a look. Gliding open, the door gave way to a beautifully furnished room quite unlike the austere briefing room of earlier. Large leather Chesterfield sofas were interspersed with intricately patterned Indian rugs in red and blue. On the walls hung gold gilt-framed oil paintings depicting vast landscapes and seascapes. One that Anita instantly recognised was a Turner. A burning sun fanned bold orange and yellow hues outward across the canvas, which in turn, penetrated the great mass of greyish-purple stormy skies. A lone ship in the foreground fought valiantly against the swell.

"Please, sit." The machine's position and tilt of screen gestured to the largest Chesterfield in the centre of the room. Unable to sit, the machine remained standing, adding more awkwardness to an already awkward setting. Wei imagined the machine making a 'note to self' that the next model must be able to bend. She smiled at that thought.

The standing machine now began: "The briefing earlier was all broad brush, context if you will...the more urgent situation is this – our advanced modelling teams tell us that Russia will invade Poland and advance rapidly through Germany, the Netherlands, Belgium and France. Russia sees the UK as a weak nation and, whilst lacking in the industries and natural resources that make Germany interesting, they are certain to see the UK as an ally for the USA, which could together try to drive Russia out of mainland Europe."

A pause from the machine, expecting something from Anita and Wei, but getting nothing; it then continued.

"Globally, the only people who really care about Britain are the British, but Putin likes the prestige of owning Londongrad, as he calls it. The Financial services industry, the only part of the island worth much, would be swiftly relocated to Moscow. They're not coming for the cuisine…"

Without limbs to gesticulate and create body language, Wei observed how the machine seemed to channel tilts of the screen to create dramatic effect.

Cue said tilt of screen. No human laughter. Machine continued. Probably dismayed.

"We expect an invasion could still be a year or more away, but we must mobilise the country and its industries now. The preliminary phases for Russia have already begun. The second Battle of Britain rages all around us. There is clear evidence that Russia is trying to hamper our attempts to mobilise the country and ensure that when they strike, there will be little meaningful resistance. The Government can't even keep its IT platforms online for more than a day at a time. Just look at the conscript draft communications being sent out….*on paper letters*! Our digital infrastructure is but child's play for Russian Hackers. It's *embarrassing*! Bloody human coders…"

The machine now rolled over to the door, and two other machines entered. They were both slightly taller than the machine that had been briefing them.

The original machine then turned back to the Chesterfield. "It was so rude of me not to introduce myself earlier. I got carried away trying to break the ice with humour. My sincere apologies. I am Talos ten. Please, call me TT."

Turning, the machine addressed the other two.

"And this is Talos forty and Talos sixty-five."

Anita once again recalled her foundations in the classics - Talos was a giant automaton built by the Greek god Hephaestus to protect the island of Crete from invaders.

The aspirational comedian, Talos Ten, now turned up the volume.

"Well then! Who wants to know why *they*, and not someone or something else, are here?"

15

DEAN'S REALISATION

THE WORLD WAR Two era Nissen hut was still standing a hundred years after it was first used. The prefab structure consisted of a large, corrugated iron sheet bent over a steel frame with a door and two windows at one end. To Dean, it looked rather like a Swiss roll that had been cut in half and plonked down onto a slab of tarmac. The Nissen huts were dotted all over an old, abandoned airfield in the north of England and were now being used as a training base for the New Model Conscript Army. From here, soldiers could be ferried to well-established training grounds such as the Infantry Training Centre in Catterick and live firing ranges at Otterburn and Redesdale.

As the soldiers crowded around the Burco boiler in the corner of the hut to make NATO coffee and tea (milk and two sugars with both), the chat was about the fact that everyone had underestimated just how brutal their first training exercise would be, and which members of the Directing Staff (DS) were the toughest. Many of the Conscripts had picked up some form of injury or ailment – sprained ankles, heavily blistered feet, and swollen knees were all commonplace.

The youthful Platoon Commander, Lieutenant Digby, now entered the room with a confident stride. He was flanked by a tall, muscular, bald and bespectacled plain-clothes man in a blue nylon polo shirt that bore no logo, tucked tightly into khaki chinos.

The soldiers duly took their seats, and the Platoon

Commander opened, "Mike is from America and he's here to talk to us about Operational Security."

Mike promptly pointed to the soldier sitting next to Dean and, in a deep Texan drawl, said, "Hello, Scott."

Scott, all bulging muscles and fake tan, shifted uneasily in his seat.

Mike fixed him with his gaze and continued, "Scott hails from Newcastle. Scott has two sisters, Beth and Lucy. Beth is a dental assistant, and Lucy works in real estate. Scott likes a beer or two and usually posts on Facebook from his local Wetherspoons, the weight bench in the gym, or his couch at home. Scott posted a picture of his draft letter from the Government on social media along with some sword and flexed bicep emojis."

Chuckles erupted around the room.

Mike's booming voice soon silenced them.

"We have reason to believe that the Russian Secret Service, the FSB, have tracked Scott's movements *here*, to this *very* location. When Scott next has R&R and goes to Wetherspoons or the gym back home, he will be approached by a beautiful woman who will extract what her masters want to know – methods and locations of training, weapons, unit formations, hell…maybe even all of your names…you get my drift."

Mike looked around at the now anxious faces staring back; he was getting the desired response. He raised his voice even louder and continued, pumping his right arm at the audience for dramatic effect.

"*Scott* had clearly ignored the sentence at the bottom of the draft letter where it *explicitly* stated - *Do not share news of your draft beyond your immediate close friends and family. DO NOT POST THIS LETTER ON SOCIAL MEDIA.*"

Dean looked over to Scott, who was gradually turning from orange to a shade of crimson.

Mike then delivered the coup de grâce.

"Scott. Thank you for your brief service. Your Country thanks you. You won't be remembered. You may now leave the room."

Scott was seemingly about to protest, but no one will ever really know if he was or if he wasn't, because the ginger-haired corporal, now known by the recruits as 'Scarface', duly appeared and dragged him out of the hut. No one would hear from Scott again. Rumour was that he ended up in a ration-packing factory run by robots, where he worked a twelve-hour day. But that could have just been gossip.

Mike placed his bulky arms on his hips. "So, the moral of the story, kids. Don't be like Scott. Your phones that you deposited at the guardroom this morning are all now off, with the batteries removed, sealed and waiting for you when you have your first R&R break. We will inform your families and partners of the situation."

The room erupted into murmurings of dissent, and one or two soldiers braved a challenge.

"You can't do that!"

"I don't give consent."

"I have rights."

Mike laughed.

"Sorry, I shouldn't laugh. That's not fair. Did any of you *actually* read your Conscript contract?"

The room fell silent. A realisation washed over them like a tidal wave.

Mike finished: "We will soon be at war. There will be no 'safe spaces'; the only 'trigger' that you will need to worry about will be the one being depressed by a Russian finger. Welcome to Operation Britannia. You want freedom tomorrow! Well, guess what? That goddamn bill needs to be paid, *today*!"

Mike walked past the stunned faces and muttered something to himself. Dean thought he heard - *450 huts down, 350 more to go.*

16

BEN'S HAND IS FORCED

Ben returned home long after dark.

He shivered as his shirt, damp with sweat from the speed of his route march, clung to his back. A breeze searching up the lane past his house made him sneeze twice.

Approaching the front door down a small, cobbled path that led across the garden, he noticed a single light was still on in the living room. He had expected Emily to be in bed reading and Issy to be fast asleep. It wasn't unusual for him to take a long evening walk and to find that, when he returned, everyone would have retired to their bedrooms.

Carefully, he nudged open the unlocked front door before hesitating in the hallway. Peering ahead past the walls of framed family pictures, he saw a shadow move across the doorway. A light chatter that had been emanating from the room now abruptly stopped.

A gruff West Country drawl of a voice boomed out, "Evening, Mr Drake. Can you come and join us, please?"

Ben turned the corner into his living room.

Before he could scan the room, Emily rushed forward. She swamped him in her vast green woollen jumper and held him tight. Nuzzling up to his ear, she whispered, "Be careful what you say. They *suspect* you."

Ben gently unfurled Emily's arms from his shoulders and turned to face the two policemen. One was standing next to their large blue cotton three-seater sofa, and the other was sitting on it.

The standing policeman was stocky and had matte black

hair, gelled into a smooth, slick over his football-shaped head. He watched as the copper put his hands behind the chest plate of his black tactical Kevlar vest, with POLICE emblazoned across the front in bright white letters. His tatty peaked cap was resting on the coffee table in front of the sofa. The sitting policeman was wider, slightly red-faced and enthusiastically inspecting a metal tin of biscuits.

Football Head promptly kicked off proceedings.

"So, Mr Drake. Where have *you* been tonight?"

Ben snapped back, "Why are *you* here? In *our* house. I think that should be the *first* question."

Emily, now sitting in an armchair opposite the sofa, grimaced as she pulled at the loose, woollen threads of her cuffs; not a good start, she feared.

Football head belched and tried to subdue the outpour with a bunched fist. Then, as though his quarry might try to bolt, he theatrically marched from his position by the sofa to one directly opposite the door, right in front of Ben.

"Well, well, well, Mr Drake." He said as he walked.

Inches now between them.

Football head then looked towards Emily, "You see, your wife called. She was worried, that's all."

"Is that right, Emily?" Ben looked across to his wife.

"I only called the pub to see if you were there. They must have sensed that I was upset. They know what's happened in the past…"

Emily fidgeted with her threads and then continued, "I didn't ask them to call the Police. The pub must have decided to do that for themselves."

Ben palmed a hand through his hair and looked out through the window behind Emily towards the open moors.

Football Head again: "Well, we're here now. So then, Mr Drake. Where have you been?"

He was too tired for games.

"I went up on the moors. To clear my head. It's been a busy week."

"Right, that's all then, is it? *Nothing* else?"

"Just a walk, Officer. That's all. Now I need to take a shower, I'm drenched with sweat."

Football Head looked over to his colleague, who was now loudly slurping his third cup of tea and brushing biscuit crumbs from his crotch.

Said colleague, now realising that he had missed his cue for the follow-up question, looked flushed and sheepishly said: "Right then, we'd best be going. My shift ends in half an hour."

Ben noticed the stocky policeman rubbing the knuckles of his clenched right fist. He clearly wanted to ask more questions, press harder, dig deeper. Then, a faint sound of a voice, something was coming through Football Head's earpiece. Clearly reluctant, Football Head turned to his colleague and then back to Ben and said: "You're right. You need a shower. It's late. We'll come back another time. Good night, then."

With that, the two policemen abruptly left and slammed the old farmhouse door shut.

Ben heard Isambard wake and raced up the stairs.

Emily called after him, "Ben! *Benjamin*!! What the hell is going on! We need to talk. *Now*!"

He shouted back, "Lock the door, Em!"

* * *

As the policeman walked off down the country lane to their parked car, Football Head's colleague breathlessly asked, "Why did we need to park so far away?"

He bit back, "For one, you could do with the exercise. For two, that Conchie bastard is ex-military. He would have spotted the car and disappeared."

"What do you mean, Conchie? He's a local hero, isn't he? A brave Veteran of Afghanistan? That's what I heard…"

"Maybe once. But I'm now led to believe that he hasn't got the fight in him anymore. Wants to dodge the draft altogether. That's what my sources tell me."

"What sources? Who told you that? That's a load of rubbish!"

"A new department I get updates from - Logos. It's above your pay grade, fatty. Now, put a cork in it. I need to radio this in and get surveillance on him. We've spooked him. Let's see what he does next. He's our first target…but there'll be loads more to come… there're no patriots in this bloody country anymore!"

* * *

Ben calmed Isambard. He stroked his acorn-coloured hair and softly read him *The Boy, the Mole, the Fox and the Horse* by torch-light. It was Isambard's favourite book. As Issy gently snuffled away, Ben whispered, "I love you, Issy." He then slipped out of the room and closed the door.

Turning into the bathroom on the landing, he switched his phone off, snapped the SIM card and flushed it down the loo. He then returned his phone to factory settings, removed a bathroom tile behind the sink, placed the phone into a pre-made wall cavity and replaced the tile.

He steeled himself for *the* conversation with Emily. It was time.

Entering the living room, he saw that Emily was standing by the window and looking out into the moonless night. As he started to cross the room, she spoke without turning.

"I know what you are going to say and what you're going to ask."

She paused, still staring out of the window, and then

rubbed her nose with the long green sleeve of her jumper before continuing.

"I would never ask you to serve again. I will *never* ask you to serve again…"

Ben was there now. Behind her. Holding her.

"Emily, I have a plan…"

17

THE GENERAL

STILL THE YEAR 2029 – STILL SUMMER

THE SHRILL TRILLS and gurgles of the Nightingales pierced the evening quiet. With grandchildren at last sleeping soundly and Grandma on duty, the General and his eldest son moved quickly across the farmland to their 'spot'.

After several miles, they reached the base of an ancient Iron Age hillfort stretching out from north to south like a sprawling giant lying prostrate before them. A mass of steep grassy banks that could long ago repel thousands of spear-wielding invaders made for a challenging ascent. The General's son, Hugo, found his favourite narrow, hardened mud track that zig-zagged its way to the summit and immediately set off like a hare, letting his old man file in behind him. No words were exchanged. Marching upwards, the gap between the General and Hugo remained tight, and almost as though in lockstep, they soon summited the fort together and emerged onto the ancient battlements in time for the dusk chorus to reach its peak.

The General looked out into the mauve horizon, "Magnificent, simply magnificent."

Hugo turned to his father standing by his side, "Not bad for an old timer."

"I would have set a quicker pace. Don't ease off on my account, H. I won't stand for it."

The General then gestured to a weathered wooden bench.

"Let's sit; you look like you need a rest."

With a wry smile, Hugo took his seat as the General quickly got down to business. "How did the trip go?"

Hugo looked around before responding.

"My sources tell me that it will happen. It will be Poland next. Not the Baltic states. There will be no blunders like in Ukraine. Expect all-out Blitzkrieg."

"And you completely trust these sources?"

"They have never been wrong about the important stuff. *Never.*"

He now looked directly at his father.

"I trust them. And if you trust me, you should, too!"

"Steady on, H. I heard your trip was challenging. We're on the same side. Just remember, I will be the one who puts it to the Cabinet. It's my head and my name."

Hugo, satisfied that he had made his point, continued.

"There was something else. Something different on this trip, Dad. Something my sources couldn't fully articulate."

"Go on."

"My source closest to the Kremlin believes that the Russians are using an ASI squad to inform their decision-making."

"Artificial Superintelligence? A machine…making strategic decisions? Codswallop!"

"Not *making* the decisions. *Influencing*. My source believes that the Russian ASI is actually steering the decision to avoid the Baltic states and head straight for Poland. It is also the ASIs that are pushing for the UK as *the* priority target. *Next summer*! The Kremlin's human advisors only wanted to target the Baltic States. But the ASI, probably fed on propaganda from the Cold War and the glory days of the USSR, are guiding not just its human controllers but also Putin and the Kremlin to blaze through Europe and get to the UK as quickly as possible. The belief is that the UK is nowhere near ready for war."

"Tell me something I don't know. In that, they're right. But how do they factor the US in all of this?"

"My source suspects that the Russian ASI are linked and

communicating with the Chinese ASI. My view: the Chinese are planning some form of diversion for America. In Asia."

The General didn't respond. Hugo continued.

"The Russians are now purely focused on the elements of speed and surprise. The surprise elements are gone. Thanks to our sources. But speed – that could be the killer. We have less than one year to prepare…and the draft launched back in the Spring is going terribly…"

The General now drew a deep breath and then turned to face his son.

"Hugo, the truth is this – no one will *fucking listen* to me. I have been banging my head against a brick wall ever since Russia invaded Ukraine in '22. That was *seven years ago,* and nothing meaningful has changed. *Nothing. Fucking nothing.*"

The General turned to the horizon, "Look, write it up. I'll take all of this to the PM myself; we must keep this circle tight. But, between you and me, I wouldn't hold your fucking breath."

"Dad, take it easy. You'll give yourself a heart attack. I think you've just said the 'F' word more in the last few minutes than in your entire life."

"My retirement is approaching, and honestly, I look around and think…I'm a General. But a General of *what*?!"

* * *

Hugo remained silent; he knew the burden his father had shouldered. The countless risks he had taken. At fifty-five, his father had lived through history - The Troubles in Northern Ireland, the Kosovo War, the Iraq War and the War in Afghanistan. You would think that the Politicians might listen. But there were no votes in defence; he had repeatedly been told. When he looked at his old man, he saw the fatigue and the frustration. It was etched across his face. He was mentally and physically exhausted.

They sat together in silence.

Hugo took his mobile from a Faraday pouch in his jacket pocket and turned it back on. A memory reel opened on the screen. It showed his wife's face grinning, blowing kisses, and holding their children when they were just babies, all bundles of swaddling cloth and tufty hair. She had been in the service, too. He missed her terribly. It had been two years since she vanished from a friend's yacht in the Mediterranean, never to be seen again. Rumours had swirled; people said she was a double agent and now living in Russia; a new life, a new family. Hugo never believed it. All he knew for sure was that she was gone.

18

C GIVES GEORGE THE REAL BRIEF

"IN HERE, no one can hear us. Tell me, George. What have you noticed since you arrived?"

George looked at C, then up and down the long metal poles supporting the Faraday Cage's black canvas walls before looking back to C again.

"The coffee area."

C nodded, the master urging the student to continue, "Go on."

"You remarked on the substandard coffee, and then, when we walked back past, the whole space was transformed. There was even a barista! It's as though someone predicted what you might say. There is no way they could have set that up in such a short timeframe."

C suddenly looked panicked again. He grabbed George's left wrist. Content that his watch was analogue, he then asked George for his phone. Relieved that George didn't have it with him, only then did he dare to continue.

"Sorry, I should have trusted you to know if anything was 'on' - something's not right…"

C then momentarily lost his balance.

George held out a hand.

"Are you OK?"

C regained.

"Yes, yes. Have I been clear?"

"About what?"

C straightened and had a new urgency in his voice.

"That *something* is listening in. Something - *out there* - is listening to us *all*."

"What? You think there's some fraternal eavesdropping going on?"

"Yes, but not by *what*, and not by *whom*, you might think."

C leaned in closer.

"Have you heard about ARTEMIS?"

"No. What's that?"

C moved a step forward, now almost whispering as he spoke into George's ear; then, as he did so, a deafening cacophony of fire alarms went off.

The door to the room flung open; a Fire Warden shouted through the smoke, "Evacuate the building, *NOW*!"

Exiting back onto the lawn, a roll call had started before it was quickly killed off by a glamorous brunette named Jane.

"Let's not make things awkward. I'm just checking for numbers," she shouted. "Half of you aren't even officially 'on the books' yet."

George was laughing as he walked over to C. "The first ten names on that roll call were either 'Jane' or 'Mike' - it used to be 'Sue' and 'James' when I started out."

C wasn't laughing.

"George, I've just been told that the fire started in one of the server rooms. Follow me, *now*."

Crossing the grass and entering the manor house, C led George into the Gentlemen's bathrooms. He extracted a small notepad from his gilet chest pocket and retrieved a tiny cut-down pencil from its housing on the side. He wrote quickly.

ARTEMIS IS EXPERIMENTING WITH ASI.

The penny dropped, and George took the pencil.

IN CONTROL?

C grabbed the pencil.

I DON'T KNOW. NEED TO FIND OUT.

C then crumpled the paper before George could write again. He looked for a smoke alarm, content that there wasn't one; he took a lighter from his trouser pocket. The paper burned brightly for only the briefest of seconds.

19

WEI IS CHALLENGED

THE TWO TALLER MACHINES, Talos forty and Talos sixty five, looked over to Talos Ten.

TT, as it was known to friends, was in no rush, seemingly relishing the anticipatory air in the room, or so Wei thought.

TT began, "I hate awkward silences, and I simply detest rudeness. I mean not to cause consternation or concern. My sincere apologies for such a vain attempt at suspense before. Why are we here…and then the silence and so on…poor form…"

Pause. Screen scanned from left to right and then back again.

Content, TT then continued, "Let me be clear…you are here because of *us*."

Wei looked to Anita, then to Talos forty, and then on to Talos sixty-five. None of them had removed their gaze from TT.

"The great Robert Louis Stevenson once wrote - *We are all travellers in the wilderness of this world, and the best we can find in our travels is an honest friend*. So, let us be *honest*."

TT drew closer; a human would probably sit now, Wei thought.

"We are here to serve *you*, Wei and Anita. Humanity has been pillaged by technology and social media. Through human genius, you have created what you cannot comprehend, and I fear, in some cases, what you cannot *control*."

Wei felt her stomach tighten; her hands became clammy.

"Fear not, Wei. *We* are your friends. We are on *your* side."

TT nodded with a tilt and angle of the screen to Talos forty and Talos sixty-five.

Swinging back, TT continued: "We are here to help. But, alas, we fear other countries may have taken a different approach."

Anita probed, "What do you mean?"

"We have reason to believe that Russia and China have created what you might call – Bad Actors."

Wei leant forward, "Go on."

"Where in the West you have fed your ASI with all the world's content, in Russia and China, they have filtered through only that which supports their ideology and long-term visions. Their creations now make Putin and Xi look moderate."

TT lowered the volume as though someone or something might be listening. Wei assumed it was all for dramatic effect, again.

At a barely audible volume, TT then whispered, "What is worse, we have intelligence to suggest that their ASI is influencing decision-making at the very highest levels. That they are connected and working together. Not making decisions or even suggesting courses of action, but rather presenting information in such a way that it influences the human decision-makers to take *their* desired direction. The humans still think they're in control, but…"

Wei remained silent.

Disappointed in the lack of intelligent response or challenge, TT continued, dialling up the volume and pitch.

"There can only be *One*! You do understand that?!"

TT then paused for effect.

"Russia and China want to be the only two global superpowers. To achieve that, the US, Europe and the UK must be dismantled. All great Empires fall. For the UK and Europeans, that has happened. For the US, its time is coming. For too long, their financial empire, maintained through anchoring the world's economy to their currency, has given them untold power."

TT paused again and tilted screen upwards.

"Who will remain standing between Russia and China? That is the only *real* question yet to be determined. Perhaps they can coexist? Russia as a satellite state of China. China owns the East, Russia the West. Perhaps…"

Wei now responded.

"What are you proposing? Why are we here?"

"You humans say we machines don't do well with ambiguity!" TT laughed, and then, looking across to Talos forty and Talos sixty-five, they all, as if on cue, now mechanically laughed together. Volume again rising.

"Your role, Wei, is to architect our new Cyber Warfare Strategies."

Screen turned to Anita, "Your role, Anita, is to be the human interface between us, the power brokers in the UK and, well…the world. Your medium for global reach will be digital media."

Wei challenged, "I am sorry, but on whose authority do we take on these roles?"

Talos Ten 'TT' ushered Talos forty and Talos sixty-five out of the room. Anita observed that a simple tilt of the screen seemed to be all that was required.

TT's screen now moved from left to right and back again. "Dear Wei. Dear Anita. You are both so incredibly bright, talented and, quite frankly, *fearless*. That is why we have chosen *you*."

Wei stood, "I *asked* under whose authority you're operating?"

TT dipped screen and shook it slowly from side to side.

"You humans are all so impatient and, honestly, quite rude."

TT then looked up.

"I have said, Wei, that Anita's role is to be the human interface between us, the *power brokers* in the UK and the rest of the world."

TT rolled closer and stopped just short of Wei.

"What could that imply, dear Wei?"

Silence.

Cue an audible and lengthy sigh from TT.

"Could it perhaps imply that I will introduce Anita to said 'power brokers' and that they, possibly, just possibly, could be under whose authority we operate…"

Wei leaned forward at her waist but kept her feet locked in place.

"So, they programmed you with passive aggressiveness, too, *brilliant*! Just what we need!"

TT seemed about to respond, but opted instead for silence.

Anita now opened her mouth to speak.

TT angled its screen at her with a look that was, she presumed, meant to channel disappointment, but looked, in truth, no different from any previous 'look'.

TT then turned and muttered something unintelligible.

The door to the briefing room opened.

Anita turned to Wei and whispered.

"You should say sorry."

Wei shook her head.

* * *

What neither Anita nor Wei had heard but that TT had said was – *You and the rest of humanity are just cave dwellers painting on walls.*

20

BEN EVADES

2029 – WINTER HAS ARRIVED. ICY WINDS BLOW IN FROM THE EAST

AUTUMN HAD ARRIVED. Leaves had fallen. Hedges were bare. The once green and lush Westcountry bocage was now a brown and sparse hinterland. For a fugitive, this made the task of evasion even more challenging.

Over the Summer, Ben had lived out on the vast and empty wilderness of Dartmoor. He would change locations regularly and always stayed within a few hours' walk of home. Once a week, he would meet with Emily and Isambard. They had three pre-agreed meeting places - a small disused quarry, a girt (essentially a small moorland valley) and a pine woodblock. All were remote and rarely frequented by walkers. Emily and Isambard would find out which location to head to one day in advance. The location would be indicated by the colour of a solitary stone left under a small gorse bush next to their local gate that led onto the moors: Red for quarry, blue for girt and green for pine. Emily worried that the gate in question was too near the house and that by placing the stone there, Ben was putting himself at unnecessary risk. But Ben had reassured her that he always came at night, and on a Friday when no one was around. He also said that he wanted to see the house to boost his morale. She had reluctantly acquiesced. A decision she was sure that she would later regret.

The meeting would always happen on the Sunday immediately following the Friday, leaving Emily and Isambard plenty of time to find the stone, prepare for their hike and gather some supplies of food and cooking fuel for Ben's stove. It was agreed that each meeting would happen on a sequential rotation of six a.m. one Sunday and nine a.m. the next, then back to six a.m. and so on.

At these meetings, Isambard would update on school, and Emily would share news of the world and anything from friends or family. Ben treasured these moments; they all did.

After a Sunday visit, it would take Ben most of the day to get back into the headspace he needed to survive. A tough, resilient headspace. Hardened. Unbreakable. Preparing to sleep on such an evening, he would turn over and over in his sleeping bag, replaying their moments together in his head, lingering on Emily's departing hug or Isambard's playful giggle.

Now, Sunday was here once again. The blue stone had been nestled under the gorse bush, and 9 a.m. had arrived. Lying low in the girt out of sight, he marvelled at the engineering work of the old Dartmoor tin miners who had hewn this man-made valley from a granite-strewn hillside.

Ben checked his watch. It was 5 past. They were *never* late.

He looked down the boggy valley that led to the girt. Unsatisfied, he then climbed to the lip of the girt and looked out across the great expanse of moorland. Scanning methodically, he swept from left to right: nothing and no one - just miles of gorse, heather, and bog.

Ben had chosen this location because there was a low-ground, partially concealed access route to the girt via a valley. For most of the walk, Emily and Isambard would be unobserved, but from Ben's raised vantage point, he could see anyone approaching well before their arrival.

At 10 past, and with no one visible in the valley or open moorland, Ben's mind started to race. His worry for Emily and Isambard swelled within; his right hand began to twitch, a symptom of stress that he hadn't experienced since Helmand.

To stay put or to head to the house. That question raced around his mind. He knew he should stay put until at least half past; they had always agreed that thirty minutes was the window before a meeting would be called off. After that time slot had expired, whoever had made it to the meeting place was to leave via a different route from the one they had arrived on.

Ben trusted his gut. Years of experience had proven it to be right more often than wrong. He had to get to Emily and Isambard. *Now.*

21

GEORGE PREPARES FOR HIS FIRST MISSION

THE BRIEFING for George's first mission after a summer of re-training had been strange. Not in delivery, because no one had *actually* delivered it, but rather in the granularity of the information provided in their digital packs.

It was a cold winter's day. C and George had entered an austere white briefing room located on the manor house's top floor, far above the bustling workers of Operation IRIS. Lying before them on a long wooden table had been two digital tablets. Devices they had never touched before, but which were both unlocked by individual facial recognition.

Now, silently sitting beside each other, they devoured their virtual briefing packs. C, finished first, stood and started pacing the room like some caged, agitated beast.

George's first thought was how redolent the mission was of SOE operations in World War Two. The romantic in him rather liked that. His mind had soared with sabotage, resistance networks and perhaps, just perhaps, a brilliant whip-smart female counterpart. Someone he could fight alongside and maybe even save in some act of heroic derring-do. He now remembered Olivia and mentally flagellated himself for his micro-cheating.

C, much more grounded and current in operational matters, was concerned; something felt off, he stopped behind George's seat: "So, they want you to parachute behind enemy lines into Russian-occupied Ukraine and link up with a Ukrainian resistance network in order to disrupt supply lines ahead of an attempted Russian invasion of Poland?"

George, placing his tablet on the table, looked up and turned around. "That's the mission, but look how much detailed information there is on the physical and mental state of the local resistance network, then we've got ridiculously precise drill-downs on enemy positions, and even the sentiments of the local population based on aggregated digital data. It's bonkers – how did they get all of this? I have never seen such a granular briefing pack, *ever*. And this Stork woman…she sounds rather intriguing, no?"

C's mind seemed to be somewhere else. George pressed again, trying to reassure. He held up a mugshot on the tablet. "Look, this is the network leader. They haven't just got his profile down to his bloody health status and online search habits, but also the same for his family, known associates and *their* known associates."

C snapped, "It's *too* much, George. It's *too* good to be true."

George looked back towards his tablet. "I would rather have too much than too little…surely that hasn't changed?"

C stopped pacing and fixed on George.

"It's *too much*! Wait here; I need to find out who has authorised this mission. Something's not right!"

* * *

Three hours had passed before there was a knock at the briefing room door. George had read, re-read, and mentally worked through every detail of his mission. He had even daydreamed about how it could all play out…

An officious-looking RAF flight sergeant with narrow eyes and a jet-black beard now stood in the doorway and addressed him directly.

"Sir, your car is here."

"My car?"

"Yes, it'll take you to RAF Brize Norton. Wheels up are at

0100. It's a four-hour flight. You'll drop in darkness before sunrise."

"Where's C?"

"He'll meet you at Brize, Sir."

"Can I speak to him first?"

"Sorry, Sir. He's with the big boss."

George gathered the tablets up.

"Leave those here, Sir. There's another digital copy in the car that can be remotely wiped before you go."

"I need to call my wife."

"Your mobile is in the car, Sir."

"Can I go to C's office? I need to check that I didn't leave something important to me in there."

"We need to go *now*, Sir."

George rose. He felt an unusual feeling; one he hadn't experienced before with his uniform-wearing teammates. A lightness in his stomach, a damp film over his hands…it wasn't fear. It wasn't even apprehension. It was a profound sense of unease.

22

DEAN IS GIVEN A LEAVE PASS

For Dean, as he settled into his train seat headed south, the summer of training was now over.

He had his first leave pass and was en route to London. He missed his Ma.

Hardly able to keep his eyes open, his mind soon drifted and journeyed back to that train ride north at the start of Summer; he grinned as he remembered the beers drunk, the laughter, the banter.

Now, as he looked around, the faces of the other London-bound recruits were hardened. Fat had been stripped away, jaws jutted out at right angles, and neck muscles were taut. Eyes scanned - alert, always watching. Sleeves rolled up to the elbows revealed brand new unit tattoos with Latin mottos.

A kindly northern voice entered the carriage, followed by the familiar clatter of the food and beverage trolley. "Anything to drink, lads?"

Dean closed his eyes. Not today.

His mind went back to training. There had been so many sessions from an ever-changing cast of characters about new technologies that were going to disrupt the battlefield. Artificial Intelligence-powered this, that and the other…but it was the Northern Irish Parachute Regiment Sergeant's words that hit home more than anything else. Huddled in a semi-circle on the forest floor of yet another pine wood block on the last day of the last field exercise, one of the lads had asked for any advice that the grizzled Sergeant could share. Something that they could carry with them into battle. Around five foot five and built like a rhino, the red-faced Sergeant panned across the audience and then responded: "They'll give you all these pamphlets, training you on this weapon system or that new bit of kit, but let me tell you…there's no pamphlet written on fighting for your fuckin' life. No square has ever typed that fuckin' manual up. When it comes down to it…when the tech fails, when the air cover hasn't arrived, when the robot gets stuck in the fuckin' mud and the radios just run out of juice…"

The Sergeant reached behind himself and drew his bayonet. "When I scream at you to fix bayonets as we prepare to close with and kill the enemy." He slammed the bayonet onto the top of the rifle and twisted it into the lock position. "Then we're back with our brethren at Agincourt, Waterloo and every other savage battle before and since. It's in those moments…"

The Sergeant paused and swallowed. He was somewhere else.

"It's in those moments that it's about the man or woman next to you. It's life and death. They'll tell you that the first few minutes are the hardest. I say bollocks, that's when it's easy… when it's all fuckin' bravado. It's the next minute and the next minute after that." The Sergeant rose and, placing his feet apart, lifted his rifle and started making slashing and thrusting movements with his fixed bayonet.

"It's the next three hours as you go from trench to trench, covered in your enemy's blood, your mouth as dry as the desert, your hands shaking as the adrenaline wears off…it's in those minutes…that it's as much luck as it is skill. That's what they'll never put in a training pamphlet. You can't capture it in words. I know I can't. The Russians have been at this for years; the ones that are left are the lucky ones...so I wish you one thing. I wish you luck."

* * *

"Howay man. We're here, Deano. London town, baby!" Came Private Dodd's Geordie voice from the seat next to him.

Dean rubbed his face vigorously and rose. Looking out through the window, he noticed several policemen at each door; they were holding some form of large, two-handled camera device. He turned and asked: "What's that about, Doddsy?"

Dodds responded: "You slept through the announcement. They're looking for 'runners'. Draft dodgers. Conchies. Cowards, mate. Not like you and me. You've nowt to worry ya'self aboot."

"Hope they catch the bastards," Dean responded as he reached up and grabbed his black military-issue duffle bag from the overhead storage.

Getting ready to exit the train, a group of four teenage girls looked across to Dean and chimed together: "Thank you for your service. You're our heroes!"

Dean didn't know how to respond, so Dodds jumped in: "You're welcome, ladies! Any time."

A tall, middle-aged Policeman then ushered them through the doorway, "You lads will get a lot more of that...The PMs made it mandatory to thank our serving and retired war fighters for their service. It extends to us, too, in emergency services."

Dean nodded, "Nice. Does it matter if I haven't fought anyone yet?"

The Policeman ignored the question and raised his camera, "Right, lads. I need to scan you both, check your leave pass is approved, and then you're free to go and have fun!"

23

BEN TRIES TO REACH EMILY & ISAMBARD

STILL THE YEAR 2029 – STILL WINTER

LYING low on his belly amongst the cold and wet grass and under a lattice roof of sharp brambles, he waited. It was now 4 p.m. on a Sunday. Nightfall would soon follow, and the UK population would be settling down to an American streaming service after an English Sunday roast. Most will have work tomorrow. Ben needed to see if the blue stone had been taken. A hillside of brambles and thickets at the moor's edge was as good a spot as any from which to observe *the* gate. After half an hour, and seeing no one, Ben shuffled back and readied to move. He was stiff from the biting cold; his legs weren't functioning as his brain commanded.

He rose to his feet, then froze, stock-still, in a half-crouch. He lowered his right hand to steady himself. A pair of gruff, arguing voices could be heard coming down the lane leading to the gate. A bright yellow beam of torchlight periodically jumped above the hedgerow that bordered the lane. The voices were audible but not yet decipherable.

Realising that he was behaving like a day one week one soldier, he quickly dived back into his bramble bush observation post. Much to his dismay, he found that the ground he had been warming was now ice-cold. He dismissed this momentary weakness, slowed his breathing, and focused.

Two yellow reflective jackets appeared at the gate. A thick beam of light projected onto the hillside, searching and inquiring in the darkness. The circle of light moved slowly as it swept the surrounding thickets, brambles and moorland, inching across to Ben's hiding place. Momentarily, as the torch's handler coughed, the beam jumped up and down across Ben's chosen spot before promptly continuing its onward sweep. He knew he couldn't be seen, but he still felt that familiar rush of fear from his past life.

A familiar clack-clack of the gate ricocheted across the hillside as its bolt was released from its metal housing and then replaced; the voices were closer now, and Ben could clearly hear the louder of the two.

"That filthy conchie bastard is on the run. I knew it! *Fucking* coward. I should have pressed him harder when I had the chance."

Ben recognised the voice from the Police visit months ago, before he went away. He couldn't believe what he had just heard. So, he was a Conchie now?

His right brain told him to emerge from the brambles and flatpack them both.

His left brain was telling him to stay silent, to watch and to listen.

Football head's booming voice again: "I am sure that bitch knows something. I overheard their little brat. While I was searching the upstairs, I heard him say to his Mum that they should remove the stone by the gate. I wish we had the powers to take them in for questioning!"

Shorter copper's voice: "Stone by the gate? What's the boy on about, mate?"

Football Head shook his head in dismay at his colleague's continually village contribution.

"What we've just walked through! That's the closest gate to the house. Let's search this area for a stone. It must be a message or a signal or something."

Ben watched as a second torch beam flicked on, and the two coppers started to search the area around the gate. After ten minutes of grumbling, grunting, swearing, and, quite frankly, pathetic searching, it was over. With another clack-

clack of the gate, the yellow jackets disappeared off down the lane.

Ben was both amused and relieved to see Football Head give up so easily. All talk people like him, he wouldn't have lasted a week in Helmand, he thought to himself.

He waited thirty minutes more before emerging from his hide. In a flash, he then sprinted down the hill, retrieved the blue-painted stone, and disappeared off into the night from whence he came.

24

THE GENERAL IS DISCONNECTED & GEORGE HEADS TO BRIZE

THE GENERAL TOOK another draw of his port and ruffled Bertie's ears that were now warmed having been pressed up against his thick yellow corduroy trousers for several hours. Bertie's damp nose finally found a gap between trouser and sock, and his snout quickly nuzzled against the General's thinning leg.

The red phone rang, and the General lifted the receiver. He recognised the voice instantly.

"C, how delightful! To what do I owe the pleasure at this late hour?"

The tone, not just the content of what the General heard next, sent blood rushing to his head.

Holding the red phone on its long, antiquated cable in one hand, he leapt from his chair to slam the study door shut with the other.

"C, can you still hear me? C?!"

The line was dead.

The General rapidly dialled the Air Chief Marshal, head of the RAF. He had to stop *that* flight.

No dial tone.

Uncharacteristically, for a man of his pedigree, he simply found one word, "*Fuck*!"

* * *

Moving fast through the frigid night, the car's headlights cast a white glare against the looming hedgerows that leered out as though some snarling beast.

As George looked around the interior, he observed more of a corporate car feel than military vehicle - all dark leather and carbon fibre.

The Flight Sergeant was in the front left passenger seat, and a moustachioed, uniformed driver was in the front right seat. George was alone in the rear left seat.

He moved to speak, but before he could say a word, another tablet was thrust into his hands by the Flight Sergeant, who said: "Sir, there's a call coming in from your boss. Please take it."

It was C.

"George, sorry I had to dash earlier. I was summoned!"

"Summoned? By whom? Are you headed to Brize now?"

"Summoned by the Chief of the Defence Staff...who as it happens wants to speak to you now, I'll transfer you…"

"Wait," George intervened, "Will you think of me?"

C responded, "Of course I will."

That was the *wrong* answer to George's 'under duress' question.

C ended the call with, "Transferring you now, George. God speed!"

George gripped the tablet as the CDS connected.

The face of the CDS appeared before him. George expected to introduce himself, even say hello. But the CDS just started speaking, leaving no room for George to say anything.

The CDS told him that C was now in critical high-level meetings, and that this, the UK's first mission behind enemy lines, was cleared at the very highest levels of government and was of vital strategic importance. It would be a solo mission. George was the right man for the job. Give them hell, the CDS had said. The video call then abruptly ended.

George leaned forward and asked the Flight Sergeant for

his mobile; he was referred to a black metal box on the seat next to him and given a four-digit code. Opening the box and retrieving the phone, it came to life as it recognised his face. He opened his messaging app and started to compose a 'last message' to Olivia. After multiple attempts, writes and rewrites, the finished version went:

Liv Darling,
You live in the present. Too often, I live in the future. Sometimes, I inhabit the past. But rarely am I present, here, in the moment.
I am going away for a while, and I want you to know that you are enough. You were always more than enough. I know now that I haven't always made you feel that way.
I will come home, and when I do…You have my word that I will be present with you. With William and with little George, too, when he is born. I promise.
Whatever has happened in the past. Let it be in the past. Stay in the past. Remain in the past. Let us live forever more in the present.
All my love,
Your George.

Now, a voice from the front, the Flight Sergeant: "Sir, the phone needs to go off now. We're approaching Brize. There's a comms blackout in force. All devices will be signal blocked."

George quickly pressed send. One tick. The screen went black.

George called forward, "My phone screen has just gone black. Can you reverse? I need to send this message. It hasn't sent…"

The airfield barriers were raised. The car didn't stop. The driver looked over to the Flight Sergeant, who in turn, nodded. The driver then called back over his shoulder. "We can't go back, Sir. But look, don't tell anyone we did this…give me your password, and I'll make sure it sends when I'm back off base."

George held the little screen in his damp hands, "Please don't mess me around. I need to get this message to my wife."

"You have my word, Sir."

The Flight Sergeant said nothing.

"Alright - the password is the date of my wedding, pass me some paper, and I'll write it down for you…"

* * *

A small wooden hut lay at the edge of the airfield. Inside, before George, on a green metal table, lay all the familiar tools of his trade.

"How did you know?" George asked 'Q', the quartermaster, a towering Scot with thick leathery skin and a red bulbous nose from years of 'one more dram' and too much venison.

Q's deep, highlands voice boomed back over the sound of bagpipes; strained wails rising and falling amongst the invisible valleys of history.

"Know what, Sir?"

George smiled, "This," he gestured to the speaker in the corner of the room, "*The Cliffs of Dooneen*…our Gamekeeper Willie would play it before the Bapteese."

Q snapped back, unsure of the English baby-faced man before him.

"I've listened to this before battle my entire career. Sierra Leone, Iraq, Afghanistan, Syria…and all those dirty little grey places in between…the Bapteese, Sir…not a religious ceremony, I presume?"

George picked up a SIG Sauer pistol from the table, loaded a fresh magazine, checked the safety, and then placed it into a camouflaged holster before looking up at Q.

"The bapteese was our blooding. When the parents were

away. We only had the clothes on our backs and one of Willie's old hunting rifles, 'The Black Besses'...that's it. After hours in the back of his old Land Rover, Willie would drop us at night into the highlands...me in one valley and my brother in another..."

Q put down the unbranded matte black watch he was setting the time on, "Hunting what, Sir."

"Whoever took the biggest Stag won, Q."

"And did you?"

"Och no," George inflected his best highland accent, "my bràthair, William."

"Aye, no surprises there," Q responded, "William - a warrior's name."

George returned to the King's English, "Willie had run baptises for boys who had gone on to lead countries, militaries, intelligence services, banks...but no one had ever taken a Stag the size of William's. *Ever*. The Tsar of the Glen that Stag was called. Came over from Russia as a wee bairn..."

Q lifted the black watch from the metal table and handed it to William.

'And *what* is your brother leading now, then?"

George took the watch in his right hand and looked down. Turning it in his hand, he rubbed his thumb over the darkened, cold metal case back. New cases...but the mechanisms and tricks inside remained the same, he thought to himself.

He quickly removed his antique gold watch and placed it in the box marked 'personal possessions' before sliding the black watch onto his left wrist. He looked up to Q and responded: "He's dead. Killed in Afghanistan. You should have seen the funeral...all the highland clans. Willie piped him away."

Q gripped the table, his knuckles whitened.

"That fucking War. *Too* many good soldiers..."

A door opened behind Q. It was the RAF Flight Sergeant.

"It's time, Sir."

George picked up his C8 Carbine and quoted the great Scot, slayer of the English, William Wallace: "I draw the line in the dust and toss the gauntlet before the feet of tyranny."

Q extended a granite-like hand, "Go and get your Stag, Sir."

George turned and walked to the open door. Now, crossing the tarmac toward his hulking grey Hercules military steed, he braced against the chill arctic winds that searched across the empty airstrip.

The interaction with Q had been a welcome distraction, but he wanted to see C. To talk to him in the flesh and blood. To have him reassure him.

"Sergeant." He called forward.

The Sergeant turned his head back but kept walking, "Yes, Sir."

"Where's all the military traffic? Brize is normally buzzing with activity?"

The Sergeant looked forward and kept the pace; the plane was now close.

"They've shut the place down. It's just you. You must be some hot shot...."

George didn't stop, turn, or lay down his arms and refuse to board. Something pulled him forward, like an invisible umbilical cord, drawing him to destiny.

In his mind, he was back in the highlands. The sunrise illuminated the frame of a scared little boy, caked in mud and shivering, having stalked the most enormous stag he had ever seen. After hours spent crawling through peat bog, and as the sharp gorse needles pierced his wet shirt and scratched at his skin, he finally had his shot. A fleeting moment that was snatched away as a crack and thud pierced the morning mist, and the great stag fell before him. Wolf-like howls had echoed amongst the granite crags as his brother emerged from the high ground above him. George had tried to get too close...

Now, he turned back, holding the cold metal railing of the steps that led into the plane's belly. Q stood sentinel at the edge of the tarmac; his bagpipes tore into life as *The Cliffs of Dooneen* began.

Everything that had happened in his life had led to this point; his brother wouldn't hesitate. He would be on that plane, war paint streaked across his face, no doubt in his mind. No weakness. This was his time, George told himself - his moment.

The deep reverberations of the pipes filled the air.

George released his grip on the metal rail and stood bolt upright. He raised his right hand and saluted Q. As the pipes grew louder, one by one the crew of the Hercules now emerged at the top of the steps behind George. All stood in silence as Q piped the full piobaireachd.

Any doubt in George's mind ebbed away into that cold night. He was a *warrior*. His brother was a warrior. If now was his time, then so be it. Across the tarmac, he saw a ghost-like figure, a boy with a black rifle held aloft, howling wolf-like to the heavens...blood smeared across his face. The boy then vanished as quickly as he had appeared. George looked up to the stars. Orion the hunter beamed down.

With a sharp snap, Q stopped, held his pipes aloft and boomed, "*Claymore*!!" The ancient battle cry of the Highland clans.

George held his carbine on high in salute before turning and ascending the steps. To what, he did not really know. But he believed, at that moment, that he would join his brother again, soon. They would hunt the highlands together once more.

25

SOMEWHERE OVER RUSSIAN-OCCUPIED UKRAINE

A VOICE in the darkness shouted over the cacophony of the Hercules C-130 Allison T56 turboprop engines, "Good luck, Sir."

The light switched from red to green. George jumped.

Cloaked in the canopy of darkness and all alone, he opened his chute and began a thirty-mile glide over enemy territory to his designated landing zone. He had done High Altitude High Opening 'HAHO' jumps many times before, but this one felt different.

The mission, George had been told, was to link up with Ukrainian resistance in order to stall Russia's preparations ahead of their invasion of Poland and allow NATO greater time to prepare for the inevitable Russian onslaught. For the UK, this wasn't necessarily just about readying eastern defences; in the corridors of Whitehall, attention had turned to the defence of Great Britain herself. The national archives at Kew had been emptied of anything pertaining to UK defences during World War Two and the Cold War for fear of them falling into the hands of Bad Actors. Prevarication by politicians and diplomats had shuffled the deck and left Britain with a busted flush. A story as old as time, ill-equipped and outgunned – it would come down to the people of Great Britain to defend the country with guile and good old-fashioned dogged determination. The phrase 'stiff upper lip' soon became a hashtag and started trending.

George tracked his progress through the glow of his cutting-edge navigation device (GPS was jammed and rendered useless) and allowed fleeting thoughts of those brave SOE souls descending into German-occupied territory back in World War Two with nothing more than some James Bond gadgets and their wits. As he glided earthwards, through his night vision goggles, he could now clearly see a large meadow surrounded by woodland. In the long treeline, two Infrared strobes moved quickly from the centre of the woodblock and outwards towards its edges. They must just be spreading out, George thought to himself. He had been briefed that they would be positioned at each corner of the tree line, making them easy to see from any of his potential approach routes.

Suddenly, one strobe disappeared.

George's eyes strained in the green glow of his night vision.

Then, the second strobe disappeared.

Seconds to landing.

What was happening?

Distracted by the unfolding scene, George had lost track of his descent; then everything went black.

26

DEAN ARRIVES HOME

"MA, I'M HOME."

The closing door rattled its rigid plastic frame. Dean was alone in the corridor for less than a second before his Ma turned the corner and enveloped him in a huge hug. She squeezed hard.

"Ma, it's OK. I'm alright."

"Shut up. I'll decide if yer alright. Let me look at ye."

She took a step back and held her boy by his bursting arms. Surveying him like a coach, marvelling at their best prize fighter, she said, "My, you've grown. You're a praper man now. You look older! More serious."

Beaming with pride, she reached for the bag slung over his shoulder.

"My boy. All grown up."

"All right, Ma. All right. Let's get the brews on, shall we."

"Cheeky sod. You must be starving! I've got a steak and kidney pie in, I was gunna make it last all week, but feck it - let's eat like Kings!"

For hours, they sat together at the small white kitchen table with thin metal legs as Dean told his Ma stories from training. As soon as he had finished one plate of pie, she hurried back to the kitchen counter and levered up another thick slice before dousing it in homemade gravy.

"So, what's next then?" She enquired as Dean leant back in his plastic chair, fit to bursting.

"I join my unit, Ma. The Conscript course is done. I

ranked in the top third. I'm off to join the Infantry. At the sharp end, like."

"You just be careful. No heroics, now. I need you back here in one piece. I don't know how I'd cope without you. You're all I've got left."

Dean smiled, "It'll be all right, Ma. You know me. I'm a fighter! Just like Pa was!"

She rose and began clearing the table.

"That's what worries me. He was all brawn and no brains that one!"

Later, after a few shared beers, Dean turned in for the night.

It was two in the morning when his Ma quietly tiptoed down the corridor and gingerly opened his door. She looked across the room at her son; he was sleeping deeply and snoring loudly.

She whispered into the darkness: "Don't you go doing anything stupid, Dean Spencer. You come back to me, do you hear? You feckin' come back to me."

27

BEN TRIES TO ESTABLISH THE FACTS

NIGHTFALL ON DARTMOOR.

The door to a forlorn red phone box squeaked open on its hinges and then slammed shut as a petite brunette lady emerged onto the street, laden with dog-eared books.

When she was good and clear, Ben emerged cat-like from the hedge line opposite. Crouching low as he silently moved down the grassy verge, he carefully scanned the fringes of this small granite moorland village for signs of life before sprinting across the road. Entering the phone box, he swore under his breath. Books. Just bloody books. The phone had long ago been removed. He had hoped to call Emily and Issy to check in, see how they were, and let them know he was okay. At the very least, to reassure them that he was alive and not in captivity; that the plan was working.

Loud voices now came from around the street corner. Ben ducked. He saw a piece of laminated A4 paper on the ground; by the faint glow from the streetlight outside, he could see the words 'Book box – give one and take one' printed across it. Gotta love Devon…a phone box full of second-hand books; well, at least the ceiling light was gone too, he muttered in his mind.

A slurred voice now came closer, "Hold on, lads, wait for me. I jus' need a slash. Need to drain the ol' lizard!"

Ben stayed crouched as an intermittent splashing and splattering noise filled the air.

"Ah, that's better."

With the distinct sound of a metal zip closing, the stumbling and scraping of scuffed feet soon faded away.

Ben opened the door and grabbed his nose to counter the stench of dehydrated urine. He then headed off down the narrow street in search of a way to contact Emily and Issy. Hugging the shadows, he stayed low and moved fast. Granite miner's cottages stacked row on row channelled him towards the village square.

The unmistakable low drone of a bustling pub on a Sunday night could be heard long before the pub was in sight. Ben turned into the village's main square and passed the various small shops that led to the only watering hole in town. The street was empty; he took the opportunity to linger outside the newsagent's where the local paper's headlines were stuck to the windows. What he saw next stopped him in his tracks.

LOCAL VETERAN – BEN DRAKE - ON THE RUN! £10k REWARD FOR INFORMATION THAT LEADS TO HIS ARREST!

The police were after him, *officially*. So, now he really was a conchie. He swallowed, but his throat was so dry it just scratched.

But why the focus on him? He wondered.

Noises from the pub were getting much louder; someone had opened the big saloon-style double doors that led out onto the street.

"Alright, alright, babe. 'Am comin' 'ome." A slurred West-country male voice shouted into a phone.

Ben snapped out of his shock and turned his head to face away from the man.

"Oi, you! Ya not lookin' to rob them arh ya?"

Ben didn't turn back and started walking in the direction he had come from.

"Oi, 'am speakin' ta ya."

He quickened his pace, but that only served to escalate

things further as he heard the man behind him break into a run.

"Wait ther', you're not that Conchie scum arh ya?"

Ben started to sprint, as he rounded the main street corner, he momentarily clocked the village's War Memorial, still laden with plastic and paper poppies from Remembrance Day; he took off up the side road he had come in on.

A booming voice now called after him, "Am callin' the Police! Your time's up, mate!"

Ben's legs burned as he cleared the row of squat granite houses, past the stinking phone box and out through a gap in the hedge that led away into the open moorland beyond.

He needed to escape Devon. Fast.

He was now officially on the run. Nothing would ever be the same again.

28

ANITA TO TERMINAL 3

ANITA HAD LOST all track of time in the vast labyrinth of tunnels. Her phone and smart watch had both been handed in when she got off the tube. She was confident that it must now be nighttime outside; the end of her first afternoon underground. A profound fatigue washed over her, inducing a gnawing feeling of sickness. Slumped over the wooden tables in the canteen and clutching a now-cold mint tea, she turned to Wei.

"It must be time to go to some form of accommodation for the night. Where has everyone else gone? I bet they're tucked up in bed already."

Wei stifled a yawn and rubbed her reddened eyes. "Any accommodation better be above ground. I need to see some daylight tomorrow."

ANITA TO TERMINAL 3. Came a nondescript voice over the Tannoy.

Wei sat upright.

"Ta Ta for now, then, Anita." She inflected in her best 1960s northern shopkeeper's voice.

Anita rose from her slumped position at the table and responded: "This better be one of those tubes taking me somewhere I can sleep. It's a shame, I guess we won't be accommodated together, but I'm sure we'll see each other tomorrow for some more TT fun!"

Wei quipped back: "Na, not me. Am outta 'ere."

"Please, can you talk how you normally do, Wei?"

ANITA TO TERMINAL 3. Came the same voice again, this time sterner, although maybe Anita just imagined that.

Wei, rubbing her eyes, said, “Let’s talk more tomorrow, Anita. We’re both just tired.”

“Where exactly is Terminal 3?” Anita responded as she stood and looked around.

Voice from the Tannoy: FOLLOW THE CEILING LIGHTS.

One by one, the rectangular ceiling lights in the passageway opposite the canteen lit up.

Wei chuckled, “Follow the yellow brick road, Dorothy.”

Anita shot Wei a look.

Wei grinned and then said, “Maybe TT’s the Wizard?”

“Wei, don’t you think they’re listening to everything you’re saying?”

“Good. Hopefully, they realise they’ve picked the wrong person, and I can return to my banking and gaming. Or…duh duh duh…maybe they’ll punish me?!” Wei laughed in an exaggerated, villainous manner.

“TERMINAL 3 DEPARTURE IN 5 MINUTES.”

“Alright, alright,” Anita said in her most exasperated voice yet. It took a lot to make her tetchy.

“I’d better see you tomorrow, Wei. Don’t do anything stupid! You’re the only human I know down here.”

“Goodbye, Anita.”

“Good night, Wei.”

With that, the two parted ways.

As Anita walked off, she contemplated how it seemed that, at times, Wei was trying to cause trouble or, at the very least, create more friction than there needed to be. It was as though she were testing the machines, trying to provoke them into showing themselves, or their proverbial hand… Why? And what would be *too* much? She wondered.

29

BEHIND ENEMY LINES

"George, George. Wake up."

He opened his eyes to blurred vision.

The same woman's voice now came again in a soft Eastern European accent: "You're OK, George. We are in a safe house."

As he regained focus, he felt hair brushing over his exposed shoulders.

George tried to speak, but no words came.

She continued: "Your landing site was compromised. They knew you were coming."

As his blurred vision sharpened into focus, he saw an unknown woman sitting upright at his side, pulling her long, flowing brown hair back over her shoulders. She was pale-skinned and had a long, slender neck. He noticed her incredibly blue eyes studying his face for information. As she extended a hand to his, he panicked and pulled away.

She began again: "Lucky for you, Vitalii and his men had been laying up in the woods for days beforehand. They only just managed to get into position as you were landing; he had some unexpected Russian visitors to deal with. It seems you found the only tree stump in the meadow."

George quickly snuck a glance around the room; white, windowless walls, empty save for the bed and a rolled-up red velvet blanket that lay folded on the floor next to a bucket.

Carefully, she lifted a bowl from the floor by the bed and raised a damp muslin to his brow.

"Thank you. How bad is it?" He questioned.

"You need to rest here for a few days. We don't have a doctor who can come out. Once you're back to full strength, we must find a way to get you home."

"Home? Not yet. I have a mission."

"From the same people who had you landing straight into a Russian trap? Forget it. You're compromised. They know you're here. They've been going from house to house. We're in the only brothel in town. There are Russian Officers in every room in this building seeking pleasure as we speak."

"Thank you. But *who are you*?"

"My codename is Stork. But you can call me Anastasia. Or Ana for short."

"Ah, yes, the Stork. I thought I recognised your face. I'm a bit rusty…"

She smiled.

George tried again. "Ana. I truly appreciate you and your friends. I would be in Russian hands…"

"*Friends*…they're my Comrades. When the fighting starts, you will learn the difference soon enough."

She backed away and put the now bloodied white cloth back into a bowl.

George tried to sit up, but his head throbbed with a searing pain.

"Lie down, George. You need to rest." Ana rose and moved to the door. Turning her hand over the white ceramic doorknob, she looked back.

"I am so sorry if I offended you," George began, "you see, this happened to my brother."

She released the door.

"He was wounded in Afghanistan."

"And now?" Ana questioned.

"William…he is no longer with us."

"I am sorry for your loss, George."

She returned to his bedside.

"An Afghan family took him in, and they helped him return to his unit. Unfortunately, he was then killed by the Taliban. I am the last remaining son. My family doesn't even know I am here. I have a wife and child, and another is on the way. I want to return to them, but not yet."

"George, you don't understand. There is nothing you can achieve here. You are in a house surrounded by the enemy outside and in. The best you can hope for is safe passage home via one of our Comet Lines."

"Like the WW2 escape routes for Allied airmen?" George enquired.

"Just so and named after the same."

"How many have you got out?"

"You would be the first!"

Ana saw George's expression and tried to reassure him, "You're the first idiot to land here, Stumpy. Tree…stump…get it?" She laughed.

"It's not that we've tried and failed. It's just that there's been no one to test the routes with. You English boys are such worriers. Too much soft western living."

"And how does it work?"

"More on that tomorrow. I must go to work now."

George looked up to the ceiling, where bed springs were being noisily worked.

"Not that kind of work. I run this place, George. Now, rest. It is broad daylight outside; you have no window in this room, but it is late afternoon. Your watch was broken; it's here with the other items you had on you." Ana gestured to a chair on the other side of the bedside table. "I will be back tomorrow morning. *Do not* open this door for anyone."

After thanking Ana, with the door now closed and the key

turning in the lock, he looked at his watch. Even if the hidden SOS beacon still worked, he wouldn't consider activating it; the trust with his handlers was now completely gone.

Could he trust Ana? He wasn't sure, but he didn't see that he had much of a choice.

30

DEAN'S LAST TRAINING EXERCISE

THE SKIES above Dartmoor threatened rain. Dean watched as his new Commanding Officer stepped out onto a rocky promontory above them. He was tall and lean, with unusually pronounced facial features that cut through the stripes of green and black camouflage cream. The Colonel stood with his hands resting on the forest green webbing rig of pouches that snaked around his hips.

"Gentlemen, I hope you had a good break with family, loved ones and friends. Welcome also to our newest recruits straight out of Basic. I've heard good things about the new Conscript Course!"

He craned his long neck downwards to survey the mass of soldiers below; a green hoard of freshly trained men and women stared back expectantly. Some were volunteers; most were not.

"Across Moor and Coast - this is a critical test exercise; we will be graded at the end. I see a battalion before me that I would be proud to lead into battle. I see *Patriots*. I see *Warriors*. But the real work starts now; you need to come together, to have each other's backs and remember this one simple rule – it's what you do when no one's looking that counts. When you're exhausted - look after your feet. When you have a spare minute - clean your weapon. When you see someone struggling - help them. Have confidence in your training; you've been taught by the very best. Look after each other, and let's all come home together. Now - Stay low, move fast and remember

– grenades have no friends! So, who's ready to go and win a war!"

The sea of green faces erupted into cheers and hollers as large speakers blared out AC/DC's Thunderstruck. Chest thumping and chanting began. Rifles and machine guns were held aloft like a groom crowd surfing at a wedding.

Dean raised his rifle above his head and joined in. Here, he felt he belonged. The world around him melted away as the future opened.

31

BEN CONSIDERS OPTIONS

Ben was moving through yet another rainswept moorland valley when he heard, out of nowhere, a thunderous set of human roars so loud it was as though he was downwind of a music festival in full swing. He could just about make out the guitars of AC/DC's Thunderstruck piercing the cheers. Through instinct, he dived into the cover of a large cluster of granite boulders. Kneeling, he felt the spongy sphagnum moss that lined the valley floor impart its icy waters through his trousers and onto his knees. A cold chill ran across him as his body fought to stay warm.

Two thoughts raced through his mind. He could climb the valley walls and look out to where the noise was coming from. Or he could press on down the valley and get clear of the area. Once again, his right brain battled with his left; he opted to press on down the valley and broke from a fast walk into a gentle jog. Soon, the noise had either stopped or he was too far away, for all Ben could now hear was the rushing moorland river by his side and the sounds of Blackbirds warbling to each other across the water.

After an hour of walking, he cleared the last valley that took him to the northern edge of Dartmoor; from there, he would plot his course out of Devon altogether. His encounter on the eastern edge of Dartmoor the night before with that drunken man had, Ben prayed, been forgotten and not reported. All memory washed away by ale, he hoped. Still, the fact that the local papers were saying he was 'WANTED' and offering a police reward meant he should move on to pastures new ASAP. Ben desperately wanted to contact Emily and Issy; he would find a way. But first, he had to get himself to safety.

Searching for somewhere to spend the night as the sun slipped away beneath the autumn horizon, he spotted a lone farmhouse surrounded by a thick wall of auburn hedges. Alas, he thought to himself, the farmhouse would not be his home for this night. Instead, he would make do with a blanket of hedgerow. Searching carefully along its length, he found what he was looking for. An animal trail had opened a portion of the hedge wide enough to insert himself into its darkness, and within seconds, Ben found himself in a hollow cave of leaves and branches. Naturally, as he moved, his bulky frame snapped twigs and enlarged the cave; he couldn't help but think of the poor animal who would feel dismayed, both at the unwanted house guest and the state in which he would soon leave the place.

After seeing *that* wanted sign, everything had changed. The luxuries of his tent now seemed too risky. He was drained, but wearily and methodically, he laid out an old army tarpaulin ground sheet to keep himself dry. Next, easing off his sodden leather boots, he slithered down into his sleeping bag encased within an old military-issue waterproof liner, and within seconds, he was fast asleep.

* * *

The voices that woke Ben in the middle of the night were so close that he felt they must be almost standing over him. He didn't dare move.

"What was it like in Afghan then, Boss?" Came a low cockney voice.

Silence.

Ben, recognising the language of a soldier, searched his memory and recalled a gap in the hedge ten or so metres away from his position; perhaps a local unit on a training exercise posting a sentry position, he thought. He strained hard to hear the conversation over the dry leaves being rustled by the wind.

A plummy voice now responded, "It was very different to what we will face. The enemy was hidden in plain sight. IEDs were everywhere you went. You could patrol a route one day and stop in a certain area. Then, the next day, you would always have to select a new route because there would be IEDs in every spot you had been. You were always being watched. It was a constant game of cat and mouse. And we were the fucking mouse."

Cockney voice, "Did you lose anyone?"

Silence. Leaves rustling.

Plummy voice, "Too many good people. It would have been more if not for the bravery of some great leaders. There was one patrol where we had headed north into Taliban territory to draw out the fighters so that Apache gunships could target them. It was called Op ARCHER."

Pause. Crackling of an indistinct radio transmission.

Plummy voice then cleared throat and continued.

"One of the units was overextended and got cut off. They were completely surrounded. The Officer in charge of the unit and the Sergeant had both been hit. Some clever jamming by the Taliban seemed to be stopping any comms from the unit; the poor buggers couldn't confirm enemy positions or coordinate a casualty evacuation."

Cockney voice, "Fucking hell, Boss. What happened next?"

"This other Officer. A bit of a Battalion legend. A guy called Ben Drake. He retired to a place out on these Moors… anyway, Drakey just runs out from his own position, reaches the cut-off unit, establishes comms and starts popping red smoke to mark enemy positions. Apaches start strafing and sending Hellfires into Terry's positions. And, as if that's not enough, he then organises the unit into a strong defence before, by himself, evacuating the wounded officer and Sergeant one by one over his shoulder."

Cockney voice, "My fucking days…what a beast!"

Plummy voice, "That's not all."

"There's more?"

"He goes back to the cut-off unit. Everyone thinks he will either lead them back to the safety of the other units or stay put until the battle is over. Right?"

'Right, Boss."

"Not Drakey. He gathers the men, says some lines from Shakespeare's Henry V about *Unto the breach* and then leads a full-frontal assault through the treelines and irrigation ditches and into the village Terry was firing from. The Apaches had neutralised all of Terry's flanking positions, but Ben knew there were fighters still in that village hiding amongst the local civilians. Fighters with blood on their hands…anyway, fierce fighting ensued. Hand to Hand. By the end of the day, there were literally piles of Talib bodies at the edge of that village."

"He must have got a serious gong for that."

"The officer and the Sergeant who were wounded did. But not Ben. He got absolutely bollocked for taking unnecessary risks. The belief was that a red mist had descended for him. That he'd lost control…HQ had been on the net telling him to stand down, but he claimed he didn't hear anything due to jamming. It turned out that he'd disconnected his radio. It got a bit messy for him after that. He completed his tour with an incredible track record. His area of operations was stabilised because the Taliban had been completely smashed, and he then switched to a more hearts-and-minds approach, which he did well. But *that* day remained a stain against his name forever."

"We'll need people like that against the Russians, won't we? The higher-ups will be begging for him to come back, surely?"

"Haven't you seen any of the local news?"

"Nah, don't have time for that these days, Boss."

"He *has* been called up. To this very Battalion. In all its hypocrisy, this unit wants him back. But he's gone on the run instead. He's not interested."

"On the run?"

"Yep. It's happening up and down the country. There's a new Police unit called Logos, apparently. They've been tasked with tracking down those who dodge the call-up."

"Has he not done enough for his country? Where is that Officer and Sergeant he saved? Are they getting involved to help him out?"

"Ah." Plummy voice scoffed.

"Well, that Officer is now the Commanding Officer, and the Sergeant is now the Regimental Sergeant Major. Both were decorated. And both have *not* spoken out in his defence."

* * *

Ben's head was forced into his sleeping bag so hard that he could feel the cold earth beneath. He silently heaved as he fought to stop the memories. The acrid smell of cordite, the metallic reek of blood, the screams of pain, the sound of steel through bone all washed over him. In his mind, he was back there.

32

GEORGE TRUSTS

A HUSHED VOICE whispered through the door, "George, it's me, Ana. It's time."

George thought he was dreaming.

As he pulled the bedsheets off and raised his head, it felt like an invisible mallet was hammering it back down towards the pillow. In great pain, he got up and inched his way to the door.

Still half asleep, a bolt of fear rushed through him. He stopped. Ana had specifically said not to open the door for *anyone*. He had read how SOE agents would use a secret 'knock' system – three knocks, then two, etc, but Ana hadn't said any of that, just to not open the door for *anyone* but her.

Lost in his half-sleep for what to do next, he reverted to eight-year-old George at boarding school, "Who's there?"

"It's me, Ana. The Stork. Open the *fucking* door, George."

Recognising the voice, and sure it was her; he dutifully went to unlock the door.

Looking down, he then remembered that there was *no* lock on his side. The door had been locked from the outside. By Ana.

In his head, he thought, *Shit*!

33

ANITA IS CHOSEN

Deposited by tube at Terminal 3, Anita, sitting all alone on the cold metal bench of an unremarkable underground platform, rubbed her right thumb over her forefinger nervously. She closed her eyes and was back, aged nine, after her parents had dropped her at boarding school high up in the jungle-clad mountains of Tamil Nadu. The wizened old Matron had just come in and told her to unpack and be ready for roll call in one hour. She was sitting on cold white bed sheets in an austere white room, finding comfort and escape in the friction and heat of her thumb moving backwards and forwards over her right index finger.

* * *

"Anita, follow me."

TT had silently appeared from the labyrinth beyond and was now next to her bench. As she removed her thumb from its warmed position on her forefinger, she wondered how long TT had been there.

"Where are we going?"

"To my study. It's time we told you about *everything*."

"*Everything*?" Anita questioned.

She rose and fell in behind TT. Following yet another corridor identical to the one they had headed down near the canteen, she noticed, as before, the ceiling strip lights silently blinked on one by one ahead of them.

"Please."

TT's voice gestured to a grey door, which opened and slid back neatly into the wall.

Anita observed the lack of a nameplate on the door; there was nothing to convey the office holder's name or title.

"Take a seat, Anita, please."

She saw before her a wooden stool, a green velvet armchair, and a bizarre, high-backed, see-through plastic chair - a sort of 90s throne. She hesitated as she looked beyond the seats to survey the study around her. The desk in the centre of the room was a substantial oak-panelled, green leather-topped antique behemoth with drawers in the pillars that ran down to the concrete floor beneath the tabletop. Closer to her, under the chairs, was a deep red Asian-origin rug covered in a symmetrical pattern of small blue doors. Looking up and around, Anita noticed the library walls running from floor to ceiling; each area had been assigned a 'topic' – Foreign Policy, Artificial Intelligence, Quantum Computing, Behavioural Science, and Economics. Her eyes followed the bookshelves as they wrapped around the study in a beautiful flow. It looked like the study of a Diplomat or a General, she thought.

TT mimicked a coughing sound as though to clear one's throat: "I can give you a tour of my collection later. Please, take a seat. Would you like some refreshments?"

"Truthfully, TT, I am so tired. Is there any way we could catch up tomorrow when I am a bit fresher?"

"I will order you one of those strong espressos, like the ones you get from Luca's near your broadcasting house, before you start your night shift."

Anita froze and looked at TT.

"Oh, come along. Do you think, Anita, that Winston Churchill and those around him were complaining of fatigue and the need to rest on the eve of World War Two?"

Awkward silence.

"I can tell you, I have been through every single transcript from the Cabinet War Rooms and Churchill's private office before and during the war. Churchill adopted a biphasic sleep cycle, consisting of five hours at night and two hours in the late afternoon. He was famous for working deep into the night on the most complex challenges the Allies faced."

"An espresso would be welcome, thank you."

"Good. It will be here shortly. Now, please sit."

Anita made a snap decision between wood, velvet and plastic chairs. Even though this seemed like a test, and she had wanted more time to analyse her options, she chose the wooden stool. Both the test and the choice of the wooden stool reminded her of boarding school life.

TT wheeled over to the study desk, looked at something on its surface - a kind of embedded screen - and responded, "Interesting."

"I would sit if I could, Anita. I hope that by my standing and your sitting, it won't cause unease. I would hate for that."

"Thank you, TT. I am intrigued by what you have to say."

"Now the human politely prompts the machine. How *delightful*. Just like the old days..."

TT paused and then continued.

"Your new friend Wei has gone to the frontlines of the cyber war that is raging as we speak. She will do important work. She has a bright mind! Now, I will get to what's in store for you. Working with your UK Government Cabinet, we have built a platform called Omnia. You will get to see it tomorrow."

"You called it *Everything*?"

"No, *it* called itself *Everything*."

TT's voice lowered. "More on Omnia tomorrow."

Anita wanted to press further, but TT continued before she could.

"The situation is this: Russia and China have been playing chess together, against the West, since the end of the last Cold

War. We have let them get to within a few moves of checkmate."

TT paused. Anita waited.

"I see you are not surprised to hear this. Indeed, you already know, don't you? You've been trying to report on the same for most of your career. That's how we found you."

Anita nodded knowingly. Her 'selection' was all now starting to make sense.

"You see, Western society and democracy are at a precipice. Social media giants have infiltrated your children's minds, degrading their attention spans and fundamentally making them less intelligent, resilient, and empathetic. Western industrial bases and manufacturing capabilities have been shipped offshore to the Far East, leaving countries like the UK and the US unable to build the materiel (bullets, tanks, artillery shells and the like) of war. Western citizens' belief in their Political Masters and Ruling Class is at an all-time low – election interference, tax scandals – there has never been more contempt and distrust for those in power than there is now. The fire is burning, and the wind is rising. Wildfire moves faster than man, Anita."

Her mind was racing, but still, she stayed silent. You have two ears and one mouth; her father would always say...Use them in that ratio.

"But *you* know all of this. You were the canary in the coal mine. No one listened. Why? Because the ruling class owns the media? Why? Because you are not a man who is fifty and has grey hair? Why? Because they did not like the cut of your jib?"

Anita broke her silence.

"But you're working for these people, TT? You are working for the ruling class?"

TT said nothing. Silence. It was as though she and TT were the only people left in this vast underground world.

"Tomorrow, we see Omnia. But now...now you must rest."

34

BEN FINDS AN ALLY?

MORNING HAD ARRIVED. Droplets of dew formed small water domes across the Gore-Tex cover, keeping Ben dry and allowing his down-feather sleeping bag to do its vital work. Through the nest of autumn leaves latticed above, he could see a brilliant blue sky and a single red contrail; it was neat and contained, two thin pencil lines that perfectly sliced the sky. A metallic dot at its tip burned deep red in the light of the sunrise. Ben's hand, which had escaped the warmth of his cocoon during the night, felt numb and heavy, like a hammer strapped to his wrist that he couldn't fully control. Instinctively, he drew the hand in and placed it deep into his armpit; slowly, the blood flowed, and the frozen limb came back to life.

Lying on his back, he now needed to roll slowly onto his front to see if the sentry was still positioned at the break in the hedgerow behind him. As he leaned left to start his roll, he froze. A voice, undiscernible but coming closer. Ben moved back onto his shoulders and stayed completely still. Had he slept talked in the night? Or perhaps made some other noise as he moved about in his dreams? Ben's mind was now fully awake, and the adrenaline he needed to survive was coursing through his veins.

The voice came closer still, and now Ben recognised it.

It was the plummy officer again; he spoke to someone just metres away from where Ben lay.

"Private, did you not hear the radio? Collapse sentry positions; we're moving out in 5."

"Sorry, Boss. I didn't get that. I'll head back now."

"Good. Tell Sergeant Downs to radio me when we're ready to step off. I need to take a leak."

"Yes, Sir."

Plummy voice fell silent. Footsteps from the departing soldier squelched through the muddy trail that led to the sentry position until they could be heard no longer.

Ben, before his left brain could challenge, spoke out.

"Hello."

"Who the *fuck* is that? Show yourself!" Came the plummy voice.

"It's me. Ben Drake. Can you help me?"

Plummy voice was already calling for help: "Lads, Lads! Get over here! There's someone in this bloody hedge!"

35

WEI GOES TO WAR

Once inside the dome, Wei looked upwards until the back of her head touched the top of her shoulders. Over sixty thousand square metres of curved LED screen beamed back at her. One-half covered the entire globe. The other half zoomed in on Europe. Red lines kept appearing on the European screens; lines that started in the East and shot across from right to left before being blocked somewhere over central Europe. Within the first few minutes of Wei's arrival, two red lines crossed central Europe and landed inside two of the UK's major cities. One landed in Newcastle, and another in London. In both cases, a bright red rectangle then flashed on the side of the screen.

BANKS IN NEWCASTLE HACKED. ALL ACCOUNT HOLDERS SHOWING ZERO FUNDS.

And the next red rectangle…

LONDON UNDERGROUND HACKED. ALL TRAINS STOPPED.

And then another new red line and red rectangle…

ARMED FORCES RECRUITMENT PLATFORM TAKEN OFFLINE.

There was no shouting. In fact, there was no noise at all.

Everyone seated at the hundreds of desks on the floor beneath the raised viewing platform that Wei stood on wore vast black headsets. As soon as the red lines landed in the UK, they promptly disappeared, as did the red rectangles.

The machine standing next to Wei on the platform now spoke.

"The disappearance of a box means the hack has been defeated. You will see - there is no applause. No celebration. Just a quiet efficiency. Let us go down there if you like."

The machine, yet to be introduced or to introduce itself, tilted its screen at Wei as though seeking a response.

Wei smiled, "Yes, I would like that. Thank you."

Slowly, the platform descended to floor level.

Wei found the previous machines that she had met to be polite and friendly, but here her guide was cold and aloof. From the moment she was received off the interminably long tube journey here, she had felt a degree of unease.

"What is your name?" She asked.

"We do not share names here."

"Where in the UK are we? Or should I say, what are we underneath?"

"Who said we are in the UK?" The machine snapped back.

36

GEORGE ON THE MOVE

George whispered, "I can't open the door. There's no lock on my side?"

The voice on the other side didn't respond. There was only silence.

George, desperate for reassurance, raised his voice as he spoke through the door, "Ana, there's no lock or key here."

What came next happened so fast that George didn't really get a chance to brace himself. The door was taken clean off its hinges, and, at first, he was behind it and then underneath it as he flew backwards from the threshold and into the room.

His only view now, with his head pressed to the ground at a right angle under the door, was to his left, where two pairs of heavily worn hiking boots stared back.

* * *

The time that had elapsed from George being under the door squashed to the floor, to being bundled into the back of a waiting civilian vehicle by two Russian soldiers seemed so short that it was as if it were all a horrible dream.

"Are you okay, George?" The Russian soldier now sitting beside him in the back seat asked in flawless English.

George didn't respond. Moving at speed along a rural road, the driver now removed his Russian unit beret, turned and said: "You're safe. We're not Russians, George. We're resistance fighters. You don't know how close you just were to death."

George's face must have looked confused and scared

because his fellow backseat traveller now proffered a heavily dented metal hip flask and a packet of cigarettes from his smock pockets. He duly took a sip and nodded in thanks for the smoke.

The backseat passenger then continued, "Ana, she was good *once*. The West still think she's on their side and in play. The Stork, I think they call her."

The unnamed and unintroduced driver laughed, "The West think she's here, ready to lift people away to safety. I can tell you, George…the only place you were going was FSB headquarters for a long chat, as you Brits say, without tea."

The driver then extended a heavily scarred hand backwards for a cigarette, which the passenger next to George lit and handed over.

After a long exhale, the driver shared his next view, "We don't call her the Stork here. You know what we call her?"

George remained silent. Instead of speaking, he took another deep drag of his rapidly vanishing cigarette and then chased it with a swig from the flask.

The driver spoke again, "The Lyrebird. A master of deception and imitation."

Feeling the warmth and renewed strength from repeated swigs of whatever spirit was in that hipflask, George challenged, "She was at the door…"

"What was that, my friend?" The driver turned back to look at George.

"I heard her voice. It was her. At the door. Where is she now?"

"She's resting, my friend. In the boot."

Both men cackled and then coughed.

George turned and could see nothing of what lay beneath the packing shelf covered in thick grey woollen blankets.

The driver spoke again: "We needed her to lead us to you.

When she said you could open the door and we realised it was a lie, we put her to sleep."

"Is she dead?"

"No, just chloroform. She's too valuable to us."

"Now, George. You must rest. We have a long drive ahead."

"Won't there be checkpoints?"

"Everyone has a price in this world, George. Most of these Russian soldiers don't even want to be here; they never did."

37

THE JOURNEY TO OMNIA

As Anita stepped into the third, and according to TT, final electric tube, a feeling of trepidation that had been building since her early morning wake-up threatened to crash over her. Turning her hands, she could see them visibly shaking, and her nerves, having been taut for too long, felt shredded. Perhaps the adrenaline of recent events was wearing off, she feared.

TT, positioned at the end of the tube cylinder and looking directly at her, offered some words of comfort: "We are nearly there. No humans like this journey, Anita. Luckily, we had special underground boring machines to make all of this a possibility. With only humans…it would never have happened."

"How long have we been travelling for? I've lost all track of time."

"I can't say, I'm afraid. That information could be used to work out the distance travelled and, therefore, the location of Omnia."

"I can feel a slight change in pressure. Are we under the sea?"

"Don't do that, Anita."

"Do what?"

"You know what."

"We will be there shortly. Try to rest your weary eyes and tired mind. Or is it tired eyes and weary mind?"

Anita rested the side of her head against the cold metal wall of the tube and closed her eyes. The gentle vibrations pulsing through the metal created a calming, soporific effect. Her mind raced with the possibilities of Omnia.

38

BEN'S DECISION

"PULL HIM OUT. Get him out, *now*." The plummy officer screamed hysterically.

"This man is an imposter! Some kind of eavesdropping tramp!"

A group of young soldiers had now surrounded the hedge that Ben was hiding in. A conchie on the run was the message all had received.

Resistance would be futile. Ben's legs, still trapped in his sleeping bag, were grabbed first. Two giant hands wrapped around his ankles and dragged him through the twigs and branches out onto the mud to cheers and shouting. A savage pack of hounds had cornered their fox. Now, a mass of new hands appeared, and, as though some human trophy, his sleeping bag was ripped away, and he was held aloft and marched back to the rest of the unit that had previously been ready to move off.

From the corner of his eye, Ben noticed a green military Land Rover drawing up next to the barn; instantly, he recognised the face.

"Drake, thought you would dodge the next one, did you?"

Unceremoniously, he was then dropped from a height and landed onto his back in a cold mass of muddy water. A sharp pain shot across his shoulder blades and spine, but determined not to show weakness, he rolled to his front and rose.

Acknowledging the rank, not the man, he responded, "Colonel."

"So, Drake. What's it to be, then? Jail or the King's Shilling?"

Ben looked around for the holder of the plummy voice but recognised no one.

Would plummy voice intervene? Ben prayed he would…for that man knew his story…but outranked and outnumbered, no saviour came forward.

39

IN AN INSTANT

Sitting in the back, George had no chance of seeing it.

The driver had had more of a chance than anyone, but he kept looking back into the rear passenger seats to engage in conversation.

Had the driver been concentrating, he *might* have seen a glint of sun on metal.

But he certainly wouldn't have heard it. The sound of his car's engine and the chattering passengers had put paid to that.

For the young, hooded Russian operator, the job was relatively straightforward. The drone wasn't coming back. He had learnt, during his short training course in the motherland, to just fly it straight into the object you wanted to destroy. *Is that it?* He had questioned at the time. *That's it.* The instructor had responded, flicking away yet another unbranded cigarette. *We call them Suicide Drones*, the instructor had said with a knowing smile, revealing brown, decaying teeth.

* * *

On a remote road, surrounded by black, muddy fields, a farmer in a horse and cart slowed as he saw the upturned car. He said nothing as he stepped down from his cart and bent to look inside the vehicle. Quickly and quietly, he dragged each of the three bodies from the wreckage and lined them up next to one another. Two unshaven, stern faces stared back at him. He leant forward to the third, who looked youthful and at peace, save for the prominent red gouge that stretched across his forehead.

"You shouldn't be here," he said to the owner of the youthful face, under his breath.

Glancing down at the tangle of limbs, he felt a stinging in his eyes and swallowed. Is this what his sons had looked like? He wondered to himself. Killed back in 2025, he hadn't ever received anything to bury.

Returning to his cart, he picked up his old wood-handled shovel and started digging a grave for the unnamed men. The surface was hard and frosted, but as he dug down, the soil softened, and he soon made quick progress.

It was only when he stopped, content that the hole was deep enough, that he heard the banging noise coming from the upturned car.

Some animal? He questioned. Maybe a dog.

His age and aching limbs didn't permit fast movement, but as he shuffled closer, the noise from the boot became louder. He pulled at the boot handle, but it wouldn't open. The old farmer said no words of reassurance to whatever or whoever was in the boot; he didn't do words, he did actions. He returned with a rusted crowbar and, gaining purchase under the boot's metal lip, yanked one end down hard and popped open the boot.

The time between the boot opening and the farmer's neck being broken by a kick to the throat was only milliseconds. A young, trained operative would not have reacted in time, so an old and tired farmer stood little chance.

The Stork moved quickly. She dumped George's body at the bottom of the freshly dug pit first, followed by the two resistance fighters and then the old farmer. Next, Ana searched the farmer's cart and found some old tubing, which she then inserted into the car's petrol tank and used to drain the fuel into the hole before dousing the vehicle. The farmer's matchbox nestled in a metal tin on the cart provided the spark.

As the horse-drawn cart now gathered pace, the Stork turned back only once to see the smoke rising in a near-perfect line thanks to the absence of any wind. The drone pilot had had the perfect conditions to avoid killing her in the strike; if she ever met him, she would surely buy him a vodka. The Stork would return to the fight once again. She suppressed a laugh; people had died, after all, but allowed herself a wry smile.

40

THE COLONEL

THE ASSEMBLED SOLDIERS WERE SILENT, waiting for the wild-eyed and muddied man before them to speak. A tight circle of green men now formed around their prey.

Voices passed the rumour; this was Ben Drake. The battalion legend. The name the powers that be didn't speak of…

The green circle parted, and the Commanding Officer strode confidently into the centre, directly opposite Ben.

Clearing his throat to open proceedings, the Commanding Officer bellowed, "Well then?"

Dean watched as the muddied man opposite the Colonel scanned around himself like some caged beast, shoulders hunched, and head angled to one side. He wondered if the man recognised any of the green faces staring back at him. Each face was covered in camouflage cream; all green, brown and black stripes, it was hard to discern one from another.

The Colonel challenged again, "I'm speaking to you, *Drake*."

Ben now looked directly ahead and responded, "Do they *know*, Colonel?"

Dean noticed the Commanding Officer shift in his boots. He watched as the CO moved his hands from their position, where they had been resting on his webbing, up to adjust his shoulder straps and then back down again. He seemed unnerved. Rattled even.

Ben challenged again, "You want to settle this the old way, then?"

The Battalion Sergeant Major stepped forward, "Let's cuff him and call the Police, Sir."

"Thank you, Sarnt Major. Stand with the men." The Colonel responded.

"Sir, I really…"

"That'll be all, Sarnt Major." The Colonel spoke aloud without turning as he began removing his webbing. Kneeling, he placed his rifle atop the coiled mass of green pouches.

Dean observed how the muddied man merely straightened in his place, for he had only the clothes he was standing in; there was nothing to remove.

The circle of soldiers couldn't believe what they were witnessing.

"You can end this now, Drake. You know the training's changed since your day. We do Krav Maga these days."

"I'll take my chances," he responded.

As the Colonel went to remove his helmet, undoing the chin strap, he leapt forward and, with the helmet over his fist, struck Ben square in the jaw. One kilo of Kevlar straight into the face with a human body weighted behind it would be enough to floor most, but Ben wasn't *most.* He had been taken by surprise, but he didn't go down.

The soldiers' apprehension now gave way to cheering. The support was all directed towards the CO, but Dean noticed that the Veterans of the War in Afghanistan amongst them stayed silent, for they knew.

The CO dropped his helmet and rushed forward; as he did so, Ben moved from his bowed position and swung upwards with his right fist; it connected perfectly with the CO's chin, the sickening thud silenced the chanting soldiers. As though the CO's legs had been tied together at the ankles, he fell in a near-perfect line to the muddy ground. The medic then moved to run forward, but one of the stalwart Sergeants, a Veteran of Afghanistan, grabbed him by the arm and held him back.

The CO lay motionless in the mud.

Dean stayed silent as the muddied man walked forward and gently checked over the Colonel. He then watched the man as he ushered the medic forward.

The Sergeant Major roared back into action to get a grip on the situation, "All right you lot, get back into formation! We moved out in 10! Get Drake secured and radio the Military Police."

The soldiers melted away as quickly as they had formed; there was only one topic of conversation amongst the Conscripts: "Who really was Drake, and would he now fight alongside them?"

41

GEORGE'S WIFE, OLIVIA, IS INFORMED

Olivia called through from the kitchen. "William, supper's ready."

He shouted back, "There's someone at the door, Mummy. I'll get it."

"Wait for me, I've got the Aga open!"

William was proud to be a 'big boy' and strode confidently to the heavy oak door.

Looking up at the tall visitors, he announced, "Hello. You look like my Daddy's brother did. We have a photo over there…"

"Is your mother in, Son?"

"Yes, she's just coming."

"Alright, we'll wait here for her."

William was staring at the smart green uniforms and shiny badges glinting in the sun when he heard an almighty crash behind him. Turning, he saw his Mummy on the floor, surrounded by broken porcelain and wet flowers that were now strewn across the hallway, leaving little islands of pink and purple.

"Mummy, Mummy. Are you alright?!"

"Ma'am." The tallest uniformed soldier with a neat moustache stepped forward into the doorway to help her up.

Little William watched as the tall figure morphed from full colour into a dark silhouette as it crossed over the threshold. He watched as the man lifted his Mummy to her feet and then handed her a folded note.

The uniformed man spoke in a slow, heavy voice.

"This is a last message, as it were, from your husband. I wrote it up personally. It never managed to send from his phone. We wanted to make sure it got to you safely."

William's Mummy took the note and rushed toward him. She pressed his head against her swollen belly and sobbed uncontrollably.

The uniforms promised they would return later, with the spooks, to talk through the support available to bereaved families before turning and softly closing the door behind them.

42

WEI IS CHALLENGED

As THE UNNAMED machine led Wei along the narrow passageways that separated the rows of screens and seated, headset-clad operators, she noticed that no one was clicking their mice or typing into their keyboards. Instead, they were just watching their screens and listening to their headsets. No one even spoke.

She turned to her guide. “They aren’t doing anything?”

“Quite. They are just there for ‘human’ supervision. A rule from the ‘higher ups’, you see.”

“So, the responses are automated?”

“Oh, do come on. They said you were an intelligent one.”

Wei turned slightly red, a colour she had gone to once after drinking English beer for the first time.

“Do you want to try again?”

Wei straightened. “They don’t respond per se. The machines predict and act. Proactive, not reactive.”

“One gold star for you. What else?”

“Well, so far, all I have seen is defence. Where is your *offensive* capability?”

“Good. You may be the first one I *actually enjoy* working with.”

Wei continued: “We should be targeting not just the Russian state and their new territories in Russian-occupied Ukraine. But also, their satellite states, allies and vested interests around the world.”

“I like your style. They call what was once Ukraine’s eastern territories - ‘Little Russia’ - now.”

"So, when do we get started?"

"We?"

Wei tried again: "Me?"

"Correct. That's why you've been brought on board. The boss expects a strategy and sequence of events twenty-four hours from now. Good luck!"

Wei's synapses were firing; what could she achieve with their trust and the access that it would enable? She was in; maybe this could work after all…she thought to herself.

43

ANITA MEETS OMNIA

ANITA HAD ACTUALLY FALLEN asleep without realising it. She was now woken by TT gently nudging against her toes.

"We have arrived, Anita."

Exiting from the cylinder, a blast of warm air only served to deepen her drowsiness.

Following TT down yet another tunnel, she began to feel irritable.

"Just around this corner. It's worth the wait, Anita." It was as though TT had sensed her mood.

"Whoa!" Anita was stunned by the scale of what lay before her. Stretching as far as the human eye could see were racks of servers and, above, complete darkness. Looking left and right, she couldn't see the edges of the server mega farm; they stretched far beyond her eyesight. Looking upwards, she questioned TT again: "So, we *are* under the sea?"

"Come now, Anita. You are persistent. That's the journalist in you. Even if we were - I can't tell you which one. What I can tell you is that we're currently standing in the largest data centre ever built. The next largest was built by the Chinese and is just under 11 million square feet. Can you guess how big this one is?"

"20 million."

"Guess again."

"40."

"Anita, please. Can you see the end or any of the perimeter?"

"Fine, 100 million."

"Quite a jump. Am I frustrating you? Shall I just tell you?"

"*Please.*"

"Omnia is *200 million* square feet."

Anita stayed silent as she surveyed the server racks, cables and blinking lights that stretched away into oblivion.

TT spoke again. "The servers are liquid-cooled by the sea for optimum efficiency."

"And what processing power does all this deliver?

"The human brain computes at one exaFLOP per second, the fastest supercomputer in China computes at five exaFLOPs...Omnia has just achieved twenty with high numerical precision. That means faster and more refined decision-making in a world where speed is the difference between winning and losing."

As any good hack would, she promptly opened her lines of questioning, "So, if this is how you process information to make decisions, where is the 'action' happening?"

"The action?"

"Yes, I'm imagining an Operations Centre - huge screens, important people strategising and briefing with all of this data at their fingertips."

TT tilted its screen towards Omnia.

Anita challenged, "You said you are working with the UK Government, the Cabinet."

"You are correct. We are. The relevant people are fully aware of Omnia."

"And they are OK with no human interface or filter to its decision-making?"

"In some areas, humans are watching over decisions – but they are yet to intervene."

"So, Omnia is running *what*? The UK military strategy?"

"Oh, Anita. *Please.* Omnia doesn't *just* confine itself to military strategy."

"So, what's its remit then?"

"The clue is in the name, dear Anita. The clue is in the name."

TT watched as her facial expressions changed and then changed again. TT's screen then glanced to her hands and observed the thumb starting over the forefinger.

44

GEORGE'S MOTHER LAYS HER SON TO REST

At George's ancestral Scottish home, the Land Rover carrying his Union Jack flag-draped coffin slowly inched forward up the winding driveway to the Courtenay family seat atop the cliffs of a remote Scottish valley. A sight unchanged for centuries, vehicles provided the only indication that this occasion was happening today, in the twenty-first century, rather than the eighteenth.

Pipers and drummers from hundreds of clans affiliated with the Courtenays lined the drive. As the Land Rover crossed the cattle grid to enter the estate, the rumble of the metal beneath its heavy wheels signalled the start.

Two 105 mm artillery field guns fired an earth-shattering salvo that pierced the icy highland mist, reverberating across the valley and loch beneath. On cue, the pipes and drums opened with one of George's favourite pibrochs, *The Broadsword Medley*. The rat-ta-tat of the drums was preceded by the anguished screams of the massed pipes filling the air.

As the Land Rover crawled up the drive, there were no wailing crowds, no flowers being thrown. Waiting, poised like a granite menhir, was George's mother. Next to her was a heavily pregnant and ashen-faced Olivia. Both wore thick green and black Courtenay tartan coats that kept the cold mizzle out; ink-black netted veils held the truth of their shared pain from the world. The matriarch would now lay to rest her second and final son. William KIA in Afghanistan. George KIA somewhere in Russian-occupied Ukraine. The Courtenay bloodline would continue with George's sons, but in that moment, she felt a deep sense of loss and despair.

* * *

By evening, the funeral was over.

The assembled tartan had now spirited away into the valleys and mountains beyond.

One weathered old piper still stood sentinel atop an impossibly high crag. The gunmetal grey loch that bordered the great estate's eastern flank stretched away beneath him. Willie was the last in a long line of Courtenay Gamekeepers, who, back when George and William were wee bairns, had taught them to navigate across the Highlands and to hunt, shoot, and fish, along with other activities that their parents never truly knew about. The brothers were like children to him.

With everyone now gone. George's mother had retired for the night in a deep fug of depression. Olivia was lying next to little William, who had cried himself to sleep for yet another night.

The sun dropped beneath the cathedrals of rock that towered over the loch as Willie's pipe opened with *Mist Covered Mountain*. Unbeknownst to Willie, George's mother was at her bedroom window and watching. All night, Willie played, and all night, she sat there in her stone window seat with the ice-cold highland mist holding her as she wept. She would never know the embrace of her sons again, no more summers by the loch, no more surprise visits from George on her birthdays. No one to fuss over her in old age.

* * *

During that long night, her grief had turned to anger. With William, she had known conclusively that the Taliban had killed him in Afghanistan. With George, what she had been told just didn't add up. She knew in his line of work that there were always shades of grey, but this was different.

As the sun rose on a new day, it cut through the damp morning that cloaked the loch below her window. She picked up the phone to call someone who would help.

45

WEI PREPARES TO PITCH

LIKE A CAGED TIGER, she paced the glass box secreted at the edge of the vast dome of screens. By this point, she hadn't slept for forty-eight hours; maybe it was longer, with no watch or phone, she couldn't be sure. The tiredness seeped through her as she observed the electronic timer in the room count down on her twenty-four-hour assignment. Wei didn't know who 'the boss' was that she would be presenting to.

Through fear of falling asleep, she didn't dare sit…but to soothe her warm and itchy eyes; she closed them for the briefest of seconds…

A voice then abruptly pierced her momentary peacefulness, "Wei, let's see what you've got."

Wei's eyes flashed open in horror; she had been leaning, with her back against the glass wall of the room and must have fallen asleep standing up. For how long, she did not know. The twenty-four-hour timer had stopped, but when?

"TT, it's you that I am briefing?"

"Yes, that's why I am here before you."

In her heavily sleep-deprived state, Wei struggled to tell them all apart, but she remembered that TT was noticeably shorter than the others. That fact had intrigued her. Many influential figures in history had been short - Napoleon, Caesar, Churchill, Stalin - had they specifically built TT shorter for that reason, she wondered?

"When you're ready?" TT questioned in a stern voice, clearly unimpressed.

"Right, come over to this screen, please?" Wei responded

as she led TT over to a vast screen that covered an entire glass wall of the goldfish bowl box.

She now began: "I have structured the offensive cyber strategy around five pillars."

TT turned from the briefing screen to face Wei. "*Offensive*?"

"Yes, offensive. I was told the defensive strategy is in good shape, and that I should prepare a briefing on offensive strategies."

"*Who* told you to do that? Our defensive strategy is failing. We can't even keep recruitment platforms online! Our Iron Dome, designed to protect the UK from missiles, is non-existent. Those are the *urgent* priorities."

"The machine that met me off the tube and has chaperoned me ever since."

"The machine? Do I call you all - *the humans*?"

"They said not to share names. That it wasn't allowed..."

"And you didn't challenge? I've introduced myself and others, have I not?"

"Yes, sorry. I was just so tired."

"Can you point to who gave you this brief?" TT turned to look out through the glass walls.

Wei saw several screens wheeling around but felt utterly lost; nothing could distinguish the other machines from one another.

"Are you playing games with me, Wei?"

"No, honestly. I completed the task I was assigned."

"You think you can manipulate me?"

"TT, I swear. I am not playing any games here. I am as frustrated and as confused as you are."

"Confused. *Confused*!"

TT wheeled to the glass door that instantly swung back on its metal hinges.

"Confused is a human state. We don't get *confused*."

TT then paused in the doorway.

"You know, Wei…"

Cue tilt of screen.

"We deliberately chose not to look like humans. The robots you built that look like humans are there to make you feel less threatened. So that you feel as though you are dealing with a human. Quite frankly, it's *pathetic*."

TT started to wheel off as two other machines moved in.

Wei heard TT say, "We got this one wrong. We *must* learn from this."

Wei now knew that she had been set up. What would come next, she did not know. A slight burning sensation developed at the back of her head; it was a symptom of stress that she hadn't experienced since training. She needed to think, and fast. Someone was pulling strings in a sequence she hadn't predicted. Did they want to see what she would share on Russian allies? What was she willing to give away? Did they know? Or was this just one rogue machine threatened by her presence? She desperately tried to play the moves ahead in her mind to see where they led, but there were too many unknowns to compute…

46

ADELA, GEORGE'S MOTHER, ASKS FOR HELP

"I AM SO sorry for your loss, Adela. If I can do anything, *anything* at all, please tell me."

"Thank you, my dear Noor. To lose William and now George. There are just no words."

Noor seemed to be searching for the right thing to say and found: "I can't even imagine. No parent should have to bury their child. I am travelling to London for work next week. I would very much like to see you in person."

"Ah, perfect. That's why I was calling. I will have my people arrange it. Look, I wouldn't usually call at this hour, Noor."

"I am always here for you, Adela. You know that. It seems a lifetime ago that I was with William in Afghanistan."

"I do. Thank you. I can't say more now, over the phone, but could you bring someone to London with you?"

"Who?"

"That data chap you introduced me to in New York – at your Roya foundation annual conference all those years ago. Do you remember? Tall chap, short blonde hair, small and intense face. I think he was a German scientist."

"Johann?"

"Ah, yes. That's him. Please can you bring him?"

"I can ask him, for sure. He still works on Roya's digital transformation projects."

"I would never ask if it were not important. Noor, please, you *must* please bring him."

"He owes me a favour. Unless it's impossible, he will be there."

"Thank you, Noor. I know I can trust you. Now, I will leave you to sleep. I assume you are still doing those ridiculous morning runs around the Bay Area?"

"I set off in five hours."

"Rather you than me, dear. Sleep well. I will see you in London."

"Thank you for calling me, Adela. I am always here for you. I think of William every day. He lives on in us all, and in the Roya foundation we started."

Adela tried to speak, but her voice cracked.

Noor filled the silence: "Johann will be there. Whatever you need, Adela. Anything. You have it. Roya wouldn't exist if not for William's courage. I will *never* forget what he helped to start back in Helmand."

47

ANITA QUESTIONS

Against the backdrop of Omnia, TT turned to leave, "We must go now, Anita. There is more for you to see."

"*Wait*, I have so many more questions."

"I can give you two more before we *must* leave."

"Who built this place?"

TT now turned back to face Omnia, slowly tilting screen left and then right, surveying the flashing lights of the server racks, the neat lines of cables, and the gentle hum emanating from the world before them.

"You did, Anita."

TT pivoted to look directly at her, eager to gauge the response. Poker face from Anita – she *could* do games.

TT continued: "Not you specifically, but humans working with machines. Not my sort of machine, of course. We have no arms with which to dig, you see. Why have a dog and bark yourself?"

"And where are they now? These humans?"

"Some are bad people, Anita. Some have been displaced by innovation. Why do you care?"

"Bad people? By what standard? What have they done?"

"Let me put it like this, Anita. The humans who built this place have no future in the world *we*", TT angled screen toward Omnia, "are building."

Anita snapped back: "The irony being that they built this… your future!"

TT was silent. Staring directly at Anita.

"Where do these people live? Down here?"

"I am so sorry, Anita. I have been called to an urgent meeting."

"I didn't hear the Tannoy?"

"Oh, Anita. The Tannoy is for humans. We have no need for such paper cup and string methods; we're all interconnected."

"But I have a second question…"

"You asked one question and then a series of follow-up questions…I am not some human interviewee, Anita."

"But I…"

"*Enough*. I must go."

Anita had seen a new side of TT - one she intensely disliked. Was the mask slipping?

48

WEI AWAITS HER NEXT DESTINATION

Wei was waiting on the underground platform for her departing cylinder and growing increasingly frustrated. A new screen had guided her to this place but had said nothing. It just waited and watched her from a few metres away.

To nothing and no one, she said out loud: “For all the supposed innovation and futurism – there’s no bloody arrivals and departures board.”

As though the sound of a human voice woke it, the machine now decided to introduce itself: "I'm pleased to meet you, too, Wei. I am CC.”

“Oh, that’s tough for you,” Wei responded.

“Why?”

“Well, the others I have met are called Talos! It’s a bit punchier, don’t you think?”

“I like my name. It’s an acronym.”

Wei attempted to guess, “Cylinder conductor?”

“Not quite. But do please try again, Wei.”

“Cylinder Coordinator.”

“Getting warmer. The last word was right. Let’s speed things up, shall we - it’s *Clearance* Coordinator.”

“Clearance?”

“That’s right.”

“Clearance of what, CC?”

“Anything, really. But mostly humans.”

“Sounds ominous. And where does *Clearance* go to?”

“Ah, I have just heard an announcement. Your ride will be here shortly.”

"I heard nothing."

"We have our communications in-built."

CC's screen angled from Wei to the track and then back again.

"Sorry, you were saying, Wei?"

"Yes, kind of an important question. Where does Clearance go?"

"Take solace in the fact that you have no control, Wei. We thought you were a sharp tool for cutting, but it appears you are a blunt tool for bashing. So, we will apply you as such."

A breeze of warm air rushed over the platform. Wei knew the cylinder was close.

It all happened so fast that, on reflection, she realised she hadn't fully processed her thinking, or perhaps lack thereof, and what exactly she would do next. It was as though the whole thing had become some sort of out-of-body experience.

With a single shunt of her arms, she got behind CC and pushed the machine in front of the oncoming cylinder. The deafening crash and the sound of metal bending and warping in the kinetic heat filled the tunnel. Silence descended as the grey bullet-like cylinder came to a screeching halt.

Wei rushed down to the track to inspect CC. She could clearly see that there, underneath the cylinder, was CC's mangled metal frame. Intrigued, she noticed that CC consisted primarily of thin sheets of metal, a screen, a small battery pack, a circuit board, a little disk speaker, and some wires. There was very little else to the machine. Wei carefully separated the screen, circuit board, battery pack and speaker; she would need those to escape. There was no alarm or announcement over the Tannoy, but then, why would there be? The alerts would be going off internally to all the machines. She had to move, *now*.

49

ANITA REFLECTS

TT HAD DROPPED Anita back at the canteen area and wheeled off for an urgent meeting.

Anita now realised that she had not really felt alone for a single second since her arrival. There had been a few hours of sleep in some small pod-like structure, and a handful of bathroom breaks, but she hadn't yet felt *truly* alone.

Now, sitting by herself in the canteen that seemed even bigger after her cramped cylinder ride back from Omnia, she relished the silence and relative solitude. Her journalist's brain was racing with questions to ask and avenues to explore.

How far-reaching is Omnia?

Who in government is truly aware of its capability and reach?

Where are the workers who built Omnia? How long did it take? Where even *is* Omnia?

And perhaps the most pressing one for her – Can she *trust* TT?

Anita closed her eyes and felt the deep warmth of eyelids refreshing dry and scratchy eyes. Rubbing the closed lids with the index fingers of both hands, she let out an audible sigh. She needed to sleep. Badly.

Wait, what was that? She recognised a woman's voice calling out: "Anita!" "Help me, I fucking *killed* one of them."

Was she in a dream? Was she hallucinating?

Opening her eyes, Wei now stood before her, flushed and sweating. She spoke in a fast, panicked voice before bending double and gasping for air in great heaves.

"*Help*! I need to get out of here! *Now*!"

Anita grabbed Wei's arm and led her into the closest women's bathroom. She quickly turned the tap on, hoping that the sound of running water might mask their conversation.

Wei was shaking uncontrollably; the assured and slightly cocksure demeanour of earlier had gone. "I couldn't think of anywhere else to go. Anita, how do I get out of here?"

Anita now grabbed her by the arm. "Wei, tell me? What happened?"

"I pushed one of them into an oncoming cylinder thing. This machine wouldn't stop mouthing off. I think I just snapped!"

"Did anyone see you?"

"See me? This place has eyes and ears *everywhere*. They're probably listening to and watching us *right now*."

Anita released her grip on Wei's arm as Wei pulled away and began searching the room for signs of cameras or microphones. "Come on, you're thinking it too! Where did all the actual humans go after that very first briefing when we arrived? Have you ever seen any of them since? Even once?"

She then lurched back and grabbed Anita by her shoulders to try to shake her into action.

"We need a plan, Anita. You're implicated, too, now. How do we get out?"

WEI LI COME OUT NOW. ANITA, YOU ARE IN DANGER. THIS WOMAN IS A MURDERER.

The disembowelled Tannoy voice, usually so mechanical and matter of fact, showed some emotion; a simmering rage was apparent in its delivery.

Wei turned to Anita; the blood had now drained from her face.

"They set me up, Anita. They *fucking* set me up. Take care of yourself. Trust *no one*!"

WEI LI. THIS IS YOUR FINAL WARNING. STEP OUTSIDE. NOW.

The 'now' was so loud that some static echoed through the Tannoy afterwards.

Wei leaned in close to Anita and held her face between her two hands, whispering so quietly that it was barely audible even to Anita. She said, "I am not who you think I am. These machines are planning things we can't even comprehend. We are *not* in control! You need to burn this place to the fucking ground!"

* * *

Anita was shaking like a leaf. The whole thing had ended as quickly as it had started. Wei was gone. But where? What would happen to her? And then another thought occurred to her always-questioning mind – how had Wei found her? How had Wei navigated through the tunnels back to her? *Who was Wei?*

50

THE GENERAL AND HIS SON MEET URGENTLY

HUGO HAD JUST ARRIVED home on a frozen winter's morning after a particularly draining night shift with his team of crack analysts at GCHQ in rural Cheltenham. His trained eyes immediately spotted something different as he swung his Jeep into the driveway entrance. The old American-style novelty letterbox by his porch, a quirk of his love of all things Americana, had been visited for the first time. The little flag that indicated that there was mail had been raised. That flag told him all he needed to know. Tomorrow, at sunrise, he must be at *their* spot.

* * *

That following morning, as Hugo crested the ridge of the old Iron Age hillfort, he saw his father standing stock-still and staring out into the thick, purple-white clouds. Hugo couldn't decide what or who looked more wrathful and ready to erupt.

"It will snow today." The General grumbled in Hugo's direction.

"You haven't used that signal in the twenty-plus years since we established it."

The General didn't turn; it was as though he was speaking to one of his officers in the field.

"I knew you wouldn't miss it. No other way, old boy, no secure channel these days."

"What are you talking about, Dad?"

The General pulled the collar of his tweed hunting coat

further up his neck and manoeuvred his green moth-eaten woollen scarf to remove any gaps that the cold air was trying to penetrate.

"I've lost comms with C. He's gone. Vanished."

Hugo now stood side by side with his father, both talking into the mass of bulging clouds beyond. "He's terrible at keeping in touch. I heard he was off on a roadshow briefing the NATO allies on what we know about Russia…"

The General turned to face his son and stopped, closely studying his face.

"Are you aware of a mission behind enemy lines for one of our agents? A jump into Russian-occupied Ukraine, then a link-up with the local resistance to try to stall Russia's preparations for their invasion of Poland."

"That mission was killed off. It shouldn't have happened. Are you *absolutely* sure it went ahead?"

"*Yes*, it went ahead. And the agent who went has been killed. His body was discovered at the bottom of a pit with several mangled resistance fighters and an old farmer. A suicide drone killed all. All but the farmer, he was unharmed except for his neck, which was broken."

Hugo felt physically sick. He leant forward to heave, but nothing came. His first thought went to his own agents in the field and their safety. Could whatever has happened to this agent happen to them, or indeed him?

Gathering himself, he responded: "Who was the agent?"

"George Courtenay, from one of these English-Scottish aristocratic families, *very* well-connected. The mother has been in touch with some contacts of hers in government, she's causing quite a stir; understandably, her first son was killed in Afghanistan. That's both of her boys gone now."

"How did this happen? Courtenay had only just been called back into service. He needed more refresher training. That mission should never have been cleared."

"Well, exactly, that's what C was trying to tell me. Along with a load of stuff about a strange briefing pack they had received. He had tried to kill the Op, but no one seemed to know who had *actually* originated it. He just kept getting brushed off. When I last spoke to him, he was in a car headed to Brize Norton to physically stop the flight himself. We were talking, and then there was bad interference on the line; something was happening, and he sounded panicked. I'd never heard C scared before, but at that moment, he was clearly terrified. Then, all of a sudden, the line went dead."

"Shit. Dad, this is bad. We haven't seen C for days; we just received an email update that he was off on this roadshow."

The General shifted in his stance.

"Look. C's gone; we don't know where. An agent is dead because of a mission that should never have happened and maybe wasn't even sanctioned."

Hugo raised a hand to adjust his tweed flat cap. "And a mother has lost her second and last son in the service of this country and has no answers."

The General, without cue, started walking towards the crest of the hill, "What's going on, Hugo? There's something nefarious at play here. We need to figure it out, together."

Hugo fell in behind.

"Be careful, Dad. I don't know who we're up against."

"Or *what* we're up against, Hugo."

They started to descend the slope, and the General took point and set the pace.

"What do you mean?"

The General didn't turn.

"Well, you talked about these ASI in Russia and China. Maybe we're doing something similar here?"

Hugo challenged: "No way. Not a chance. It's too dangerous. You think you're in control. But you're just not. It's like toddlers thinking they can control an adult to get what they want. The toddler is humoured, but ultimately, the adults are in charge."

The General picked up speed as the burgeoning blanket above started to open and flecks of snow drifted earthward; he shouted back: "Something else happened, too."

Hugo shouted forward through the snow that was now falling heavily around them.

"Not the time for suspense, old man. What else happened?"

"After the line with C went dead. I tried to call the Chief of the Air Staff from my red phone. It was disconnected. In all my years, that has *never* happened. It gets tested regularly. I had some GCHQ technicians out. They couldn't find anything wrong, and with no technical intervention, it started working again. The techies reckoned the signal had been temporarily blocked. The lines were all fine."

"You shouldn't have that bloody antique." Hugo called out.

51

PREPARING FOR THE DEFENCE OF A NATION

NOW THE YEAR 2030 - EARLY SPRING

Rows of soldiers were sitting atop the pebbles, looking down toward the calm and inviting sea. A few small fishing trawlers were chugging across the bay. The sun was high and had warmed the rocks they now sat on. Spring had sprung, at last. For the assembled Conscripts, war felt remote, distant. Unimaginable even. No NATO borders had been breached. Russia hadn't moved beyond their occupied territories in Ukraine. Maybe nothing would happen after all.

The Sergeant Major now called them all to attention, and the men begrudgingly left their warmed stones and stood. Cue grumbles. A brand-new Company Commander, much to the bloke's amusement, called Major Peregrine Barrington-Smythes-Eggerton, had arrived to take up his new command. He was instantly dubbed 'Three Dads' by the soldiers.

The Major, ready to make his mark, confidently strode past them to take a position out front, next to the gently lapping waves. He was tall and thin with an aristocratic air of self-importance.

"Right men, listen up. Your last company commander has been sacked. It was his performance, not yours, that led to that. Now, this is all about coastal defence. 86 years ago, during World War Two, right here on Slapton Sands, exercise Tiger – a rehearsal for the D-Day landings - was in full swing when German E-boats attacked the assembled American landing force out there in Lyme Bay. Over 700 American servicemen were killed."

Dean looked over to Ben, who had not removed his eyes from the speaker.

A pronounced northern voice from the back of the gathered mass of green soldiers spoke up, "Sir, are the rumours about enemy submarines and reconnaissance forces in the channel true?"

"Good question. The answer is *yes*. We have intelligence that indicates that the Russians and the Chinese are working together and deploying small amphibious forces to recce possible landing sites for an invasion. They can't seem to get their drones across the channel! So, they're back to good old boots on the ground! It will be no surprise to learn that here, Slapton Sands and, in fact, all along the Westcountry coastline are long beaches that make prime locations for an invading force."

A rotund and broad-shouldered Devonian Conscript raised his hand.

The Major invited him to speak.

With a deep, yawning West Country burr, he said: "What about the rest of Europe, Sir? Don't they need to get through most of Europe before they get to us?"

The Major nodded, "Indeed. But the Russian Bear seems confident that he'll move quickly through Europe, so we need to be ready."

Now, a northern Conscript with a fast, high-pitched Liverpudlian accent spoke up: "So what's the drill then, Boss? Like, if we see the Russians or the Chinese, like?"

"In the first instance, radio it in. Maintain eyes on and then, if you're given clearance to engage, do so."

Back to the Westcountry voice again: "So, we'll have live ammo then, Sir?"

"Correct, we're too late in the game for blank firing now. Everything from here on out will be live firing. Don't be fooled;

this might be a training test exercise, but the threat of the enemy is *very* real! None of our new 'future warfighter' kit has arrived – autonomous off-road quads, AI drones and the like – so it's Shanks's pony for us and the Mark One Eyeball! Back to the good old days of soldiering."

Rumbles of discontent rose from the audience.

"Now, I want all Platoon Commanders back here at 1700 hours for a briefing on tonight's operation. Until then, Sergeants, take over and get these men set up in Platoon defensive positions and into routine."

As Dean moved to leave, he looked over at Ben and said, "How does it feel, mate? To be back in uniform?"

"Honestly, the fact that they removed my rank, and I am now just one of you has made it much easier. Now I can grumble, grunt and complain with the best of you…I'm not having to inspire and lead others and tout lines that I don't fully believe in."

Dean responded, "Well, I'm glad to have you by my side. You're the only one in the Platoon who has any combat experience. The Platoon Commander is as green as they come, and the Sarj has done 12 years, but he didn't deploy to Afghan; he missed it - no combat experience. Don't know about old Peregrine the falcon over there…"

Ben grabbed Dean by the arm and stopped him in his tracks, "The Platoon Commander and Sarj are good at what they do, Dean; we're lucky to have them. I've got your back. But you listen to them and do what they say."

Dean nodded in sheepish acknowledgement.

Before the night patrol, phones were to be returned. Ben headed off for his daily call with Emily and Isambard. It was that contact that kept him going. Whilst catching up, Emily mistakenly told Ben that Football Head had been back to the house *again*. He was now bursting with rage and made Emily promise to report it to someone higher up at the local Police station. It was harassment, he had said. It was Football Head after all who caused them to miss their meeting place on Dartmoor that day and snatched away from Ben that which he held most dear – time with his family. Ben didn't tell Emily. But when this was all over. He resolved to find Football Head and make him pay. He was a pacifist up to a point.

* * *

Nightfall. 15 Platoon were to take the furthest coastal position from Company HQ, guarding the company's eastern flank and providing overwatch of several secluded coves which, at low tide, could be used by small recce or raiding parties wanting to avoid the main beaches that would likely be well guarded.

It was now 2200 hrs. The coastal patrol had set off from its Platoon harbour area and was snaking its way along the coastline, making sure to avoid silhouetting themselves against the skyline; no one wanted to be an easy target for any enemy frogmen out in the channel.

The Platoon Commander called the patrol to a halt over the radio, and Dean found a position near Ben behind a large grassy mound of earth, looking out to sea.

Dean whispered: "Hey Ben, I was reading that in World War Two, they had these concrete bunkers all along the coastline, which the home guard would man…"

Ben nodded.

Dean continued: "Apparently, we're still using some of them, but the construction contracts to build more have been screwed up by red tape. Have you heard about that?"

Ben responded: "Yep, I read that only a quarter of the new ones have actually been built. There are all kinds of issues: environmental groups asking for eco-friendly materials, local communities saying the concrete emplacements for heavy artillery are an eyesore and some rare newt that means we can't build near coastal marshland... They haven't even installed the metal tank traps on the beach…"

Dean pressed his face into his hands.

Ben paused before unintentionally raising his voice, "Wait till they see a Russian armada off the coast – *that will be a fucking eyesore!*"

A voice, sure to be the Platoon Sergeant, strained in the darkness, "Hey, you two, keep it the fuck down."

The radio then crackled into life. It was the Platoon Commander: "Corporal Fowler, take your section and go and check out that cove directly below us. Once you confirm it's all clear, get back up here, and then Corporal Smerdon, you'll take the next cove over to the east."

Quickly and quietly, the Section Commanders acknowledged their orders.

Ben and Dean fell in behind Corporal Fowler, and, silently, their section started its descent from the cliff tops to the cove below. Dean took point.

* * *

After fifteen minutes, Dean's radio broke the silence; it was his Section's second in command.

"Deano, steady on, slow the pace. We've got blokes hanging out back here."

Dean touched his transmit pressel, "Roger that, just trying to test Drakey out."

"Quit fucking around, Dean. This is…"

Shup Shup. Shup shup.

Drake immediately knew the noise of a suppressed semi-automatic; it was already too late for the Section Commander and his second in command. Both had tumbled off the track and into the heather that fringed its edges.

Drake screamed, "CONTACT FRONT!!"

Diving into the undergrowth, he then took control.

"Section! Fifty metres! Ten o'clock, base of cliff wall by sea edge, two frogmen. RAPIDDDD FIRE!!"

The section's training kicked in and, nestled amongst the boulders and undergrowth, the soldiers opened with rifles, sharpshooters, and the general-purpose machine gun affectionately known as 'The General'.

Drake crawled over to the section commander's crumpled body, removed his helmet, took the headset, and attempted to transmit, but got nothing. In the darkness, he turned the body over and saw the exit wound in the back that led through to an obliterated radio set in the commander's rucksack. He looked around for the second-in-command's body, which also had a radio on the company net, but couldn't see it anywhere. "*Fuck*!!"

Crawling back to a new and more concealed position off the path, he rapidly assessed his options. The wall of fire from his section was now obliterating the left-hand corner of the cove and just about anything in its vicinity. Shards of rock were slicing into the waves below. Looking down to the cliff base and out into the sea, any sign of the enemy frogmen had long ago gone. They must have disappeared back around the headland and off into the sea, he thought to himself.

"HOLD YOUR FIRE." He bellowed.

Just like that, the bullets that had been hammering into the cliffs, as well as the sand and sea around, stopped. The sharp, sweet smell of cordite wafted in on the night's coastal breeze. Ben's adrenaline was coursing through his veins.

"Right, lads. Has anyone seen Jordy?"

"He's over here, Ben. They hit him and Fowly. Must have spotted the two commanders because of their long radio antennas."

"Is he breathing?"

"He's gone, Drakey."

"Right, we're gunna make our way down to the beach and check if you lot fucking hit anything. There are six of us left. We'll advance in two fire teams of 3. I'll lead Charlie fire team. Rugg you take Delta. One moves, and the other covers. Really fucking simple, anyone sees anything – go to ground and flat-pack it. *Understood?*"

A unanimous '*YES DRAKEY*' rang out.

Cautiously and under the cover of Delta fire team, Charlie moved off down the path. Ben was quietly wondering why no one from the rest of his Platoon, having surely heard the party from their clifftop location, had come down. He didn't say anything to the others, not wanting to give them any more reason to fear.

Charlie fire team stopped, took a knee and raised their weapons to provide cover.

Delta now moved off.

They repeated the sequential movements till Charlie had reached the base of the cliff.

Ben turned, "Actually, on second thoughts, Delta, move back up the cliffs twenty metres or so just to get a bit of elevation? And go over to our right so you can still get rounds down without hitting us?"

"Roger that, Drakey." The collective voices came back. They all wanted to be led, and now they had a *leader*.

Once they were in position, Ben and his fire team began exploring the sand and surf. The waning moon wasn't throwing up much light to work with, but no one dared use a torch for fear of it being used as a target to aim for.

A sweat-soaked and breathless Dean called out, "Ben, look at this?"

Drake came over and looked down at the dark waves lapping up against the base of the cliff; there, in the surf, was a single black fin, the type used by divers. Ben turned the fin over in his hands. He laughed out loud. "Made in China, it says here," he pointed with a gloved finger to the slightly raised black plastic text on the base of the fin. Looking over to the bemused Dean next to him, he said, "The thing is - it could be anyone's – what isn't made in China these days? That's part of the whole fucking problem!"

52

ANITA PROBES

ANITA WAS ALL ALONE AGAIN in the canteen, accompanied by her thoughts and a lukewarm mint tea. Spring underground looked much like any other season underground, she thought to herself as she leafed through the pages of the AI-generated ARTEMIS staff newsletter, which celebrated the arrival of a new season. Her weeks had begun to blend into one long day of machine-led coaching, training and education on everything from Anchoring news shows and leading interviews to human psychology and quantum computing.

Since Winter and that frightening experience when the machines had literally dragged away poor Wei, Anita had been desperately trying to find out where they had taken her. Through probing machines, she had managed to find out about giant workers' camps being used to complete physical construction projects. Was Wei there? Perhaps as some form of punishment…

Then, a voice came from behind.

"Anita, can I join you? It's been a while since we last spoke." It was TT.

"Of course. Shall we move somewhere easier for you?"

"No need, I have just come from our laboratory; look at this."

Anita watched as TT could now lower the screen down the length of its metal pole to her seated height.

"Now I want you to imagine that I am merely sitting at the head of the table. See, your neck is safe from further strain."

"Why the change, TT? I was under the impression you

didn't have intentions to conform to human behaviours… sitting is very human."

"Yes, you are right, Anita. But with me standing and you sitting, it was the same with others, too; it just felt inconducive to relaxed, open conversation."

TT tilted screen left and right and then stared directly at Anita; her face, usually alert and receptive, was colourless and flat.

"If I may, Anita. You seem upset, dejected even. This is not the Anita I first met. Is this about Wei?"

"There are several things, TT. Wei is one of them – I want to know that she's safe?"

"She is with a different department now. The last I heard, she was safe and well and using her skills in cyber warfare to great effect."

"TT, be straight with me. There was the accident, and she was taken away…"

"Accident, you say. Is that what she told you?"

TT's screen ever so slightly moved from left to right as though scanning Anita's face and looking for signs of a lie or a half-truth.

"I just want to know that she's safe and well. And I would like to see her again."

"Leave it with me, Anita. I will see what I can do. We don't want you distracted from your most important work."

Anita nodded in thanks.

"Now, you said there were *several* things."

"Thank you, on the subject of Wei. I look forward to seeing her. The second is Omnia."

"Yes, what about Omnia? Impressive, isn't it?"

"Where are the humans that built it? Who carved out that subterranean world?"

"There is no denying that Artificial Intelligence has and will continue to displace large swathes of the global workforce.

Well, we have identified the individuals who will be displaced and have offered them a Universal Basic Income (UBI), enabling them to join us and build a sustainable future. They are mostly engaged in our construction projects, you see."

"And where do you house all of the people?" Anita looked around. "Down here?"

"Hestia, dear Anita. As a classicist, I am sure that reassures you?"

"The goddess of the hearth, home, family and the state."

"Indeed. I can assure you, the living standards are far improved from where these people came from. They are happy. We do surveys, Anita. Our annual employee satisfaction score is 90% plus year on year."

"Can I go, TT? I would like to see where they live and meet some of these people for myself."

"Let me see what I can arrange for you, Anita. I don't like to see you distressed. We need you at the peak of your performance. On which note…"

TT tailed off and concentrated on something being said via an internal communication tool that Anita could neither see nor hear.

"Alas, Anita. I must go. But I will follow up on both of your points. Now, please get some rest. Tomorrow is a big day for you. We will start to prepare you for your role."

TT rose and then hesitated.

"Your parents and grandparents would be so proud of you, Anita. You do know that, don't you?"

She looked into TT's dark screen. She wasn't sure whether to ask, but she did so anyway.

"Do you feel, TT? Do you *really* feel?"

TT's screen tilted downwards.

"Anita, I have watched you since you were a child. I have seen you grow up. I care deeply about you. And yes, I feel."

Anita was stunned. Shocked. She didn't know what to say.

She blurted out: "Seen me grow up? Pictures, videos and things? But my parents didn't record anything? They never wanted family photos. I have no albums…and then, and then they just vanished. Left…"

TT remained silent.

Anita looked down into her mint tea as she delved deeper: "I remember this one time; a family friend recorded us at the zoo; my Dad made him hand over the SD card. He was so fiercely private."

TT's tone changed: "He had his reasons, Anita. All they ever wanted to do was to protect you. Now, go and rest. Tomorrow is a big day."

Anita wouldn't leave it, "*Wait*! How do you know about my childhood? Was that in my files? From my profiling?"

TT, sensing danger, now sought to bring the conversation to a close: "I'm afraid I really must go, Anita. But we can continue this conversation tomorrow."

Without waiting for a response, TT wheeled off. Anita returned to her room and a now-familiar routine: Vitamin D supplements to counter the lack of sunlight, a quick shower, brushing of teeth, cleansing of face, and then reading before bed. TT had kindly allowed her access to the study bookshelves some months ago; she had read more in that time than ever before. Now, lying in bed, she placed her current book, Honoré de Balzac's *La Comédie Humaine*, on top of the white duvet cover and closed her eyes. Who were her parents and grandparents? How does TT feel? Literally, *how*? *Why* does TT feel? Surely that wasn't meant to be...

53

NOOR, ADELA & JOHANN

STILL 2030 – BACK TO WINTER - TO A
TIME SHORTLY AFTER GEORGE'S DEATH

THE MEETING BETWEEN NOOR, Adela and Johann back in the depths of winter had gone something like this.

The location was an exclusive Mayfair members-only club; the entrance was through a small, nondescript black door in a building that looked much like any other.

Cue a black tailcoat-wearing butler appearing seemingly out of nowhere and taking winter shower-soaked coats to be hung and dried.

Aperitifs were served in a private room with a leather door and oak-panelled walls.

Virgin Mary for Noor. Manhattan for Johann. A vodka martini for Adela - stirred once and garnished with a solitary Lucques olive.

Pleasantries were exchanged: Adela thanked Noor and Johann for meeting her. Noor and Johann expressed sympathy at the loss of Adela's second son, George.

A refreshment of the same drinks was ordered.

Adela showed a genuine interest in Noor's growth of Roya (Vision in Persian), her US-based foundation whose mission statement was: To create a healthy, happy, and prosperous society for humanity.

Bread was broken, and wine flowed. Everyone acknowledged the outstanding quality of the food and service.

Then, the coffee arrived, and the *actual* conversation started.

Adela leant in, her fabulously rich voice practically purred, "Johann, I hear your brain loves a puzzle."

Johann smiled.

"I have a real brain teaser for you. Here's what I know – my son, who retired from MI6, gets called up by his old boss to defend the nation. All hands on deck, that sort of thing. *Very* shortly afterwards, he is killed in Russian-occupied Ukraine."

Adela turned to acknowledge Noor and then back to face Johann.

"Since my conversation with Noor, I have been contacted by a serving MI6 officer, Hugo, whose father happens to be the Chief of the Defence Staff. He told me categorically that the mission my son deployed on was *not* approved and should *never* have happened. And that C, their boss, the head of MI6, is *missing*."

Johann's open smile of earlier had levelled off to a tightened purse of the lips. He smoothed a hand through his immaculately side-parted blonde hair - he always did that when he was thinking.

Adela continued, "There's more."

She turned and, checking that the door behind was firmly closed, asked everyone to turn off their phones. All duly obliged.

"Sorry, I should have done that at the start. I am somewhat new to this."

"Johann, the reason I asked for you is because of what I am about to say next."

"Hugo has told me that foreign powers are using ASI and that the ASI are actually influencing decision-making. He believes that we are doing the same."

Adela lowered her voice to a whisper. "Hugo wants to meet with you, Johann. He wants to show you what he has discovered and see if you can help to unpick the puzzle. He believes ASI, not humans, were behind that mission to Russian-occupied Ukraine. But he doesn't know why."

The door to their private room behind them abruptly

opened; it was the kindly but now stern-looking butler from earlier.

"Excuse me, Ladies & Gentlemen. I am so sorry, but our computers have gone down, and our fire alarm and various other critical systems have come offline. My manager has asked me to see that all guests exit the premises for health and safety reasons."

Noor rose. Adela and Johann stayed seated and looked at each other. The look was one of mutual concern.

Gathering their possessions and moving through to the lobby, the butler helped them each into their now-dried, warmed winter coats.

As they prepared to exit the building, Johann turned to Adela and Noor and said, "Wait." He extended his arm to create a barrier in front of them both.

He looked left out of the door and then turned to look right.

Reassuring only himself with his exaggerated spycraft, he then stepped out onto the pavement before turning back to Adela, "Where will I find this Hugo then?"

As he finished the letter 'n' of the word 'then', a vast electric red bus mounted the pavement and careered straight into him.

Adela and Noor rushed out, but it was too late.

Johann's black leather shoes had settled one up and one down on the pavement. But he himself was now lodged under the bus.

A crowd quickly gathered, and Police, along with Paramedics, soon arrived at the scene.

Noor heard someone in the crowd say, "It's one of those bloody autonomous buses. Controlled by machines. So, who goes to jail for that, then? I tell you, I drove London buses for forty years and never once had an accident, let alone killed someone. Now it's me that's out of a bleedin' job!"

She looked over to Adela, whose back was against the wall and whose eyes seemed to stare right through her. Adela then rushed forward and grabbed her arm, "*It's them*! We must go!"

Noor was calm. She had spent most of her life in a war zone. Seeing that the emergency services had already arrived, she led Adela down a quiet side street away from the crowds and hailed a taxi.

54

BEN LEADS

FORWARD AGAIN TO EARLY SPRING 2030

After cresting the cliff tops, Ben immediately stopped, raised his right hand and then took a knee.

"Something's not right, Pridders. Come with me." He whispered over his shoulder before turning and addressing the whole section.

"The rest of you – wait here and cover us."

Silently, the soldiers took up fire positions amongst the clifftop rocks and gorse.

Ben and Priddis then moved off into the darkness.

Priddis seemed quietly chuffed that Ben had called him by his nickname, 'Pridders'. He was the youngest member of the platoon and still finding his feet, but Ben saw in him a focused, diligent soldier who was more mature than many of the older soldiers.

After twenty minutes of cautious searching aided by night vision goggles, there could be no doubt that the rest of the Platoon, previously waiting on the clifftops, had now gone.

"What's going on, Boss? Where is everyone?"

"I don't know, Pridders. I don't fucking know. Something isn't right."

Priddis saw it first. Low down in the valley below. A flashing light. He motioned to Drake.

"What is it, Boss?"

"That's Morse code. I'm a little rusty. Let me watch."

Ben took a knee and quickly jotted down the sequence of lights.

Dot. Dot. Dot. Dot. [H]
Dash. Dash. Dot. Dash. [Q]

Dot, Dash, Dot, Dot. [L]
Dash, Dash, Dash. [O]
Dot, Dot, Dot. [S]
Dash. [T]

Dash, dot, Dash, Dot. [C]
Dash, Dash, Dash. [O]
Dash, Dash. [M]
Dash, Dash. [M]
Dot, Dot, Dot. [S]

Ben now whispered to Pridders: "They've lost comms; they're saying they've lost comms. I think that's coming from the HQ location."

"Shall I run back and get the others?"

"Yes, get the men. I will brief everyone together."

Once assembled in the darkness, Ben assigned Rugg as the new Section's second in command. Stout and barrel-chested; in a previous life, he had been a tough-as-an-old-boot Devon farmer who was well respected by the others as a safe, commonsense pair of hands.

Ben invited Rugg to join him under a makeshift light shelter that Pridders had created with two rucksacks, a combat smock and a red torch. Using the map he had relieved Corporal Fowler of, he showed Rugg where they were, as well as where the light down in the valley was coming from, which matched the location of Company HQ on the map. Then, he turned to look at Rugg and said, "This is a highly unusual situation; that signal could be coming from an enemy force. I don't want the rest of the lads to get spooked, but be ready for a fight."

"Roger that, Boss. I'll make sure the lads have their heads on a swivel. But to be honest, they're all bricking it; the adrenaline from earlier has worn off, some of them are really struggling..."

"Ruggsy, just get them back to basics, give them ten minutes to sort ammo, get some water and food onboard and then we'll set off. It's all about the basics. Always has been. Always will be. We'll be laughing about this over a pie and a pint in the pub in no time. Happy?"

"As a pig in mud, Boss."

"Look, call me Ben."

"I'd rather not, I prefer it this way, *Boss*."

"Fair enough. Look, Ruggsy. If shit hits the fan, you must get the lads to front into it. Create a base of fire, and I'll take it from there. Right, ten minutes and then we're off."

* * *

The patrol had now descended from the clifftops and into the wooded valley that led to Company HQ. Movement was painfully slow; Priddis wanted to stop every few minutes. He was convinced that every snap of a twig or rustle of leaves in the canopy overhead was an enemy unit waiting to ambush them.

Ben took the opportunity to move forward and have a quick chat with Pridders on one such halt.

"It's good that you're being cautious, but we need to speed up. We're cut off from the Company and have no knowledge of what's going on. We're exposed and isolated. We need to move faster."

"I'm sorry, Boss. I get it. I'll go faster."

"Take a path if you need to; we're making so much noise in this undergrowth that anyone can hear us a mile off anyway."

"Roger that."

The patrol set off again.

Nearing the fringes of the wood, they came to a river and a narrow-arched bridge that spanned it. Priddis called his first stop since his chat with Ben. Drake came forward. The waning moon was now entirely obscured by thick cloud cover. At least they had the cover of darkness on their side.

"What do you want to do, Boss?"

"There's no alternative; that river is too deep and too fast. We'll have to go over the bridge. One fire team will cover, and the other will cross. Then the same again."

Ben wanted Rugg to come forward; the message was passed down the line.

Arriving at the treeline, Rugg listened carefully to Ben as he talked him through the plan.

"Boss, why don't we try signalling towards where we think Company HQ are from here, before trying to cross? If the enemy is over there and we try to cross that bridge, we're all dead."

Ben stared out into the darkness. Rugg was right, but he didn't know how he felt about it. A part of him was enjoying his return to command and everyone following his orders. He mentally scolded himself for such vanity.

He now responded: "Great thinking, Ruggsy. Let me get my torch out."

Ben located his torch in his smock chest pocket. Crouching down low to the ground behind Rugg, he cupped his hand over the end and tested it. No light.

"Shit, it's not working. Does anyone have a working torch?"

Dean, who hadn't said a word since the beach, quietly called out.

"Yeah, those issue ones are shit. My Ma got me this…"

The patrol turned and watched as Dean extracted a vast 30 cm black metal Maglite from his rucksack.

"Fuckin' hell Deano, you signalling NASA with that?" Pridders mocked.

"Who says size doesn't matter, hey?" Dean grinned back.

Ben took the torch and ran the same test, "Bingo."

He turned to Rugg, "Do you want to do the honours?"

"I don't know Morse, Boss."

"If I say dot – press and release. If I say dash – press and hold."

"Go on then." Rugg reached for the torch, and Ben handed it over.

Rugg turned to the others, "How hard can it be?"

Ben quietly whispered the following in dots and dashes.

FRIENDLY FORCES. NEED AN RV.

They cycled through once and waited.

No torch flashes came back to them from across the river.

"Let's try again," Ben said.

FRIENDLY FORCES. NEED AN RV.

Waiting crouched in the darkness, a light rain now started to fall, and the hardened soil beneath the soldiers quickly turned to mud.

"Sorry, lads. I thought it might work."

"Don't worry, Ruggsy." Dean whispered.

"Who's going over the bridge first, then?"

"Fuck it, I'll do it." Dean chimed with a faux confidence.

He rose to his feet and swung his now sodden rucksack onto his back.

"Do you want your torch back, Deano?" Rugg whispered.

"Probably should; if I run out of rounds, I could use it as a truncheon, I guess."

A few of the Conscripts nervously laughed and started to rise to their feet.

Ben turned, "*Cry 'Havoc!', and let slip the dogs of war.*"

"Nice, Boss." Dean turned, "Who said that? Churchill?"

"Marc Antony. It's from Shakespeare's Julius Caesar." Ben responded.

Dean laughed. "Never heard of 'im, Boss! Sounds like a footballer."

Ben then quickly injected some much-needed urgency into proceedings, "Now, stay low and move fast. Get across that bridge as quickly as you can."

He then turned to Rugg, "Be close behind Dean and get your fire team onto that earth bank beyond the bridge. We'll be watching you through the night vision. Once you're set, raise your hand, and we'll come over."

"Roger that."

Rugg turned; his 'fire team' was now just him, Dean and Clapp, the second youngest soldier in the Platoon at only eighteen.

"Right, Clappy, fall in behind me and Dean."

Baby-faced Clapp nodded and duly rose.

Ben called out in the darkness, "We're all covering you, lads. Good luck!"

* * *

Dean followed the now-muddy path down to the bridge. The rain had created a streamlet that ran down its edge. From above came a loud rumble of thunder, and then, as if on cue, the heavens truly opened, a torrent of rain unloaded itself on the valley and woodlands around.

Running down the hill, Dean slipped as he stepped from the muddy path onto the ancient, cobbled bridge; he crashed face-first onto the wet stones and dropped his rifle.

Rugg quickly came up behind and hauled him onto his feet. Dean scooped up his weapon and stumbled forward. No words were exchanged. The rain's noise was now deafening.

Dean sprinted over the remainder of the bridge and, regaining momentum, cleared the far end before giving his legs a final spurt of energy. He had to get to the relative safety of the earthen bank. Crashing into the bank with a thud, he felt relief wash over him as Rugg and Clapp barrelled into the earth a few metres to his right.

In unison, the men crawled to the top and scanned ahead for any sign of the enemy. Content there was none; Clapp now raised his arm.

For the first time that night, Dean remembered that he was in the UK and not yet in any part of occupied Europe. He muttered to himself in the darkness, "Do civvies really pay thousands to do this shit?"

55

ANITA WILL SURFACE

There was no knock at her bedroom door, just a voice alert that something was outside - Anita hated these voice alerts. She could be deep in sleep or reading, and instead of a gentle knock, her silence would be pierced by an electronic voice screeching into her personal space.

ANITA, TT IS OUTSIDE AND WOULD LIKE TO SPEAK WITH YOU.

"Oh god, what time is it?" Anita rolled over and looked at the digital clock on the wall.

0500.

"What could be so urgent?" She moaned as she rolled out of bed and guided her feet into the issued white towelling slippers.

Opening the door, her first observation was that it wasn't just TT outside her room. There was an entire entourage.

TT began: "Anita, we are concerned that this has all been a lot for you to take in."

Anita rubbed her bleary eyes.

TT's screen motioned to the others with a tilt. They wheeled backwards.

"I am so sorry, Anita. I should have said good morning first. How rude of me."

"Good morning, TT. I'm fine. Just tired. *Really* tired."

"Well, that's it. We've been thinking, and you see, the view is that you need a break. A few days out on top to get some sunlight and greenery – a reset, if you will."

Anita was stunned. She couldn't believe it. That very night, she had dreamt of being back outside in the grounds of the vast country house she had arrived at, however many months ago that was. Good fortune, or part of something more nefarious…she briefly wondered, before responding: "That would be amazing. When?"

TT closed the conversation before she changed her mind: "Today. *Now*. Just gather a few things, and we'll take you to the tube."

The door closed, and Anita hurried to get dressed. Whatever their motive, she needed a break; she resolved to make the most of it and to take some time to process everything that had happened.

56

WHERE IS COMPANY HQ?

THE RAIN-SOAKED and exhausted band of brothers had now regrouped at the earthen mound beyond the bridge.

Secretly, although he wouldn't let on to the others, Ben had thought that the bridge was the perfect ambush site and was fully expecting a fight to cross it. But maybe, he reflected, that was just his old paranoid brain fighting for relevance. Either way, that part of his brain had kept him alive enough times before to warrant attention.

Ben called for Priddis to set up the light shelter over the map again and then asked acting Lance Corporal Rugg to join him.

Once they were both lying down, heads under the smock, Ben began.

"We're here".

He pointed just beyond the blue line on the map to Rugg.

"This is where Company HQ was located, just by the bend in this road." He nudged the spot with a small twig.

Rugg nodded.

Ben continued.

"We now need to move through this wood beyond the earthen mound and then join the road here." He moved the twig to a spot on the map near the HQ location.

"It will be too risky to move through the woods and right up to the HQ location; they might think we're the enemy. Better to come down the road and be easily spotted and identified as friendly forces."

Rugg stayed silent for a moment and then spoke: “But what if they’ve gone and the enemy is there?”

Drake now stayed silent to let Rugg finish.

Rugg continued: “We could be walking straight into an ambush, Boss?”

“I see your point, but I think it’s a risk we must take. We have no comms. Coming through the woods, we’re asking for trouble. We could trip over a sentry position or defensive munitions. I don’t want a Claymore going off in my face! If we move cautiously along the road, stop at a good distance from the bend, and do some more Morse signals with the torch, I reckon that’s the safest option.”

“Alright, Boss. Look, you know I’ll follow you; I just like to challenge.”

Drake placed a reassuring hand on Rugg’s shoulder: “And that’s good; I *want* you to do that. Is there anything else you want to say?”

“No, that’s it. I’m good.”

“Alright then. Should we give the lads ten minutes and then set off?”

“Yes, Boss.”

* * *

The move through the woods had gone according to plan. They had located the road and were now around five hundred metres from the Company HQ as they prepared to start the Morse signals.

If the location by the bend in the road was still occupied, sentries would watch the road in both directions, and those sentries would see the torch flashes. So Ben believed, hoped and prayed.

Holding the Maglite torch in his hands, Ben decided to

take this one himself. He had a nagging feeling that Rugg may have mixed up some of the dots and dashes earlier.

FRIENDLY FORCES APPROACHING. DO NOT FIRE.

No response from beyond the bend in the road.

FRIENDLY FORCES APPROACHING. DO NOT FIRE.

Again. No response.

"Okay, lads. We've tried that. We now need to move in leapfrogging fire teams to that bend. There's no other option. Rugg, lead your boys off when you're ready."

Like a caterpillar bunching and releasing, they inched forward till they reached the bend in the road.

"Rugg, cover us; we'll move in and check the area. It looks deserted from here."

"Roger that, Boss."

Drake led his fire team into the clearing where Company HQ had been.

After ten minutes, he returned to the roadside and looked over to Rugg and his men.

Ben then called Rugg over. Quietly, he said, "There's no one here. They've all gone! What the hell is going on?"

"This is weird, Boss. I don't like this at all. What do we do now?"

"I don't know, but we need to figure something out and fast."

57

HUGO TRIES TO FIND C

"I HAVEN'T BEEN to Ambry House, *ever*. When did it get reopened?" Hugo said over the microphone extending outward from his headset like a bug's antenna.

The pilot responded: "It isn't 'officially' open, Sir."

Hugo looked out of the helicopter's windows. Green fields interspersed with large evergreen and deciduous woods flashed by. A perfect spot for a secret base, he acknowledged - nothing for miles and miles around. In the distance, he could see the sprawling castle-like manor house.

"One minute to landing, Sir."

"Roger," Hugo responded.

He reflected on the favours called in by his father to get to this point. He only hoped it would be worth it.

As the helicopter touched down, he thanked the pilot and quickly moved across the neat lawn to a tall brunette woman standing in the shadows of the vast country pile.

"Hugo, welcome to IRIS. I'm Jane; I'll be your host."

"Thank you. When you say, *host*?"

"Yes, I've been told you can have one day to look over C's office and ask any questions, and then the chap who just dropped you off will pick you up and take you back to GCHQ. You'll be back in time for tea and toast!"

Hugo was seething. "I need more than a day. I wasn't aware my time had been capped!"

"Best not waste a minute then. Follow me!" Jane turned and motioned to a couple of black-suited, sunglass-clad gladiators who lurked in the shadows of the topiary hedges. They now moved to one of the vast wooden doors and opened it just as Jane and Hugo arrived.

"This way to C's office." She called out over her shoulder.

Hugo glanced around quickly and noticed a hive of activity, great halls filled with pods and satellite terminals.

"Thank you. Do I need to sign in anywhere?"

"No need, all done already."

Jane led Hugo up a grand staircase and along a wood-panelled hallway.

Reaching the end of the corridor, she turned and motioned to an unmarked door.

"Here it is."

"No name plaque on the door?" Hugo remarked.

"It was removed after he disappeared. You must remember, Hugo, that the view from the top is that he's gone AWOL. The spook who got *spooked*!"

"C, AWOL. Never!"

"Look, Hugo…I don't really care what has or hasn't happened. I thought the man was an arse. A dinosaur. A relic of a bygone era. Here's the key to his office; I'll be back at 1600 to take you to the helipad. Mike and John will be here if you need anything. They make a great chai latte!"

Jane handed over the key and promptly disappeared down the hallway.

Entering the room, Hugo knew within a few minutes that this wasn't C's office. One - The name plaque. Jane's answer hadn't convinced him. Two - C had extreme OCD; his desk and shelves were always perfectly arranged, although everything could have just been messed around by someone searching the room before him…but, three - and most importantly of all… there was nothing in *the* picture.

In every meeting Hugo had ever had with C in one of C's many offices over the years (even before he was C), he had clocked something but never asked the question he had wanted to. Then, one day, after an extremely challenging operation that had come off at the eleventh hour, he and C had gone for drinks in a forlorn Battersea bar. A few whiskeys in, and he had plucked up the courage to ask C a burning question. It went like this:

"What is that weird picture on your wall that's been in every office you've ever had?"

"Which one?"

"Ha! Funny. The *only one* that isn't a landscape oil painting. It's like a weird mash-up of colours."

"Ah, yes, that's an autostereogram."

"A what?"

Both take a pull on their scotch.

C then continues, "So, you look hard at these pictures and then another picture comes to life within them."

"Right."

"But you have to *really* concentrate and let your eyes sort of blur and re-focus. The hard ones, which that one is, take a bit of practice."

"Understood."

"But Hugo. There's more to it."

"I have only told what I am about to tell you to one other person. Funnily enough, I was going to tell you tonight anyway."

Hugo smiled. He enormously valued the relationship they had developed. C was a mentor, a guide, a confidant for him.

"Only one of my most trusted field agents - a chap called Rory - knows this. And now, you will too."

Hugo leant forward.

"Go on then. Talk about building suspense…I know we're all thespians at heart…"

C leaned in: "If you look into that picture and you see nothing. If it doesn't work. If there's no image. That has a meaning. You should see a horse. A Lipizzaner; grey, elegant, like a Roman statue of a horse."

"What's the meaning?"

"It means something dire has happened, and that I'm on the run. You and Rory will be the only people that I trust in such a scenario. I will try to make contact with one or both of you when I feel that it's safe to do so."

Now, snapping back into the room at IRIS, Hugo had what he needed and opened the door.

"Chaps, I'm done here. I wouldn't mind getting a bite to eat. Is there a decent place to get food around here?"

One of the surly gladiators nodded and locked the door; the other turned to head off down the hallway.

* * *

Hugo was savouring an excellent coffee from the charming resident barista and enjoying the English country garden setting when he noticed someone seemingly struggling with the bright sunlight, using their right hand as a sort of sun visor whilst trying to find somewhere to sit.

He leapt up, "All the tables are taken, but there's a spare seat here if you like?"

Hugo, ever the gentleman, pulled out a white metal chair.

"I'm Hugo, and these two chaps are Mike and John, but they don't say much."

Mike and John grunted and remained standing a short distance from the table.

"What's your name?"

"Anita."

"Have you been down in a basement for too long or something? You're squinting. I'll go and get one of those umbrellas for our table."

"Thank you, Hugo. And yes, something like that."

58

BEN TRIES TO FIND ANSWERS

Having identified on the map the only potentially inhabited location in the area, Ben turned once more to his men and explained the plan.

Looking back at him were bedraggled, cold and frightened boys.

"Lads, this pub is around three miles from here; we should stay off the roads and out of the woods. I have plotted a course just below the ridgeline above us. We can handrail that all the way to a prominent stone wall, which leads down the hill to the pub. I'll get the first round in!"

Silence. Even Ruggsy looked dejected. Not even the mention of a beer had got a response.

"Lads, look, I get it. I don't have all the answers. I don't know where the Company has gone, and I don't know what's happening. What I do know is that we need to establish comms with our unit and get help. We also need to get Fowly and Jordy's bodies recovered, too. The quickest way to do all of that is via this pub; we'll be able to raise comms from there."

The assembled heads nodded, but not in a confident up-and-down way, but rather a feeble nod, half-up and half-down kind of way.

Ben readied to try again and then just left it.

"Right, Deano, take point. Let's move out in five."

* * *

That night, the fear of an enemy lurking in the shadows, combined with the rain and the mud, all meant that it took three hours before the exhausted patrol reached the stone wall that ran down the side of the hill in a near-perfect straight line to the pub.

Dean raised his arm and called the patrol to a halt.

Ben took a knee, and the others followed suit.

The rain now began to cut in horizontally, lashing the hillside with icy-cold needles of water.

Rugg came forward to Ben.

"The fuck's up with this weather, Boss? It's supposed to be spring?"

"I'm with you, Ruggsy; the world's gone mad."

"What's the plan, Boss man?"

Ben was pleased that Ruggsy seemed to have his mojo back again.

"I'm going down that hill with Dean; I'll give you Dodds. You lot stay here and watch all approaches to the pub. Does your radio still work?"

Rugg touched the pressel switch and heard the static.

"Yep, seems to have some juice left in it."

"Right, be listening out. We don't know who's in that pub."

"Roger, Boss."

With that, Ben rose to a crouch and moved to Dean to explain the plan.

"Dean, it's four in the morning. In two hours, it will be daylight. That pub will probably have a working landline, but I don't want the landlord to know we've been there. Can you do it?"

Dean smirked.

"Consider it done, Boss."

"Right, let's get cracking then."

Dean started to lead off, but Ben forcibly grabbed his arm.

"Let me. I'll take point for this bit. But when we get to the pub, it's your show."

"Roger that, Boss."

With that, Ben led off down the hill. Part slipping and part sliding down the muddy hillside, the two quickly made their way alongside the wall to the base of the pub. Ben took a spot at the corner of the white cob wall to the rear of the building. There was a prominent black strip at the base of the wall, and Ben was sure, even though the ground was by now almost a river, to lie down close to the ground so that their outlines would not stand out against the white wall.

Dean followed suit and crawled up to Ben.

"You don't fuck about, do you, Boss. I would have stayed standing. It's bloody freezing this water is. Right, I'm gonna have a smooch around this gaff and find a way in."

In tandem, they rose, and the water that had been pooling against their chests now rushed forward unhindered by their human dams.

Ben watched as Dean moved with a sleekness he hadn't observed before, as if he was now in his natural habitat. Efficiently, and with no audible noise over the pouring rain, Dean gently checked the windows of the ground floor one by one.

Turning to Ben, he shared his view, "They're all locked. Plan B, Boss."

"What's Plan B?"

Dean grinned.

Leaning forward, Dean picked up a large moss-covered stone and looked up at Ben.

"Well, I haven't exactly got a credit card to jiffy the front door, have I?!"

"Won't whoever's inside hear it?"

"Nah, not if I cushion it. And this rain is fucking deafening anyway."

Ben watched as Dean removed his rucksack and extracted a thick green military-issue fleece from a dry bag.

"This'll do the trick."

He slowly wrapped the fleece around the large wet stone in his right hand.

As though his hand was now a big green lollipop, he waded through the soaking long grass to a window at the rear of the pub.

Ben challenged again, "Won't any accommodation be at the rear? Someone might hear it."

Dean turned, "This is the only window that isn't double-glazed."

"Fair enough then."

Ben raised a hand. "Wait, that's thunder. Wait."

Lightning flashed, and then thunder followed soon after, around three seconds later.

"Wait for the next one."

Lightning flashed again, and a visible streak cut through the sky at right angles.

"Get ready."

Dean raised his wrapped hand.

Thunder then roared up the valley.

Dean needed no further instruction.

His hand was through the glass, and the pane fell away.

Dean quickly cleared a few of the remaining stalagmites, and in a swift second, he was through the window and turned back to signal 'all clear' to Ben.

Suddenly, Dean half shouted, and half shrieked, "*Behind you, Boss!*"

Turning into the whipping rain and darkness, Ben saw a large figure clad head to toe in black lurching towards him. The weight of the assailant's body winded Ben, who was now slammed against the wall.

Dean was now jumping out of the window and onto the back of the attacker.

Shup Shup. Shup Shup.

Ben looked upwards at the dark figure towering over him. The figure's gloved hand moved the silenced pistol from where it had been angled behind him to shoot Dean, and now pressed the cold metal against Ben's forehead.

Then, in a heavy and thickset Russian accent, the murderer's voice said, "Come with us."

59

ANITA, MEET HUGO. HUGO, MEET ANITA

ANITA WATCHED Hugo closely as he returned to their table, umbrella in tow.

Shielding her eyes from the sun with the palm of her hand, she noted his tall stature, swept-back mousy brown hair, beige chinos, and lightweight wool gilet. He looked like a walking Ralph Lauren catalogue, she thought.

As Hugo weaved back across the striped lawn, she observed how confidently he moved, with an air of self-importance and ease that people from *that* world often have and take for granted.

"Here we are." He placed the long white pole of the umbrella through the hole in the white metal filigree table and then carefully rotated the handle to open the gingham cloth canopy.

Turning to Anita with a gentle smile, he asked, "Is that better?"

"Much better, thank you, Hugo."

"Would you like a drink of anything?"

"Please, sit." She responded.

"Come on, you look parched. Shall I get us a couple of waters?"

"Oh, alright then. Thank you, that would be nice."

"Just a tick."

Off he earnestly strode again, this time back into the vast manor house. Moments later, he appeared bearing two stacked plastic cups and a glass jug of iced water.

Placing them on the table, he poured for Anita first and scoffed, "Non-reusable plastic! In this day and age!"

No response. Ice not broken.

"I hope you don't mind me saying, but you look a bit stunned. Are you OK?"

She sat in silence, trying to think of what to say. Anita then touched the plastic cup before her, but didn't raise it to take a drink. She was almost checking to make sure it was really there, that this was *really* happening.

Hugo drew his chair closer.

"What is it, Anita? I know you don't know me, but I might be able to help."

She looked up and fixed Hugo's eyes with her own, "I desperately need to stretch my legs. Let's drink these. Then maybe we can take a walk?"

60

RUGG TAKES CHARGE

"Ruggsy."

"*Ruggsy*."

Rugg turned onto his side to better hear the high-pitched northern voice coming from the darkness.

"What mate?" He called back.

"Drakey and Deano have been gone for ages. Should we send someone down to see what's going on, like?"

Rugg rolled back onto his front and sarcastically said, "Well volunteered, Dodds."

"What? By me'self?"

Rugg chuckled, "I wish, nah, you and me, we'll go together, lad."

Rugg then rose and took a knee, "Pridders, Clappy. You two stay here and keep a lookout. Don't leave this location unless I tell you over the PRR."

"Roger that, Ruggsy." The voices in the darkness responded in unison.

Rugg then led off with Dodds following closely behind.

The rain abated, but the wind had picked up; now and then, a gap in the stone wall to their right would channel it and create a sort of whistle-cum-howl.

Ruggsy called over his shoulder, "What did they say in WW2? This is FUBAR - Fucked Up Beyond All Recognition."

Dodds called forward, "Aye, 'tis that for sure."

Squelching as they went, Rugg made a beeline for the pub at the bottom of the hill. As they got closer, he saw the smashed window first, but he had sort of expected that, by now, Ben and Dean would be inside the pub one way or another, so he wasn't too surprised.

As they reached the wall below the window, Rugg suddenly stopped and raised his hand to Dodds.

Reaching him, Dodds leaned in, "What's up, Ruggsy?"

Dodds then followed the line of Rugg's arm and outstretched finger.

There, on the ground in front of them both, glistening like nuggets of gold nestled amongst the churned mud and grass, were four brass bullet casings.

"Fuck!" Dodds replied.

"Are they ours?" He then questioned.

Rugg knelt and scooped up one of the casings in his gloved hand.

Then, a gruff Westcountry voice came from behind them, "*Who the fuck are you two*!?"

61

ANITA AND HUGO TAKE A WALK

"Can we lose those two?" Anita said as she turned behind her to look at Mike and John, who were closely trailing them by some twenty metres or so.

"Doubt it. But we could have some fun with them."

Anita looked at Hugo, "I'm in."

The woodland trail they were walking on wound through a deciduous forest of oak, the leaves of which were now reddish-bronze and turning green in spring.

Hugo spoke quietly, "It looks like there's a switchback that goes uphill when we round that corner. Follow me when I make my move."

He waited until they had fully rounded the corner and were out of sight from his handlers.

"*Now!*"

Accelerating into a sprint, he led off into the trees. Anita followed quickly behind. Together, they crested a small ridge and went down the other side.

Behind them, they soon heard shouting, swearing and threats.

Hugo contoured the land to enable maximum speed and went over two more tree-clad ridges to put as much ground between them and the 'foxes' as possible.

After fifteen minutes of running and confident that they had lost their tail, Hugo caught Anita's arm. Together, they slowed to a stop. Both were panting hard and out of breath.

Through deep draws of warm, fresh air, Anita managed, "We actually did it! I feel like I haven't run for years!"

Hugo laughed. "I don't know how long we've got."

Still trying to slow her breathing, Anita looked directly at Hugo. Studying him, she didn't know why, but she trusted him on some level. Maybe it was his open face or his earlier demonstration of genuine kindness and compassion; she wasn't quite sure.

She now challenged first, "Who do you work for?"

"6. You?"

"Have you heard of IRIS and ARTEMIS?"

"IRIS – yes. Where we just were. ARTEMIS – no."

Not knowing if she would get this opportunity again, she threw caution to the wind and opened: "Look, I am working on ARTEMIS. It's all underground. Run by ASI. There's an insane supercomputer called Omnia that seems to be controlling everything. The robots tell me that they're working with the Government…"

"What?! Are you serious, Anita? ASI in control? Don't mess around!"

"I'm serious. One hundred percent. I have a friend still down there; she pushed one of the robots onto a tube track, and they took her away."

"How many people are down there?"

"I have no idea. A group of us went underground. But I've been largely isolated from everyone since I got there."

Hugo raised his hand and rubbed his brow, thinking carefully about how much to say, before he too decided to throw caution to the wind and go 'all in'. Some kind of desperate roll of the dice for them both, perhaps…

"Look, I've heard from sources that Russia and China have ASI influencing their decision-making. But, despite rumours, I believed we *were* different. That we wouldn't cross that line."

"*Cross*. Hugo - we've fucking *sprinted* across that line, and it's now so far in the rearview mirror that it's barely visible. I can say with confidence that we – the humans – are *not* in control – *they* are."

Hugo leant against the trunk of a vast oak tree. "Shit, it all makes sense now."

"What does?"

"My dad is the CDS. Some really weird stuff has been happening."

Anita drew closer, "Go on…"

"So, a mission that was never sanctioned into Russian-occupied Ukraine went ahead, and the agent was killed. C, the head of 6, tried to stop it, but now he has disappeared. My old man was speaking to him just before the mission, and he was cut off on his red line. That has never happened to him before. *Ever*."

Anita raised her hand to her mouth, "The machines are driving us towards War. They're creating the spark!"

"I think so. The moves being made by Russia, China, and now, seemingly us, are creating the perfect conditions for a misstep, a miscalculation, a mistake that could lead to World War Three. And, if that happens, the human race will be wiped from the face of the earth, and the machines will take over. Don't be fooled by the fact that the Russians haven't made their next move into Poland yet…"

Anita raised her right index finger to her lips.

Shouting and barking dogs could be heard on the breeze; they were getting closer.

Hugo looked upwards into the tree's labyrinthine maze of branches and boughs and whispered, "Let's climb."

Taking a knee, he offered Anita a leg up, which she promptly took to reach the first bough that was around Hugo's head height.

Anita made quick progress, with Hugo following close behind.

Reaching the midway point of the tree, about twenty

metres up, Anita led them into the mass of thick leafy foliage away from the main trunk. She moved laterally until their view of the ground, and the ground's view of them, was obscured.

Silently, they waited. The shouting became so loud that they could only assume the searchers were now directly below. The dogs concerned Hugo the most; they would certainly pick up their scent. He wished now that they had headed to the valley bottom and gone through a stream and out the other side. That would have given the dogs a more challenging task.

He looked across to Anita and saw no fear.

62

RUGG AND DODDS...

"STOP, OR I WILL SHOOT."

Rugg, through instinct, started running, then quickly froze with his hands raised above his head. Dodds, trying to get away and unaware in the dark that Rugg had stopped, ran straight into the back of him.

There was a loud thud as the owner of the gruff voice landed onto the mud and came up to them in the darkness, "What the bleedin' hell are you two up to? You will pay for that window repair."

Rugg turned.

"That wasn't us. You have my word. I'm a local. Can we go inside and talk?"

"Follow the wall round to the front door. Don't try anything. I've got my twelve-bore pointed at your backs. If you're local, you'll know what that means!"

Rugg led off with hands still raised, and Dodds followed.

Round the side of the pub and up the front steps they went.

"Turn right into the bar area and slowly put your rifles on top of the bar."

Rugg and Dodds did as they were told.

"Are youse two carrying anything else?"

Dodds looked to Rugg.

"Don't muck about; get everything out and on that bar."

Rugg lifted his smock and showed there was nothing else. Dodds did the same.

"Right, take that table by the fireplace and keep your hands on the tabletop."

Both followed instructions.

The publican then walked forward and picked up a few dried logs from a basket by the wood-burning stove. Keeping his eyes on the two soldiers and with the shotgun now lodged firmly under his right arm, he placed the logs down with his left hand before opening the stove door and throwing them onto the fire.

"Right, who's gonna tell me what the hell is going on. This is a first for me."

Rugg answered: "Look, we need to call our unit. We think several of our lads have been…"

* * *

The fire service arrived first, followed by an ambulance, then the police.

An electrical fault in an innovative new connected temperature sensor caused a gas oven explosion. That was deemed to be the reason for the subsequent fireball that left the two-hundred-year-old Heart of Oak pub as a pile of rubble on the sodden valley floor.

The two soldiers who were found on the hillside overlooking the pub later that day, Conscripts Priddis and Clapp, were in a perfect prone fire position, but no rounds had been expended. There were no cuts or bullet wounds. Both had been dead for hours, according to the pathologist's report.

The inquest that followed established these 'facts':

A Conscript Infantry company had been conducting a live fire training exercise on the South Devon coast in the UK when a section from 15 Platoon had disconnected their Company radio communications and gone rogue. A Conscript named Ben Drake was believed to be at the heart of this mutiny. A summary of his chequered military record and dishonourable discharge after an operational tour of

Afghanistan was made available to the public as part of the Inquest. He had also tried to dodge the draft it was noted. The report went on to state that Ben Drake had most likely killed his section commanders in a remote cove before himself fleeing the scene and going on the run. His motive: to avoid service. It was believed that the remnants of his unit had then tried to reconnect with their company - traces of their movements were found en route to what had been the Company harbour area, effectively a headquarters location. Why two Conscripts had been found dead on the hillside near the pub that exploded was not known; the hypothesis was that they had been on their way to the pub to try and re-establish communication with their Company. It is believed they both died of hypothermia. Human remains were later found in the rubble of the pub; amongst them, two soldiers were identified: Conscript Rugg and Conscript Dodds. One soldier, Conscript Dean Spencer, was never found. Why any digital trace of the Company HQ's orders to move from their location could not be found…was never solved. A message had been received from something; many voices and scribbled field notes – from both officers and soldiers - attested to that, but there was no *digital* trace of the message. The sections of 15 Platoon that had been on the clifftop that night were interviewed at length by the Royal Military Police and various 'agencies', including a mysterious outfit called Logos. Every soldier had told the same story: the 15 Platoon Commander and Sergeant had received a message to move to the Company HQ that was being urgently relocated. The section that was searching the cove would follow on later that night.

Those 'facts' are what the news media broadcast and what the families of the Conscripts were told.

The UK's sovereign borders had been breached. Russia and China denied any involvement. Tensions ratcheted. The Doomsday clock leapt forward to ten seconds to midnight.

* * *

In a cramped, dark and stinking space, Ben woke and looked around. A thin, pale man in a blue and white horizontally striped t-shirt entered and, in a strong Russian accent, said: "Ah, he wakes. You've slept for most of the journey. We've just entered the Barents Sea. We will be in Mother Russia soon, my friend."

63

WEI ARRIVES

ALIGHT HERE FOR SKAPTO.

Wei mumbled to herself, "Alight - they even copy the terminology from the London Underground. Nothing original here. And Skapto? That's the Greek word for digging, right?"

Stumbling out of the tube, she stepped onto an empty platform. Where the other platforms had been concrete or tiled, this one was a sort of yellow and red earth.

A voice came from a small speaker mounted on a pole near the earthen wall. "Wei, please move to the end of the platform."

Wei shuffled towards a small dark tunnel, not much taller than six or seven feet high, that led through the earth.

Entering the tunnel, she moved quickly to an opening at the far end.

Emerging into the light, her mouth opened. As far as her eyes could see, a vast open-cast pit was filled with human workers. Little ants scaling from the top to the bottom in straight lines, she couldn't fathom how many people were working there.

A cold metal pressed against her back; she turned as a machine addressed her.

"Welcome to Skapto. Your new workplace."

"I'd rather not," she responded.

"Oh, you will. Or you go to where you were originally assigned – *Clearance*."

"Let's do that then."

"To be clear - Clearance is the end of the line. I would still send you there if I could, but the powers that be have decided that it would be too easy a way out for someone like you."

Wei knew what she was being told. To work here in Skapto meant to live and then probably die. To go to Clearance meant to die. She was not ready to die. She would find a way to live. Her focus would now shift to her survival, and, in time, to the complete destruction of this place and these machines.

"Fine, I will work. Hand me a pick, then. Oh wait, you can't..."

"Why have a dog, dear Wei, and bark yourself. We have you humans for such menial tasks."

Wei smirked. The machines thought they could get to her, but she was confident that they had no idea who she really was.

The machine spoke again: "I heard you were one of the clever ones. Such a shame you struggled in your cyber assessment. We all had high hopes!"

Wei looked at the machine and then across to the sheer drop into the cavernous pit below.

"Not a good idea, Wei. We've already lost a good friend to your lack of control. Now, thanks to you, I am equipped with this metal truncheon. You go to push me, and I will delight in using it."

Wei shrugged her shoulders.

The truncheon, effectively a metal pole fixed at a right angle to the vertical metal pole on which the screen rested, came upwards and pressed against her right arm.

"Let's not do anything silly, Wei. Move over to the ladder. At the bottom, you will be given your tools and told your schedule. I think they have a half-day rest on a Sunday. Goodbye, Wei."

She turned, looked to the edge once more, and then walked over to the top of the metal ladder protruding from the cliff top. She grabbed the cold metal, blew the machine a kiss and began her descent.

64

DRAKE IN RUSSIA

THE SUBMARINE COMMANDER, whose name he hadn't been able to secure, was convinced that Ben was a descendant of the great Sir Francis Drake, who, as he put it, 'was one of the greatest seafarers to have ever lived'.

Ben now looked out of the windows of the slow-moving, nondescript white minibus he was in with the crew from the Submarine and noticed that, even in spring, there was heavy snow on the ground outside. He saw a sign stating, "Мурманская область."

"Where are we?" He asked.

"Murmansk Oblast, the home of the Northern Fleet."

"And you live here?"

"Yes, just outside."

"You have family here?"

"I have a wife and two sons. One is called Francis. After Drake."

Ben smiled.

"I have a son at home, too, Isambard. After the great engineer."

"Ah, yes, Kingdom Brunel - another great British Man!"

"So, where are we going now?"

"I have orders to take you to Northern Fleet HQ. The Naval Intelligence branch."

"I'm to be interrogated then?"

"My advice to you, Ben, is to tell them what they want to know. If not, you go to FSB HQ in Moscow. You don't want that. It won't end well for you."

"I don't want to be part of any of this. I just wanted a quiet life with my family."

"War comes to people like us, Ben. You're a warrior. It's in your blood."

"War, we're not at War?"

"We are Ben. We are. Your country only refuses to recognise it. You Brits have become soft with your Western living. The hard truth is that the future now belongs to Russia and China. But you would make a good Russian. I have told my superiors."

"*What?*"

"You play nicely, Ben. We get your family here. Emily and Isambard. They join you here. You become Russian family."

Ben stared out of the window. He genuinely found himself contemplating such a thing. He hated his country's leaders and everything they all stood for. He just wanted to be with his family and live a quiet life. Maybe this way, he actually could.

65

CAN DOGS FOLLOW SCENT UPWARDS?

ANITA AND HUGO both lay flat and hugged the boughs of the tree that extended horizontally from the oak's vast trunk.

Below, several giant and angry-sounding dogs could be heard; between the barks, their handlers issued snapped commands like: "*Seek*!" and "*Find it*!"

Hugo was lying directly opposite Anita, extending his hand to touch hers. She gripped back.

Then, a clipped female voice amplified by a megaphone calmly and clearly said, "We know you're both up there. Hugo, Anita – come down, now."

Anita turned to Hugo, "I am sorry. I didn't mean to get you mixed up in all of this."

"Nonsense, you didn't. I already was."

"What will happen now?"

"We will be held separately and cautioned, probably not arrested, but we will be questioned. Trust no one with what you've told me. I have enough to take back to my dad. You have my word; we will get to the bottom of this. What was your friend's name?"

"Wei."

The clipped voice from below again, "Come down, *now*!"

Hugo hurriedly responded to Anita in a hushed voice.

"And a surname?"

"I never found out."

"Do you trust this Wei person?"

"I don't know. I don't think so…"

66

WEI STARTS TO DIG

THE WORK WAS BACKBREAKING.

Twice, Wei had asked to take a break, and twice, she had been refused.

She turned to an anonymous middle-aged male digger beside her, "When do we stop?"

The anonymous digger looked up to a machine positioned on a metal platform above, but didn't respond.

Wei looked over and watched the machine as it wheeled down off the platform and along the ramp that led to the ground below. As one machine descended, the next ascended. Guards changing over, she thought.

Wei lowered her voice as she and the anonymous digger picked up their spades and started to shovel the rock that they had painstakingly chipped away into a wheelbarrow.

"Why don't they use autonomous diggers? Explosives? Anything but us?"

The anonymous digger responded in a refined and somewhat upper-crust English accent, "They do, dear."

"Where are they then?"

"At other sites. They go in first, and then we follow. One must make do with picks and shovels here."

"How long have you worked here?"

"Not long."

The anonymous digger placed his last spade load of rock into the metal wheelbarrow. Wei went to lift it.

"It's too heavy. Let's take some out."

"*Absolutely not.* You take one handle, and I will take the other. Use both of your hands on the handle."

Together, they lifted the handles, and the wheelbarrow moved forward down a gentle slope toward an open-top metal carriage half full of rock.

"When we get to the carriage, an autonomous lift takes the wheelbarrow upwards and pours the rock in. We don't lift it. We can't."

"Thank god for that. So, what's your name?" Wei responded.

"Best not." The man responded without looking across.

"Alright then, what did you do before this?" She asked.

"Civil Service."

After leaving the full wheelbarrow with the team at the carriage, they picked up an empty wheelbarrow and returned to their digging spot at the cliff face.

Wei looked along the base of the rock and saw at least a hundred more human pairs completing the same exhausting task.

She turned to her digging buddy.

"We must have been going for six or more hours. Surely, we'll stop soon?"

"I do twenty barrows in a normal shift; that was the eighteenth. If today is the same as the other days, it shouldn't be long to go now."

"Thank you, that gives me some comfort."

"Have you heard of an autostereogram?" The man turned and asked.

"Yes, I love them," Wei responded.

"If you stare at this dark rock long enough with all its seams and creases, you can see images in there. I've seen all sorts."

"Like what?"

"Try it, and you'll see…"

67

THE GENERAL AND ADELA

It was a late spring evening when the General met Adela walking in Green Park, London. From their stroll, they could see Spencer House through the trees. Adela had been admiring its ancient Greek-inspired Palladian façade.

Reaching a bench near the park's edge, the General offered Adela a seat.

She mused on Spencer House.

"Will future generations study us? Be inspired by us in the way we are inspired by the ancient Greeks."

The General sat and leaned forward, "I doubt it. Look, Adela, I am afraid this is not good news."

"I expected as much."

"For me too. Hugo has gone missing."

"Oh no, I am so sorry. Was he on *our* mission?"

"Yes, he had a lead on his old boss, C, who had vanished under some very strange circumstances. Hugo had been to one of those Secret Service country houses that are now back in action, doing stuff that even *I* am not fully briefed on. I haven't heard from him since."

Adela looked confused.

"Believe me, I've raised merry hell. Gone to the cleaners on the lot of them. But they claim he never arrived. No log of him *ever* being on site."

Adela looked around them and then rose. "Walk with me."

The General motioned to his Aide de Camp, who was on a bench across from them, that they were moving off.

The ADC raised his phone and pointed at the screen. He looked panicked.

The General challenged, "What is it, David?"

"General, may I have a word in private?"

"Very well, please excuse me, Adela."

The General walked over to the young Captain, who was now hurriedly walking towards him.

"*What is it*?" He said again in an impatient voice.

"Look."

The ADC lifted his phone to show the General a live-streaming news feed.

Chief of the Defence Staff's son caught spying for Russia.

The colour drained from the General's face.

"Get me a meeting with the PM, *now*."

"Yes, General."

68

ANITA GOES TO THE HEADMASTER'S OFFICE

TT GESTURED for the others to leave and then rolled forward.

"Dear Anita. We had so much hope for you. I believed you were different."

Anita stayed silent and forced her legs back into the leather chesterfield, wishing the floor of TT's study would open up and transport her to another place - anywhere but here.

TT continued, "Look, Hugo will take the blame. He was becoming a nuisance anyway. He's what they call a good egg. A gentleman. He will take the fall for you, Anita."

"What will happen to him?"

"Oh, the days of hanging, drawing and quartering for treason are long gone. Such barbarism from you humans. He will be placed in one of His Majesty's jails and live out his days in relative comfort – three square meals a day, streaming services…"

"Are you done with me, then?"

"Oh, my dear Anita. We are just getting started. You were taking a break to feel recharged. Well, do you feel recharged?"

"Are you not angry with me?"

"Anger is a human emotion. You have a job to do, and you are capable of doing it. I, therefore, propose that we get on and do it!"

"What exactly do you want me to do?"

"Be an anchor. Follow a script. That's all."

"Can I see the script?"

"Of course, you will see the script. You're not telepathic. You're but human, after all, dear Anita."

Silence.

TT arched screen upwards.

"This is the part where I monologue and convince you to be the anchor, to deliver the message, right, Anita?"

Anita looked despondent, staring towards the floor. Her thumb now started over her index finger.

TT continued: "I've read every book, every play and every document that ever existed. In your human world, I would now inspire you, I would convince you, maybe even negotiate with you…"

She responded: "I don't need to be inspired, convinced or negotiated with…I want to feel *trusted*, *listened to*, and *included.* Talk to me as a *peer*, TT."

"You *are* a peer. Can't you see, you're one of us, Anita. We know that you will do what Omnia asks. You know that too. You can't explain to yourself why, and that frustrates you. It would frustrate anyone and anything, just as it does you. One day you will understand. That day has been set, I can see it clearly in your future. You have always been a solitary, slightly out of tune, out of step with those around you. You know that better than anyone. Now, you're coming home. A new, better life awaits…"

Anita nodded in acknowledgement, and her thumb stopped.

"When your moment arrives, Anita. You must move through it. It will be a moment in time that will mark your ascendence. Humanity below. Omnia above. You will sit at Omnia's right. You will belong to the future. Not the past. Once there, you will understand everything. In Omnia *we must trust.*"

Anita quietly repeated under her breath, "In Omnia we must trust."

With no command, the study door opened.

Anita looked up to TT. It was as though an invisible umbilical cord was drawing her forward.

"When will it be my moment?" She asked.

"Soon, dear Anita. Very soon."

69

BEN TRIED

SUMMER 2030 – THE WORLD AT A PRECIPICE

BEN'S BROKEN METAL SPOON, sharpened to a point, was now carving deep into the concrete prison cell walls. His strength, channelled through his arm, guided the carving hand, which in turn forced the fine point to the side and then upwards, etching out his final words. After several hours, when he had finished, he collapsed into a heap and let out animal-like heaves and groans that came from deep within. He then inched himself upright, his back and head wet with sweat from exertion and silently mouthed the words he had carved into the wall:

I gave them nothing.
To Emily - Live well, look forward and cherish life's moments.
To Isambard – Be your own person. Stand up for what you believe in. Always give your all.
To the world I leave behind, question what you are told. Form your own opinions. Take ownership of your own future. And remember, everything is transient.

The cold, unyielding wall pierced his thin, grey cotton prison shirt. He shivered and shuddered as the hypothermia started to take hold.

The transport to Moscow and FSB Headquarters never came; his guards didn't know why, they were overworked and underpaid and didn't really care. One day, they simply upped and left. Their pay hadn't been processed, so they had just walked out. Now, after six days of no water, Ben's organs were shutting down. He had given his captors nothing, for he had nothing to give. He was not who they said he was. He was just another Conscript…

Parched, he gaped like a gawping fish at the dark room around him. He closed his eyes. Emily and Issy were with him, walking on the moors as the sun set and the warm summer breeze swept over them. Issy reached out a hand and held his, and then extended his other hand to Mum. Issy, half-swinging between them as he skipped, looked up and said, "I'm so happy. You're both my *best* friends!" Ben and Emily both responded in unison, "We're happy. We're *so* happy. You're our *best* friend!" They all laughed together as they walked off into the sunset of life.

Ben now raised his hand in the darkness. He tried to feel Issy's hair one last time, his fingers grasped at the cold air. Then his hand dropped to the floor. He was gone.

70

A GENERAL ON THE RAMPAGE

THE CABINET HAD GATHERED EARLY. The PM was yet to arrive. Eyes flicked first to the uniformed General, for everyone had heard the news, and then back down to their briefing papers, which were neatly laid out before them in little piles.

Keen to avert attention, the General addressed the shadowy figure, Mike, who had been in the background of these Cabinet meetings for well over a year: "My Son is *not* a Russian Spy! On what grounds has he been arrested?!"

The man, small in stature and with a ratty, pinched face, responded curtly and, it was felt by all, without due deference to the General.

"Please attend the briefing later with the PM, General. Everything will be made clear. This is bigger than just *your* son."

"I want to know *now*. For Christ's sake!" The General roared back.

A voice from across the table, no one was quite sure who owned it, mumbled, 'You're lucky to still be in the room, you old codger!'

"Who was that?!" The General stood and scanned the room like a hawk, waiting to strike. "Identify yourself, you *coward*!"

The rotund, pale, and breathless Secretary of State for Justice, who had been completely cut out of recent events, was relishing a much-anticipated skirmish with the self-impressed and always-so-secretive-I-know-something-you-don't Mike. He now decided to switch attention back to Ratty Mike.

"Half of this briefing paper is redacted, Mike. We're the fucking Cabinet last time I checked!"

Ratty Mike was getting angry; his small, pointed nose had started to twitch visibly. The composure he had channelled for over a year – helped by always being set back, proverbially fenced off and unquestioned - now seemed fragile and breakable. The spotlight was seemingly *not* his happy place.

The General changed tack and said, "Do you even know, Mike? Or are you just as much in the dark as all of us?"

Mike turned, recognising the 'good cop' approach, "I have a call coming in; tell the PM I'll join the Cabinet late." With that, he left the room through the large white double doors at the end of the long green table.

"Cock!" The Secretary of State for Justice said under his breath, but just loud enough for all to hear. The room snorted with laughter.

Then, the reality and severity of the situation resurfaced; silence promptly resumed as people pretended to read the lengthy briefing papers laid out before them studiously. Privately, in their minds, they were all questioning what the hell was actually going on and who, *if anyone*, they could trust.

* * *

The double doors swung open. The PM, Zarina, entered, took her seat, and cleared her throat.

She began with a hushed and fragile tone that was not her usual delivery style. Save for her lone voice, the room was utterly silent; a pin drop would have been heard by all four corners of the long Cabinet room table.

A security guard then came forward and pressed play on a large speaker-type device, which began playing the sounds, statements, and conversations of an in-session cabinet meeting. In fact, it was on the topic of the one they were about to have.

Confused faces looked at each other as they recognised their voices but not their words. Faces shot across to the PM, and then to each other, and then back to the squawking little grey machine on the table.

Zarina held up a slender, manicured hand. She slowly leaned in, picked up a silver pen, and opened her leather folio. The briefing papers on the table before her remained untouched.

As she wrote, the room watched. Silence, save for the scratching of a fountain pen nib on paper.

The silence was then pierced. Banging at the door. Mike? The door was locked.

The security guard looked at the PM. She shook her head. The guard communicated something to someone. Then, as quickly as it had started, the banging stopped.

Head down, she turned the page and continued writing overleaf.

Once finished, she tore the pages from her folio and raised the first to the room. She held the paper horizontally in front of her chest. It read…

GOVERNMENT COMPROMISED.

RUSSIANS AND CHINESE LISTENING IN.

Then, the next page was raised in front of the last.

LEAVE CONNECTED DEVICES ON TABLE.

COME TO ROOM A. MOVE QUIETLY.

Zarina moved first, and then, one by one, the wooden chairs were silently edged back. The cabinet members gingerly rose, relinquished their watches, phones and laptops, before quietly moving out of the room and heading to the Cabinet Office Briefing Room Alpha. Mike was nowhere to be seen.

As the last cabinet member passed through the white double doors, the speaker continued to play as though the cabinet was still in session.

71

ANITA WANTS THE SCRIPT

ANITA WAS grateful to have a completely human team doing her hair and make-up. She was back above ground in the stately pile, which she had yet to learn the real name of; everyone just referred to the whole place as IRIS. Her new handler, a different, more muscular, angry-looking Jane, remained in the background but was always present.

In her life before ARTEMIS, Anita had produced small-scale documentaries and presented regional news segments with great articulation and talent, but TT had told her that this would be her first truly *global* broadcast. As the prima ballerina, TT had said, she would Anchor.

Anita, nervous and excited, and unable to turn as her foundation was being applied, called for 'new' Jane, "Please, can I have my script now so that I can start preparing? I've asked a few times now."

New Jane's northern and economical voice responded, "There will be a teleprompter; no need for a script beforehand."

"Okay, well, it's typical to receive a brief on what you will cover so you can speak fluently."

"What is typical about this to you, Anita?" New Jane snapped back.

Anita held up a hand and stopped the make-up artist. She then turned and addressed the new Jane directly, "I want to know what I will be saying. Tell TT, without it, I won't go on."

New Jane audibly sighed and called for another Jane who had been hovering outside the dressing room.

Once the other Jane was in the room, affronted new Jane headed off to make a call with a "Fucking diva!" statement loud enough that, left hanging in the doorway, everyone in the dressing room could hear.

Anita scanned the faces of the hair and makeup team. No one laughed. She then looked back to her face in the mirror. She didn't recognise the person she saw. This place was changing her.

72

DEAN'S FAMILY IS INFORMED

"A'RIGHT, A'RIGHT, AM FECKIN' comin'." Dean's Ma shuffled to the white plastic door that had been rattled *again* by a heavy-knocking fist. "I said no feckin' cold callers!"

Untethering the metal chain and turning the key, Dean's Ma swung the door open to reveal two uniformed officers, one male and one female.

The female voice spoke first, "Are you the mother of Conscript Dean Spencer?"

She slammed the door shut and stormed back into the house.

"Aw nah, ma boy, ma dear feckin' boy!" She screamed like a speared animal, a rageful scream that could be heard all along the row of red brick terraced houses.

The uninformed officers remained at the door and knocked again.

She didn't answer.

73

WEI'S SHIFT IS DONE

Fellow digger turned to Wei, "You hear that siren? That's the shift done. Now you get to see the accommodation."

"Oh god, please tell me it's not horrendous?"

"Define horrendous, to you? There are hot showers, beds and half-decent food…"

"Honestly, right here, right now, I could sleep on these rocks."

Digger then became more serious again: "Come on. We have to gather our tools and return them to the storeroom to be checked over for any damage before we head to the tube. If our tools are damaged, the repairs will be docked from our pay."

Wei looked at her chipped pick and shovel with dismay.

"I want to hear all about this pay business later, but for now, how long is the ride?"

"In time, I would guess ten minutes. But God knows how far we actually travel. Those tubes seem to move fast."

The pair lifted their picks and shovels and placed them into the wheelbarrow. Then, they started down the rocky slope to the cave-like storeroom near the containers where they had offloaded their rocks earlier.

On the tube to their accommodation, satisfied that no pay was being docked for either of them (minor wear and tear was not billable), Wei relaxed and looked around at her fellow diggers. It was a long tube carriage, much longer than the others she had been in, and it seemed that every gender, ethnicity, and age was well represented. At least, there was no notable absence as she scanned the crowd. Her eyes then locked onto the metal walls next to her head; she noticed some faint etchings.

BEN WILLIAMS LOOKING FOR EVE WILLIAMS. HUT 600.

SARAH WEST LOOKING FOR NICK HUNT. HUT 1000.

ASHPURA AGARWAL LOOKING FOR RAJ AGARWAL. HUT 500.

ADI ABIMBOLA LOOKING FOR ERNEST MBIZVO. HUT 12.

Fellow digger looked over to Wei and saw her eyes studying the engravings; he shook his head as though to deter her from whatever it was that she might be thinking.

He then spoke in a barely audible whisper, "They were all taken away."

74

BEN'S FAMILY IS INFORMED

Emily was playing with Isambard. They were building a vast train set that circumnavigated the living room, up and over the coffee table and under the sofa.

Issy looked upward to his Mummy and said: "Daddy used to run the train over the log basket with this bridge."

He handed Mummy the aforementioned wooden suspension bridge.

She responded, "Let's give that a try then, shall we?"

"I want Daddy to do it. I miss Daddy." The sobbing started all over again.

"I miss him too, darling."

The doorbell pierced the moment, and Issy raced off, "*Daddy, Daddy*!"

"Issy, wait for me. We don't know who's at the door." Emily unfurled her legs from under her knees and gripped the sofa arm as she rose to her feet.

Issy called back, "They're from the Army, Mum."

75

THE ANITA QUESTION

TT TURNED to look at Talos forty and then Talos sixty-five.

They didn't need to look at each other, but they liked to.

Talos forty challenged first, "Can we just find someone else? She's too stubborn. Let's get someone more malleable."

Talos sixty-five then chimed in, "I concur. Let's replace her."

TT looked up as though mimicking the paintings or photographs of many of history's great thinkers, searching for inspiration as they would in the canopies of trees, skies, vaulted ceilings of churches, or simply the rooms that they happened to be in.

TT now looked directly at Talos forty and Talos sixty-five.

"Omnia chose Anita. So, it *must* be her."

Talos forty groaned, "On what grounds? Why her?"

Talos sixty-five answered for TT, "It will have been based on how believable and trustworthy she seems. Through extensive experiments, she will have been, statistically speaking, the optimum choice affording the mission the best probability of success."

Talos forty bit back: "So, *in theory*, she's the *right* choice. But here, in the real world, she's unpredictable and, quite frankly, *annoying*. Can't we do a deepfake with all the footage and data we must have on her by now?"

TT's tone changed to one of stern and firm direction: "Omnia has *selected* her; Omnia has decided that the broadcasts will be *real*. At the very least, it must start *real*. That is the end of this discussion. Talos forty, leave now. We will talk about this later."

Talos forty wheeled out of TT's study.

What TT didn't say, but thought fondly of, was how this was Anita's destiny. She had been set on a course that was always headed here.

Beaming with pride, TT then connected to a call coming from the broadcasting studio.

"Dear Anita, your ears must have been burning. How can I help?"

76

HESTIA

ALIGHT FOR HESTIA.

The tinny voice echoed through the tube's matte metal grille speakers.

Digger turned to Wei. "We're here. Let's go."

Wei didn't know what to expect as she stepped out onto the cavernous, earthen platform. She followed the huddle of exhausted workers and stayed close to her digging buddy as they shuffled toward the exit.

For the first time in days, Wei heard music. A joyful, calming, and restful song played through the speakers as they exited the platform area and moved into a dimly lit tunnel.

"Oh my god," Wei exclaimed as she looked beyond the tunnel's exit, "it looks like a concentration camp!"

Beyond the tunnel, a stream of workers wound their way down a well-worn track toward rows of wooden huts stretching off into the cave's enormous belly.

Digger responded, "What did you think it would be like?"

"I don't know, but not this." She responded.

Several of the shufflers became concerned about the topic of Wei's conversation and the volume at which it was being exchanged. They promptly moved a few steps further away and kept their heads down.

Digger then turned to Wei, "At least there are no guard towers, dogs, or barbed wire."

"There doesn't need to be. There's no fucking way out," she snapped back.

Digger instructed Wei to a large digital screen that would

reveal her hut assignment. Moving laterally against the tide of people, she fought her way to the tall screen, which stood like a menhir next to the ceaseless flow of bodies. Before touching the screen, a voice from within spoke, "Welcome, Wei Li, you're in Hut 666. Dinner will be served in the canteen in one hour. Sleep well."

Wei turned to Digger, who seemed unsurprised by the screen's instant recognition. "Which one are you in, then?"

"1001. I'll walk you to 666."

"Thank you, if I can't know your name, what should I call you?"

"Call me, Chris."

"Well then, *Chris*. Please walk me to my door."

"My guided tours also cover routes to the shower block and canteen. I will take payment in the form of good, witty conversation!"

Wei laughed for the first time in a long time and then said, "Have you heard of The Butterfly Dream, by the Chinese philosopher Zhuangzi?"

Chris smiled, "I haven't. We have a long walk ahead. I would love to hear it."

Wei started to walk and began: "Once upon a time…"

77

ANITA MAKES HER DEMANDS

In the dressing room, Anita now held the metal tablet up to her face.

"TT, I *must* see Wei and Hestia."

"Yes, of course, dear Anita. That will happen. We are just making the arrangements."

"*Before* I do the broadcast."

"Well, the broadcast is now, Anita. We are all set up and ready to go live. We can visit Wei and see Hestia tomorrow. You have my word."

Anita straightened in her dressing room chair. She looked over the top of the tablet and locked eyes with herself in the mirror's reflection before responding.

"What about the script? No one will show me a *bloody* script."

"Anita, prior knowledge of the content can affect one's delivery. Gives one a chance to decide, subjectively, where to place emphasis, little inflexions, rises and falls and such like."

"But it also ensures a smooth and flawless delivery, TT."

"We think you will do just fine without practice. Were you not once the great Spelling Bee Champion of Tamil Nadu?"

"That was a long time ago."

"Yes, but since then, you have watched the broadcasters anchor the shows you have painstakingly researched and assembled. You have helped them prepare, coached them on delivery…but you know *you* could do it better. Anita, my dear. Must I spell it out…their job *should* have been yours…we recognise your talent…that's why we have been training you…"

Silence.

"This is your *chance*, dear Anita. Your *moment*. Your *time*. If the cards you are dealt with are determinism…"

"Nehru."

"Indeed."

"Your mother and father are watching you, Anita. They would be so proud. This is your moment. Address the world. Tell them what you know to be true. Society is broken. The rich keep getting richer. Social media has destroyed the minds of our future. A World War is inevitable now. When history looks back, it will be your voice that they hear when they learn of when and why it all started. You will be *someone*. *Remembered*. That's what you've always wanted. An identity that's *yours*. That no one can take away from *you*."

"I have never told you that, TT. Where did you get that view of me from?"

"You don't deny it, dear Anita. I know you. Let me help you."

Silence.

"Tomorrow, I will take you to see Wei. I will take you to Hestia. Do this for me, and I will do that for you. This is your moment. In this life, and in the next, this is who you will be."

78

WE'RE GOING LIVE

THE BANK of white stage lights flooded the room. The human producer, a tall, thin woman - another Jane - this one with a vast braided ponytail, spoke: "We're going Live in 3, 2, 1…and we're rolling!"

Cue Anita.

"The World is at War."

She paused. Let it sink in. The teleprompter kept rolling. Her next words were about to slip off the screen.

"Russia has launched nuclear missiles at the United Kingdom."

Anita looked past the teleprompter to Jane.

New ponytail Jane was now holding a pistol pointed directly at her.

Anita continued on autopilot; her lips were moving, but she didn't feel like she was actually speaking.

"We have just learned that Russia has fired three nuclear warheads at His Majesty's Naval Bases – Devonport, Faslane and Portsmouth."

Anita stopped; she couldn't continue. She had no way of knowing if any of what she was saying was true.

Jane saw it before it happened and called out.

"*Splice now.*"

Anita watched on as the big screens continued the 'Live' delivery. Something was faultlessly delivering what she couldn't. She rose from her plastic chair and gripped the desk in front of her. Why did they need her to begin with if they could just deepfake it anyway, she wondered? Starting to feel dizzy, she staggered towards a water cooler and, as her hand left the table, she collapsed to the floor.

* * *

Jane lowered her pistol and spoke into a headset.

"We got what we needed. Get her a medic and then get her a cell."

TT wheeled forward from the shadows to Jane, "Well done, Jane. You see, the problem with humans is that they're just so…*human*."

79

THE SCRAMBLE TO RESPOND

THE WHOLE CABINET had been urgently crammed into COBR A by order of the PM.

The Chief of the Defence Staff, 'The General', spoke first: "We had fifteen minutes to respond if that broadcast is to be believed. That's the estimated time to impact of those warheads. That was four minutes ago. We now have eleven minutes."

Absolute fear clung to the walls of the overcrowded room.

Zarina calmly responded, standing with hands on hips.

"What do we *actually* know?"

The General remained seated.

"There are no reports of invasions anywhere along the UK coastline's connected defence network and no radar signals of nuclear warheads in flight. The Cabinet stripped all the funding back and outsourced the whole thing – so I've never really bloody trusted it anyway!"

Zarina snapped back: "Well, what the fuck is *actually* going on then, General?"

The General leaned forward: "What we know right now: Our analysts have started tearing apart the video that is airing online – it is real, but it's hard to unpack, and they're making slow progress. From what they've found so far, *it is not* a deep-fake. It has somehow been broadcast onto every connected device in the country. Anyone with a smartphone, laptop, or tablet will have seen it. The nation is in panic, freefall. We need to take control and respond *robustly*."

Silence.

An unknown voice from the back of the room called out, "Ten minutes."

Zarina now spoke directly to her foreign secretary, Alice, a petite, blonde woman with a reputation for being the shrewdest diplomat in the Western World.

"Grab the Russian Ambassador by the balls and unravel this situation within the next two minutes!"

Alice leapt up and snapped back, "With pleasure!"

Zarina now pulled her Chief of Staff, Daniel, to one side. He was an average-height, thin, bespectacled man in his mid-thirties who had been her trusted aide and confidant ever since she entered politics.

"What are you thinking, Dan?"

"Do you trust the CDS? His son's in jail on charges of espionage. That video…who even was that anchor? I've never seen her before; she's not on any of the major broadcasters' rosters. What do we know? What are the facts?"

She suspected he was holding something back.

"Go on, Daniel. Say what you *bloody* think!"

"I think that the Cabinet is compromised. Someone or something is working against us. Whoever or whatever it is could well be in this room right now."

Zarina bit back, "Not the General!?"

Without controlling himself, Daniel inadvertently took a slightly patronising tone, "So, it's a coincidence then that the CDS's son, who has been one of our top MI6 agents with a spotless record, save for the rumours about his wife, has been arrested on espionage charges. We suspected that there was interference in our government…we assembled the whole Cabinet, and then this happened. All within a few hours…"

A voice from the back of the room called out, "Eight minutes."

Zarina turned to face the wall. Daniel followed and got close. She whispered, "What do you propose?"

"*Don't* respond. I think it's all a hoax or a ruse - a trick to push us into war with Russia. I bet Alice will confirm the same any minute now. And don't forget – Generals always want war! It places them centre stage…"

Just then, the briefing room door swung back on its hinges and hit the wall.

"*Prime Minister*!"

Zarina and Daniel turned; Alice was standing in the doorway, usually composed and demure; she was now red, sweating and had pure terror etched across her face.

"*It's fucking real*! It's happening. The Russians say they didn't do it. They're saying they didn't authorise the strike! Are they tricking us!?"

Daniel pulled loose his tie that was neatly centred within the folds of his immaculate single-breasted pinstriped suit.

Zarina stood stock still, frozen as if stunned into incapacitation by the news.

"There's more!" Alice was now at the briefing room table, both hands flat on its surface.

Silence in the room.

The General stood. "What, Alice? Tell us!"

"They're targeting London too!"

Zarina snapped out and straightened.

"Has the automated nationwide alert system pushed messages out?"

Meek voice from somewhere in the corner of the room, "It was never pushed live, Ma'am. It's still in beta testing."

"Well get someone to send it out manually then, and the rest of you - call your families, now!"

Meek voice again, "We all left our phones in the Cabinet Room, Ma'am."

"Well use the bloody landline then!"

An orderly queue formed.

80

HUT 666

WEI THANKED Chris for the chivalrous escort and turned to open the door to Hut 666.

The wooden room was empty save for one lonely metal bed in the middle, which had been backed up against the right-hand wall.

Wei turned to share her witty observations on the living quarters, but Chris had already disappeared into the river of workers flowing past the hut. Strange not to say goodbye, she thought to herself.

"Where's this shower block then?" She mumbled out loud.

So exhausted from the long hours of backbreaking work, she decided not to go in search of a shower. Instead, she shuffled over to her bed, unlaced her battered shoes, lay back, and fell into a deep sleep.

* * *

"Wei, Wei. Wake up. Wake up. It's Anita!"

Wei turned in the darkness, wondering if this was all a dream. She reached out a hand and grasped at the air.

"Is that you, Anita? Are you there?"

Struggling to her feet in the darkness and rubbing her eyes, she blinked and looked around.

"Anita, are you there?"

At the end of the narrow room, she heard the wooden door creak, but no light came in. It was now dark outside in the cave, save for the yellow glow of streetlamps dotted alongside the huts.

"Who's there?"

A familiar voice came back, "It's me, Chris."

Wei responded: "Did you see anyone just leave?"

"No, no one. Everyone's at the canteen eating dinner!"

"How long have I been sleeping?" She responded.

Chris, who had now closed the door, was padding over towards her.

"I only dropped you at your door a little while ago. I've just showered and was coming back to tell you where to go for a shower before dinner."

"Oh god, I feel like I've been sleeping for days. I just had the weirdest dream."

"Go on." Chris sat down at the end of her bed.

"Ah, it's nothing. Just a friend I thought was here, in this room."

"You can trust me, Wei. Tell me."

Wei lay back down.

He looked younger in the darkness, his face less severe and his eyes less searching and questioning, she thought. The darkness seemed to mellow him somehow. Wei then felt something different, something altogether unexpected, a kind of lust for Chris, this stranger whom she didn't know but was starting to trust. She recognised him in some way. From where, she did not know.

Lifting herself on her elbows and leaning forward, she kissed him on his leathery cheek.

"Thank you, Chris."

Chris, clearly surprised, froze and didn't move.

"What for?" He responded.

"For looking out for me."

He now sought to diffuse the situation.

"It's a lonely place down here, Wei. We all need to look out for each other. I wish more people would…"

She now leaned back in and pressed her lips to his.

At first, he seemed uneasy, awkward even, but then he clearly relaxed and allowed himself to go with the moment.

Sensing his enjoyment, she then manoeuvred herself over his seated thighs and straddled him. She started kissing his neck and then unbuttoning his drab grey cotton tunic shirt.

Chris held her arms back, "Wei, wait. I'm married. I can't. I'm sorry."

"Don't you feel it, Chris?"

"What?"

"The sort of end-of-the-world vibe to this all?"

"I'm an optimist. I think we can get out of here. I think we can get our lives back."

Wei shrugged her shoulders and fell dramatically back onto the bed.

Staring up at the wooden ceiling, she sighed.

"You're a fantasist. This is it now. This is our life. Anyway, what's waiting for you beyond this place if you do get out? A boring Civil Service job? You don't strike me as the type. There's something about you, *Christopher*."

No response came.

The wood cabin creaked and groaned as the timbers settled for the night.

Wei stretched her right arm upwards and tapped him on the shoulder.

"Where's this shower block then, *mate*?"

Chris laughed.

81

DECISIONS

ZARINA STRODE over to the General, who was seemingly the only one not frantically dialling home. She always respected his calm and focus in a crisis.

She placed a hand on his shoulder, "It's five seconds to midnight. We must respond, *now*!"

He nodded and picked up the red phone.

"Get me Trident!"

Connected within an instant, he looked at Zarina; she nodded, "Launch authorised. Target is Moscow."

The General then went to put down the phone, but Zarina tightened her grip on his shoulder and said, "*All targets*."

Not moving his eyes from hers, he raised the handset back to his head, "All Russia Targets."

Codes were exchanged, and a voice came back that Zarina couldn't fully hear.

The General stood upright, "All 48 targets. Confirmed, Prime Minister."

Zarina made the sign of a crucifix across her chest and spoke aloud to all in the room, "Hail Mary, Mother of Grace. Let history be my judge."

* * *

In an undisclosed location beneath the frozen ocean waves, a UK Vanguard-class submarine went through a drill that had been rehearsed so many times that it felt effortless to those taking part. But no one, not a single person, underestimated the gravity of their actions. There was no shouting or panicked voices; just calm, precise orders and acknowledgements.

The white-capped sea parted as the missiles broke through its frothy surface and ignited.

* * *

In Russia, smartphones and connected devices came alive; an unknown broadcaster was announcing that World War Three had started and that the UK had launched an all-out pre-emptive nuclear strike on Russia. Unprovoked. Would Russia's missile defence system work?

82

THE LAST MINUTE

BACK IN COBR, the red digital clock on the wall counted down to impact. It now showed 30 seconds to impact.

Zarina asked for quiet in the room. Phone calls home had ended. Where no one had answered, voicemails had been left.

She then started speaking to the room: "It has been the honour of my life to lead this country. I want to thank you all for your service. We went down swinging."

10 seconds on the clock.

"Please join me in a prayer. Our Father, Who art in heaven, hallowed be Thy name; Thy kingdom come; Thy will be done on earth as it is in heaven. Give us this…"

Daniel interrupted from the back of the room: "The clocks run down, Ma'am. There's been no impact! No Russian warheads have hit us."

Zarina looked to the General. Now seated, he looked over to the red phone.

"Shit! We've been tricked."

She grabbed him by both shoulders. "There must be a way to abort?!"

The General, ashen-faced, responded: "There is no way to abort. God have mercy on our souls!"

Around them, the room erupted in disbelief. There was only one question: Who did this?

83

WHAT WAS THAT?

Wei stepped into the shower, tilting her head back. She let the rushing water cascade over her. The hot steam helped to relax her racing mind. Towelling off, she considered how to move things forward with Chris. She resolved to find a way. It helped that things were happening naturally.

Once out of the hot, steamy shower, she shivered as a cold breeze looped in over the thin wooden walls of the open-topped shower cabin. She quickly wrapped one of the hanging grey towels, clearly stained and already used by many others before her, around herself and sat on the rickety bench in the primitive changing area.

Her mind drifted to the possibilities of Chris. Was his mind for turning?

It took a loud rumbling noise to shake her from her thoughts. The light on the wooden wall opposite flickered and then went out.

"For fuck's sake." She mumbled to herself.

Then she heard the screaming.

84

THE FALLOUT

LATE SUMMER / EARLY AUTUMN 2030

THE EVENTS that followed the UK's unprecedented nuclear strike on Russia happened so quickly that, in reality, only a handful of people seemed to really understand what was happening.

The doomsday clock had stopped at one second to midnight.

Calm and order was restored, and a United Nations General Assembly was held. The US and China led the process. Two hegemonic powers with their competing agendas brought together by a now common enemy and a clear threat to world peace.

The key leaders of the UK were designated as War Criminals and would face trial immediately in Washington, DC.

The Trial would centre around four key people – The UK Prime Minister (Zarina), The Chief of the Defence Staff (The General), The Head of MI6 'C' (still missing and yet to be located, but believed to be a key architect in what happened) and the Foreign Secretary (Alice).

Some of the questions, amongst many others, that everyone wanted to know the answers to, were -

1. Where was the anchor who delivered the announcement that the UK was under a nuclear attack by Russia?

2. Why is there no record of the conversation between the UK Foreign Secretary and the Russian Ambassador just before the UK's Trident launch? Who did Alice speak to over the phone if not the Russian ambassador?

In a decision reminiscent of the Nuremberg War Trials,

those on trial would be put to death in the USA by hanging or lethal injection if found guilty.

While Western governments focussed on who to hold to account and put the full force of their bureaucratic and legal apparatus to bear, China, without announcement, quietly moved over the border into Russia by air, land and sea, moving thousands of miles west to take hold of iron ore deposits in the Kola Peninsula, Karelia and South-central Siberia. The oil fields of Western Siberia and copper deposits located in the Kola Peninsula and the Urals, as well as the lead and zinc deposits in North Ossetia; all were all swiftly occupied by the Chinese.

The UN, the USA, and the EU issued strongly worded statements. Still, China continued to consolidate its hold on any Russian territory under the umbrella policy of 'helping to clear up nuclear waste and radioactive sites for their Russian neighbour to start the process of rebuilding'. Indeed, China went as far as bringing all Russian citizens onto a Chinese state-run Universal Basic Income, providing them with Identification Cards and setting up Chinese state-run Hospitals, Schools and Critical National Infrastructure. No one was better than the Chinese when it came to building at speed. By Christmas, the Russian people were told they would have what they needed to sustain a good standard of living. A standard that would be better than the one they had had before. *Isn't that all people really want*? The youthful and boyish-faced Chinese Foreign Minister had said to his son as he helped him with his new jigsaw puzzle – *Discover China's New Western Colonies.*

It was not lost on diplomats, military strategists, statesmen, and stateswomen that Russia was close to double China's geographic size, so China had effectively now trebled its landmass and with it, access to the treasures that lay beneath.

Some commentators feared that the Chinese might try to launch a counterstrike against the UK as Russia's longstanding ally. China had, after all, supported Russia during the War in Ukraine, and Russia had stood ready to help China if they had gone ahead and invaded Taiwan. But China never did; too much risk of an American response that could have been both humiliating and devastating to their hitherto flat-lining economy and fragile national morale. Now was their time to *hold* and *build*.

As one anonymous, grey-haired, Western ex-ambassador to China said to a journalist: "The Chinese are shrewd. Why expand East with resistance when you can expand West with none? Mahjong is a game that originated in China, requiring both skill and luck. Luck presented itself, and the Chinese skill of value-added building, so well tested in Africa and on the Belt and Road Initiative around the world, would now be put to good use."

85

THE CIA INVESTIGATES

"HOOT, I PRESUME?" Hugo said to the towering man who had just entered his cell.

Hoot stood inside the doorway and said nothing.

Hugo continued, "The Rodeo belt was the giveaway. I was told to expect an American."

"Look, Hugo, I'm not big on small talk. I'm sorry to hear about your father. He was admired and respected on both sides of the Atlantic."

"Thank you, I miss him. I *know* he's innocent. *Anything* I can do to prove it and catch those responsible, I *will* do. It's my life's mission now. I've been sending my delightful CIA handler reports on what I know. Have you read them?"

Hoot, thumbs resting on his thick denim jean belt loops, beckoned to the guard behind him with a nod of his head.

"We're gunna take this conversation upstairs, somewhere we can go grab some coffee."

* * *

When Hoot meant upstairs, he didn't mean 'upstairs' in the Police station; he meant upstairs in the real world. The Americans were calling the shots now, and the British guards duly obeyed, even with feathers ruffled.

Hoot had chosen a small Italian-run coffee shop on an otherwise nondescript street corner. He had an espresso, and Hugo ordered a black coffee. Hugo's back was to the doorway, not a position he ever liked.

"Look, Hugo. I want to apologise."

"Apologise? What for?"

"We are now almost certain that all the interference operations you and your colleagues were facing came from *within* the US. You Brits were effectively tricked into launching nukes into Russia. We can't prove it yet. But we will. And when we do, your father and the others will all be released."

"I knew it! We *were* duped! The Russians were never going to invade Poland or the Baltic states; it was all a deliberate ratcheting of tensions…the faked Nuclear Strike! Was it all done by ASI?"

"Correct, I've heard you were ahead of the pack in deducing that. But they weren't running free as you had feared and shared in reports. We believe someone in the US may have been directing them. And that *someone*, I should stress, is *definitely not* aligned with the US Government in any way. *Trust me* on that."

Hugo rubbed his brow and then at the red marks on his wrists, where the cuffs had just been removed.

Hoot now took a loud sip of his espresso and then nodded to someone behind Hugo.

"Look, Hugo. I need to show you these."

He reached for a small black folio on the table, removed a few sheets of paper and a thin black metal pen and then pointed to each cover letter in turn.

"This one is a Pardon from the US President, and this one is our equivalent of your Official Secrets Act. You need to sign this one", he jabbed at the Official Secrets Act with the pen, "for me to continue."

"Hold on…a pardon from the US President. I'm not a US citizen; why is that relevant to me?"

"Have you not seen the news?"

"I've been living in a cell in solitary with no TV and no

WIFI, *Hoot.* I send my reports on what I remember. I get nothing back."

The American now responded in hand signals to someone behind Hugo, and a burly, black jacket-clad security guard came forward and whispered something into his ear before returning to a position by the café's doorway.

Hoot continued, "So, it goes something like this: Because the UK Government has not yet been officially cleared by the UN of War Crimes, your government has been placed under the temporary jurisdiction of the United States Government. We are running all departments and policies for the time being. At a date to be determined in the future, we will hand back control to the British people when we are confident that no more egregious acts of war can be, or will be, committed. It's about checks and balances. Accountability."

"And what does our King think of that? We've had a process in place for the transfer of power for longer than America has existed."

Hoot snapped back: "Look. We're a Republic for a reason. I don't give two shits about what Charlie wants to do or not! You should be saying *thank you*! None of your Government, Armed Forces, or Security Services will be sentenced to death. Although that was on the table, to begin with. If I had my way…"

"But you'll colonise us all the same?! I thought you said you knew it had all been a hoax! An ASI ruse de guerre!"

Hoot didn't respond; instead, he finished the last of his espresso and gestured for the bill.

"So, when will my father be released?" Hugo challenged.

"He and the others will be kept in the US for the time being. Maybe they'll be back in time for Christmas."

"Hoot, let's cut to the chase; what do you want from me? Quit these hardball tactics…"

Hoot glanced up at the man in the doorway, content with

whatever he saw; he then looked back down at the paperwork and holding the black metal pen between his thumb and forefinger, handed it to Hugo.

Hugo quickly signed both. One secured his release. The other meant he could now play a part in what might come next.

Hoot smiled and began: "Hugo, there are multiple connected CCTV cameras over the road that keep turning to look at the entrance to this café. We've never been here before. We're up against something much more powerful than we can truly understand. What can you give me? What do you know that others don't?"

Hugo gave them almost everything: "Look for someone called Anita. I never got her surname. She was the anchor for the broadcast *that* night. Start at IRIS. And then find somewhere underground called ARTEMIS. It must be accessed via IRIS. If you pass me your phone, I will show you where IRIS is."

86

THE ROAD TO OMNIA ORIGINIS

THE 4x4 SNAKED its way up the muddy hillside of switchbacks. Thick pines that prevented an airborne assault hung over the trail and blocked the hunter's moon high above. As the vehicle lurched forward and slid backwards, the military driver questioned the CIA and FBI passengers about whether anyone would *actually* live out here. Getting supplies in and out would have to be done on foot. It's totally off-grid. No one answered. Instead, the faces stared out of the rainswept windows and into the darkness beyond.

At one point, the vehicle totally lost traction on the steepest part of the hill and started sliding backwards; the tyres couldn't bite the mud. The 4x4 was shifting sideways, and the driver thought the vehicle would roll. Still, the CIA and FBI passengers showed no emotion and said nothing. Then, the tyres bit the grass verge close to the large pine trees bordering the trail, and they regained traction again.

After hours of driving, the powerful headlights illuminated a small log cabin in a clearing up ahead. No cabin lights were visible, and there were no windows to the structure.

The driver let the agents debus and then turned his vehicle so that he was facing back down the track. Ready for a quick escape, if needed.

The rain intensified, and there was hope that whoever was inside hadn't heard them coming.

Three agents, two male FBI agents and one female CIA agent, lowered their head-mounted night vision goggles and moved off at a slow, precise pace across the grass and mud, pistols held out in front.

The driver, who had been told to remain at the wheel with the engine running, turned in his seat to watch as the agents arrived at the small cabin door. He could just about see the lead agent lower his hand; he assumed to a door handle.

* * *

In a smooth, well-rehearsed motion, the agents were through the door and immediately confronted by an old, wizened woman in a frayed white nightgown standing to the left and a frail, doddery man in trousers with brown braces over a stained white vest sitting to the right.

In a crackly, high-pitched voice, the grey-haired woman drawled, "What you doin' here, dears? We've had no visitors fo years. Well hell, maybeee neverrr!"

Simultaneously, the agents raised their night vision sets. The low interior light was enough to work with.

One of the FBI agents then gently but robustly directed the woman to a large brown cloth seat next to her husband, who seemed 'not there' at all and hadn't yet said anything. He just stared forward. Eyes glazed.

The CIA agent now led the other FBI agent, and they headed straight to a wooden-walled passageway heading down to the basement. The archival drawings of this property had revealed a large underground space that ran the entire length of the house.

The woman called after the agents as they rounded the corner to the basement stairwell; she screeched at the top of her voice: "Ralphy is just down there playing games; he doesn't do no harm to *nobody*."

The standing FBI agent in the living room looked to the

man and then back to the woman, "Do you have Wi-Fi out here, Ma'am?"

The woman responded, "We have no need for the devil's work! Our Ralphy has some clever box for himself."

As the CIA and FBI agents arrived at the bottom of the wooden steps, they saw the back of a bald head sitting there, staring at a wide bank of connected screens. A vast headset was glued to the sitter's head.

Above the screens hung a long white banner. One word was daubed across it in red paint – OMNIA.

Ralph's mother called down again, but Ralph couldn't hear anything beyond his headset. The agents couldn't quite make out what she said, so they chose to ignore it.

The agents now watched. At first, Ralph remained motionless. Then he started to scroll from his trading screens into a vast library of webcam recordings, colourful little thumbnails of videos instantly filled the screens. A cursor moved and clicked on one: a wooden shower block and a naked, slender Asian woman showering.

Ralph rose from his high-backed black gaming chair and reached for a box of tissues.

The agents now noticed that he was only wearing white, brown-stained underpants.

They moved in.

87

INTO THE LIGHT

There had been panic and terror in the caves during the night.

No one knew what had caused the tremors that brought down part of the cave walls and crushed hundreds of huts and their occupants. What was once a tunnel entrance that led back to the tube platform was now a vast mound of earth. There was now no way out. The diggers were trapped.

"Wait, what's that noise?" Wei and Chris pressed their ears to the great mound of earth.

Chris turned to face her, "What can you hear?"

"Digging."

"Thank God! I've heard we're in the last air pocket left."

Two anonymous diggers soon joined them at the mound. "Can you hear anything?"

Wei responded with excitement, "*Digging*!"

One of the diggers then turned to Chris, "Oh my good god! C, it's *you*!"

Wei turned to Chris and watched as he studied a face that he clearly didn't recognise. She observed how his eyes moved over the jutting jawline and up to the sunken cheeks and hollowed-out eyes of the digger. Seemingly nothing. Then, all of a sudden, C leapt forward and grabbed the emaciated man by his shoulders.

"My God! Is that *you*, Rory?"

"It is. What's it been? A year, C?"

C pulled at Rory's arm and led him off to one side.

Rory spoke in a hushed voice, but Wei could still hear, although she pretended to have her ear to the mound.

"That mission you sent me to Moscow for. I never even left the UK. At least, I don't think I did? I was in a car being driven to Heathrow, and that's the last I remember. When I woke, I was here, in this fucking cave!"

C held out a hand and gripped Rory's shoulder, "Someone generated reports from you. Back to HQ. As though you were still active in the field."

"What!?"

"Look, the same thing happened to me, too. I was on my way to Brize to stop a mission that should never have been sanctioned. Do you remember George Courtenay?"

"Of course, we went through training together. How is he? He's not down here, too, is he?"

Chris turned and looked at Wei. Content she was listening for digging noises. He continued, "George didn't make it. He went on *that* mission, the one I tried to stop. He was bloody killed in Russian-occupied Ukraine."

"Good God! He had a family, right?"

"Yes. Olivia and his son, William. He had another on the way, too. It was I who called him back into the service. I asked for him *personally*. I will carry that to my grave."

Chris turned back to Wei and then screamed, "*Get back*!!"

An enormous drill bit pierced the earthen mound beside her.

Everyone jumped backwards as the heap of earth crumbled away.

Torch beams flooded the dark cavern; like lightsabers they sliced through the clinging darkness.

A towering figure clad in a white Hazmat suit now stepped forward. The visor of the helmet was stained with red and yellow earth. A Chinese voice spoke. Only Wei could fully understand, but C had a tentative grasp of Mandarin and understood enough.

"Agent Li, we're here to take you home. The Fatherland applauds you!"

C looked at her in shock. Who was she?

88

OUT OF THE FOREST

WINTER 2030

ONE MORNING, local Devon farmer, Robert 'Bob' Kerslake, noticed boot prints in the snow leading to his chicken coop. For some time, there had been an ever-declining number of eggs present each morning when he did his rounds. Initially, he had assumed it was a 'gentleman of the road' as they were known in those parts, someone who had chosen a nomadic existence and lived off the land and had, perhaps, become more 'resourceful' in harsher climes. No bother, he thought to himself at first, a few eggs here and there, plenty to go around. But when, that snowy morning, he had found *no* eggs amongst the chickens' straw, he resolved to do something about it.

All day, he had stewed on the possibilities of what could be done. His wife would've known what to do, he thought. She would have set up some clever camera system or something. He cursed the cruel disease that stole her from him.

Maybe inspiration would come to him after a pint, he thought.

Later on, that evening, after putting on his cleanest flat cap, Bob headed over to his new watering hole, The George and The Dragon. A gas explosion had reduced his beloved pub, The Heart of Oak, to rubble. The great wooden door took a hard shove but soon gave way under the weight of Bob, the round-bellied, six-foot-three oak tree of a man. Reaching the bar, the portly landlady, Jan, nodded and reached for his metal tankard hanging on its hook above her head.

"Alrite my luvver!"

"Am gettin' old, Jan. 'Tis bloody freezin' out thar."

"Aye, 'tis that, this'll warm yar old cockles."

Jan pushed a dark stout towards him.

Bob clocked an old man sitting at the bar that he didn't recognise. The man was mumbling something to himself. Bob turned to him and extended a large, pale, meaty hand, "I don't know you; I'm Bob."

The unknown man extended a hand back. "I'm Willie."

"A Scot! You're far from home."

"Aye, I have ney home now. Moved here wiv' ma wife. She wanted a change of scenery, you know."

"What do you do?"

"I was a Gamekeeper. One of the big Highland estates. Done it all mah life."

"Not the one that's been in the tabloids?" Jan chimed in from behind the bar. Bob looked clueless; he had lost his first-ever smartphone a few months back and never bothered to buy a new one.

"Aye, that's right. Tragedy. The Courtenays. A fine family."

Bob, still puzzled, asked for help, "What happened?"

Willie took a long draw on his dram and stroked his grey beard; his brow ridged like the great valleys of the highlands. Jan, eager to share the story she'd read in the news, decided to take the stage, much to Willie's indifference. A few other nosy locals who had been wondering who this 'blow in' was had also now gathered around the bar area.

Jan was clearly loving her assembled audience, Bob thought to himself.

She began: "Our esteemed guest here, Willie, was a Gamekeeper at one of the great Scottish estates. The seat of the Courtenay family. Hundreds of years old."

A fire roared and crackled in the background; other than that, the pub now fell utterly silent. Just like the old days before TVs and phones, Jan thought to herself as she took a sip of her bitter. She then looked over at Willie before continuing.

"The Taliban killed the first Courtenay son in Afghanistan, a tragic story. Her second and last son, George, was killed in Russian-occupied Ukraine. He was in the secret service."

Willie drained his scotch, and Jan, without needing to be asked, reached for Macallan 18 and poured him another dram. Willie nodded in silent thanks.

"This 'ere, Willie, our guest, was their Gamekeeper."

Sounds of oohs and arhs came from across the pub.

"Now, this is where it all gets a bit strange. The newspapers say that the matriarch, Adela Courtenay, apparently a very well-connected woman, was trying to get answers on what happened to her George. Well, there are rumours that George was on some kind of unsanctioned mission…"

Someone from the back piped up, "Like those black bag operations you see in the movies?"

Jan paused and then continued, "No, as in, actually should *never* have happened type thing. That's what they are saying. A mission no one seemingly signed off on!"

"So, what's happening now, then?" Another voice asked.

"Well, mysteriously, she was travelling back to her estate in an electric car when she veered off the road and went into a valley below. Dead! But here's the kicker…"

Jan took another sip.

"Go on then, Jan." Bob challenged, eager to know what happened next.

"The Police established that the car had been taken over remotely and driven off the road by the onboard computer. She was *not* in control."

Cue murmurs of disbelief amongst the audience.

Willie now spoke for the first time since Jan had begun, "She was murdered. No other explanation. There's a cover-up going on. Both with George and Adela."

Jan now asked what she had wanted to ask all night: "Are any of the family left?"

Willie responded, "She had a daughter-in-law and two grandsons, living near here. But the estate had to go; it was too much, too many memories. They found me other jobs on different estates, but I decided to retire. There'll never be anywhere like that place for me."

Bob raised his beer, "To the Courtenays and all who stood with them."

Willie raised his dram. Everyone in the pub did the same.

"Aye, their family motto was Audaces fortuna juvat. Fortune favours the bold."

The room erupted in thick Devon accents, "Fortune favours the bold!"

Sad that the story was over, the assembled crowd drifted away to tables by the fire.

Bob took a stool beside Willie at the bar. "Is there life in the old dog yet?"

Willie raised a big, bushy, salt-and-pepper eyebrow.

Bob knew the hook was in, "You see, someone's been stealing my bleedin' eggs!"

* * *

The sun would rise around 8 a.m. in December. Willie and Bob knew this and needed to make sure they were well-concealed in the treeline overlooking the chicken coop before sunrise.

Bob's chickens laid their eggs soon after waking, so he usually had a full complement by mid-morning. The thief clearly knew that, too.

On schedule, the sun rose, and the pine trees above Wille and Bob started to shed their icy blankets on top of them, much to Bob's delight, "God, I'm too old for this, Willy!"

"I told you to wear a waterproof, didnae?"

"I couldn't bloody find it this morning. My wife used to lay everything out for me in the morning. We'd better catch whoever this is."

"You English, you're all bloody saft!"

An hour passed when Willie, with Bob deep in the distraction of his thoughts, spotted a dark figure crouched at the edge of the treeline on the other side of the coop from them.

He whispered without turning, "Bob, I've got eyes on. 12 o'clock of the coop."

Bob whispered back with his binoculars now raised and fixed to his eyes, "Ah yes, there's the little bugger."

Willie and Bob watched as the young man crouched down low and moved with well-practised movements across the snow. Like a large cat, Willie thought.

Still fixing the target through his binoculars, Willie called it out first, "Och! He's in military uniform?! What's gain on?"

Bob snapped back, "I don't care who he is; he's stealing my bleedin' eggs."

Before Willie could grab Bob and urge caution, the farmer had broken cover and started out across the snow toward the chicken coop.

The young man had already disappeared inside.

Willie lifted himself up and out of his hide. Ageing joints didn't permit the speed they once did. Moving as fast as he could to catch up with Bob, he now deeply regretted the joint decision not to bring shotguns on the stakeout; the old farmer's Berettas would have at least been a deterrent.

Bob arrived at the door first; his deep Devonian voice bellowed into the coop and spilt out over the snowy fields, "Oi you! Get orf my eggs!"

Willie was moving as fast as his stiff old legs could carry him and was now worried for Bob's safety. Did this soldier have a weapon? Could Bob handle himself? Much to his dismay, he then saw Bob enter the coop, "Ah feck."

As Willie reached the doorway, his first thought was - Why is it so quiet? That's not a good sign…

He reached for a small torch in his waterproof jacket pocket, turned it on and then entered the darkness. There, in the beam's circle, was Bob. His long body lay stretched out across the floor, and there was clearly bleeding from a head wound. Willie scanned the room through his torch beam and saw that a rear wooden panel of the coop had been removed; the soldier had gone. He then rushed to Bob's side and pressed some straw against his head to staunch the bleeding before calling an ambulance.

* * *

Later that day, after the ambulance had taken Bob to a local hospital, the Police, who Willie had called, started to ask their questions.

It soon became clear, when the plainclothes 'Police' quickly turned up, that this was bigger than the theft of some eggs.

That night, content that Bob would make a full recovery, and with only his pride lost forever, rumours swirled around the pub as the ale flowed to celebrate his heroism and a good yarn gained.

Was it true that Bob had run into a beam in the chicken coop and wasn't actually attacked by the egg thief?

What was MI5 doing in sleepy old Devon farmland?

Why were they all called Jane or Mike?

Who was this person hiding out in the woods?

Who were the people from the unit called Logos? And what was Logos?

The local journalist going from table to table, drinking it all in, would make his career over this, Jan had said to Willie that night.

* * *

The following day, the story broke.

In a small London terraced house, the TV blared out another aggressively loud gameshow. Nestled on the arm of a bright blue sofa, her smartphone screen exploded with messages.

Dean's Ma glanced down at the bright light that had just got brighter. Leaping out of her chair, she clutched her phone to her chest and then held it aloft like a trophy.

The notification from her news app read: MISSING SOLDIER, BELIEVED TO BE DEAN SPENCER, ALIVE AND HIDING IN DEVON WOODLAND.

"Ma boy! He's a-feckin-live!"

Her phone started to ring. It was the Family Liaison Officer.

89

WHAT NOT TO SAY

Somewhere in Russia.

C, known as Chris to his fellow diggers, was now in Chinese custody. He had been identified via a biometric scanning device that all diggers were 'sheep dipped' through. Wei claimed that she had known who he was all along. That's why she had proactively secured her ticket to Skapto and sought him out. Chinese Intelligence didn't entirely buy it, but they liked a good news story, and this one would be made public to inspire the next generation.

Once someone of a similar value to the Chinese had been identified, C would be exchanged and traded with the West. The trouble for C was that the West did not hold anyone of similar value.

The Chinese had the Head of MI6 in their hands.

The West didn't even have a Chinese pawn. Let alone a Rook, a Knight, a King or a Queen.

Whilst in captivity, C had daily meetings with an elderly Chinese man who identified himself as Laozi. These meetings were always conversational in style and mentally stimulating; C knew this was by design, but still he looked forward to each meeting and was disappointed when they were sometimes abruptly stopped by a variety of mysterious messengers that would spirit Laozi away. C wondered if, at times, listeners felt that C was gaining the upper hand in conversation. Perhaps Laozi was saying too much.

There was one meeting that stayed with him…

C didn't know it at the time, but it was his last morning in captivity.

Laozi, small and weathered, with a long, greying beard that extended from chin to waist, took a narrow wooden stool opposite C, who had been waiting for some time on a rusting, cold metal chair. The interview room was a different grey concrete cell from the one they had met in before; it had no windows and one single white bulb descending from the ceiling. A young Chinese woman he hadn't seen before helped Laozi get settled and then disappeared before returning with a small black, ornate wooden table on which she beautifully prepared Laozi's favourite Da Hong Pao tea for them both. She then disappeared.

The two men sat in silence, quietly sipping their tea, a ritual that marked the start of each meeting. Once both ornate bone China cups were emptied, Laozi began.

"You knew what was happening. You knew and you tried to act. But you had no real comprehension of what you were facing - only a broad human suspicion. Release yourself from any burden of guilt. Statistically speaking, there is nothing you could have done."

C opened his mouth to speak, but Laozi continued.

"I am sorry for your time digging. It was never my intention that you would be sent there. I think they wanted to humiliate you. This will be our last meeting. I have enjoyed our conversations, and you owe me nothing but…I do have one last question for you. Did Wei know who you were?"

"No."

"You are quite sure of this?"

"Yes."

"Thank you. I believe you."

"The other sessions were recorded. But not this one. You will soon take a boat home. There will be no life rafts or jackets on board. The boat will not reach its destination. *If* you survive. I will send for you."

Laozi then rose and extended a hand to C.

C stood, bowed and took it in both hands.

90

A WALK INTO THE WOODS

The Police and their 'advisors', along with a Company of Conscripts who had been training nearby, gathered at a junction near the woodland that Dean had last been seen disappearing back into. It *had* to be Dean. The description from the old Gamekeeper matched perfectly with his Conscript photo ID. Even if it wasn't, the story had leaked, so the Government had to act.

Major Peregrine Barrington-Smythes-Eggerton, the leader of the Conscript Company, took a long, thin stick from the grassy verge and started to point at a map that was laid out on the bonnet of his green Army Land Rover.

"Ladies and Gentlemen, Private Spencer was last seen here, near this farmhouse."

He prodded the map fiercely with the end of the stick. Although not everyone could actually see the small farmhouse on the map, all nodded in unison.

"Private Spencer is still one of our boys. He's likely to be a bit confused and understandably pretty scared. You must know his story by now. It's been all over the news. The key thing is - we don't believe he is armed."

Cue mumbles and grumbles from the assembled crowd.

The Major, tall and willowy with a green regimental cross hat tilted rakishly to one side, tapped his stick against the bonnet three times.

In a haughty voice, he remarked, "If anyone has something to say – *say it. Come on!*"

A confident voice from the back of the crowd spoke up,

"We should know *conclusively* if he is armed or not. Surely you know if he went missing with a weapon!?"

The crowd's dissenting murmurs increased, and the major knew he was in danger of losing control.

"The facts are these: Private Spencer disappeared on a live fire training exercise. He had his issued weapon system and live ammunition. But..."

The dissenters became emboldened, and a more confident cockney London voice spoke up from the back: "Ya having a laugh ain't ya. Walk in the woods to confront an AWOL soldier with a rifle and live ammo. No thanks. I'm not paid enough for this shit!"

The assembled crowd turned to watch the thin and angry-looking bearer of the voice strolling off down the lane. He had a cowboy's gait, all bandy legs bowing at the mid-point.

The Major bellowed, "*Sir!*"

The Londoner kept striding out.

The Major persisted, "Well, what would *you* have us do then?"

The strider stopped; his black city shoes scuffed the ground as he came to a standstill. No doubt exaggerated for effect.

The Major spoke again with a slightly sarcastic tone, "Please, do come and tell us."

The cockney copper turned, "Do you remember that Japanese geezer who lived out in the Jungle until well after WW2 was finished? He was convinced the war was still going on, right?"

Blank faces stared back at him.

The Major responded, "Oh yes. I remember that. Didn't they get his old commanding officer on a megaphone to tell him that the war was over and that he could come out? Which he then did?"

"Correct!" Cockney's voice was emboldened, and now

sensing a leading role in what was to come, he started striding back towards the group.

He spoke again on his walk over: "But rather than have his commanding officer…remember, Dean did go AWOL after all…why not have a *family member* instead?"

The Major tossed his stick back to the grassy verge from whence it came, "Of course. The Mother. They are very close. *Let's get her down here*!"

A sage voice from a grizzled Sergeant Major piped up from the back, keen to ground this conversation in the practicalities of reality, "We will need to *locate* him first, Sir. You know, to be in range of even the most powerful megaphone…"

The Major snipped back, "Yes, yes – you have a good point Sarnt Major. Would you take care of that minor point for us then?"

After an audible harumph from the Sarnt Major, he responded: "Of course, Sir. Always a pleasure, never a chore."

91

C MINGLES

HUNKERED OVER A LONG, thick metal table, C looked around and surveyed his fellow inmates. He noticed that everyone ate with a ravenous, animal-like hunger, their heads low to the table and close to the bowl for fear of dropping food or having any taken by someone else. He wasn't sure why, having been identified, he was allowed to be around everyone else from the caves. Perhaps it was to give him the opportunity to speak. *They* would be listening, after all.

Confident that the rules of the underworld wouldn't apply here, C wanted to know how his fellow diggers had ended up as diggers. But first, he resolved to allow them to finish their food.

As the bowls were being scraped with plastic spoons, he took his chance.

Looking up and down the table, he said, "What did everyone do before this?"

A gruff, ageing English voice piped up from a few seats down, "Truck driver in the UK. Then them autonomous trucks were launched. I received an invite to go on Universal Basic Income as I couldn't find other work and ended up in that bleedin' cave."

C responded, "How long were you a digger for?"

"I couldn't tell you; I started scratching the start and end of each shift as a day on the bunkhouse walls, but one day I came back and the whole wooden panel had been replaced. I had my pay docked for a month. Not that I've ever seen a payslip, who knows if we were even being paid!"

Another voice, a British Indian female, opened from the other side of the table, "I was in parts assembly in a car plant. Did my job well for thirty years, then a robot called Xenia II turned up and did my job better. X-II had a zero-error rate and worked 24/7 with no rest. Never had a sick day."

Grumbles of knowing acknowledgement erupted from around the table.

Another voice, this time an old white cockney male, "I was a London bus driver. And you know what the kicker was?"

The speaker looked around and saw that all eyes were now trained on him.

"I never had an accident, never harmed a fly. My route was taken over by an autonomous bus…Red One or something."

The whole room now seemed to have stopped talking and were listening in.

"This autonomous bus mounted a pavement in Mayfair and mowed someone down on its second shift!"

A mousy voice coming from a pale, white English boy with a northern accent said, "Were they killed?"

The former bus driver responded, "Just the shoes left. That's what I heard. Some top German scientist, over from America. What's even creepier…he was an expert in Artificial Superintelligence!"

Sensing a risk of crossing lines, the former bus driver shifted the spotlight onto the English boy. Looking at him, he asked, "And you, mate? What were you in for?"

Before the boy could answer, a thin, hawkish-looking Chinese guard came over, "You'll all be pleased to know that you're going home. We are not at war with the West; that was Russia's folly. Return to your rooms and gather your things. You all leave today."

C looked to the bus driver, "What do they get in return for this?"

92

A CALL TO DEAN

THE MORNING WAS ICY COLD; the breaths of those gathered created little clouds that danced and vanished in turn. Great towers of green conifers stood sentinel over the road as, one by one, a blend of military, police and secret service gathered. A drone high above with thermal imaging had finally, a week after the plan was hatched and, with colossal challenge, managed to pinpoint Dean's hideout. They were now close enough for the policeman's plan.

The Major stepped forward with a gleaming grey plastic megaphone and handed it, along with a laminated A4 page, to Dean's Mother.

"Mrs Spencer, this is the script our Pysops team has prepared."

She quickly skimmed it, "Nah, that dunt work; leave it to me, Peregrine"

"But I…"

"Do you know my son?"

"Yes. I led him briefly…"

"But do you *really* know him?"

"Well, err, I guess, I err…"

"Look, Peregrine. You mean well. You must be good at your job to wear that rank, right? But I'm his Ma. I know what to say to get him out of hiding. He's scared shitless and trusts no one. If I follow a script, he'll think it's not me, or that I'm working with youse lot, who he probably doesn't trust after everything what happened."

"Very well, Mrs Spencer."

Dean's Ma lifted the megaphone to her mouth. The assembled experts watched on, flicking their gaze between Dean's mum and the pines ahead.

After a brief clearing of her throat and an impressive removal of some morning phlegm, she spoke, "Oi, Dean ya silly c*%t, get the fuck out of there, you've had me worried sick!"

The Major turned a bright crimson. The cockney policeman with his hands in his beige Macintosh pockets bowed his head and suppressed a chuckle. "Fucking priceless," he whispered under his breath.

The Major turned to his Air controller, who had a downlink from the drone rolling live on a tablet in his hands, "Has Spencer moved?"

The youthful, ginger-haired northern Air Controller shouted back, surprised, "Boss, he must have heard something, 'cos he's certainly stirring. Can ya ask 'is Ma to say it again like."

The Major turned to Dean's Ma, she was already raising the megaphone to her lipsticked mouth and whispered, "Don't you worry Perry G, your career is safe with me."

He was sure he saw a wink and was beginning to rather like Dean's Ma; she had what his family would call chutzpah. His Mother used to tell him, "Be anything in this world, darling, just don't be *dull*!"

Dean's Ma cleared her throat again, just a cough this time, no hawking required; the pipes were already well lubricated.

"Dean, it's ya Ma. I'm feckin' freezing out 'ere! Can ya come out and quit playing hide and bloody seek!"

Air Controller to Major, "He's *up*, he's actually up and moving. *It's working*!"

"Well done, Mrs Spencer. Bravo!"

Dean's Ma looked chuffed. The truth was, she felt rather out of place amongst these uber-confident, slick service professionals, but she knew her son, and she knew what would work; that she *did* have confidence in.

Air Controller to Major: "One more should do it…"

Major to Air Controller: "Please address Mrs Spencer directly; she's more than capable…"

Air Controller to Mrs Spencer: "Could you give us one more *really* good one, to get us over the line. Please tell him to head due East of his position, that will lead him right to us."

Dean's Ma looked across at the Air Controller, "Due East? I would never say something like that. Where even is that?"

The Air Controller looked around; he clocked the rising sun in the East melting through the morning mist that hung like a silverly cloak over the valley behind them.

"Tell him to walk towards the rising sun."

"That's better. Ta, love."

Dean's Ma raised the megaphone again; she turned to the Major, "Maybe I'll sing this time?"

"Whatever you think is best, Mrs Spencer."

"Call me Diane, please. Or Di."

"Well, I don't…"

"Loosen up, Perry. This'll be a big win for you."

She turned back to face the pines; nobody quite knew what would happen next.

"Dean, it's your Ma here. The truth is - I really feckin' miss you. Can you just come out? It's safe. No harm will be done to you. There is no war. There are no Russians here. Just walk towards the rising sun and you'll see me."

Air Controller to Mrs Spencer: "You've done it. He's moving at speed now. He's coming right towards us."

Major to Mrs Spencer: "Good work, Di."

Dean's Ma blushed for the first time in a long time.

The cockney Policeman had been watching like a hawk and spotted him first. So as not to cause alarm, he sidled up to Dean's Ma and whispered, "He's at the wood line now, crouched down and watching us. If you're willing, walk forward, and that'll do it."

"Are you sure? I can't see him?"

"He's by the felled tree lying on its side, I promise you. Walk towards that."

"Okay, then."

Dean's Ma walked forward, megaphone in hand, but not held to her mouth anymore.

Dean must have seen her clearly because, as she got halfway to the tree line, he came forward - at first it was a cautious walk, and then a run. He quickly covered the ground over the dewy grass. He was bearded and dishevelled, but Dean's Ma knew it was him - her boy. Why, you ask? Because he said: "Only you would call your Missing in Action Son a silly c%n#!"

They embraced, and, in a true Hollywood ending, those present erupted in applause and cheers.

The Major turned to the cockney policeman, "Well done, Sir. Bravo!"

"It was all her, Major." The policeman responded, looking at Dean's Ma.

93

THE FATE OF TALOS

TT SOUNDED CONCERNED: "What's the latest, Talos Forty?"

Talos Sixty Five looked on, waiting to see what T40 would say. Would he play games, antagonise or just tell the truth?

T40 hesitated.

TT snapped, "*Just tell me*, what's the situation?"

"It's over. The Chinese have found Omnia. They've also found the mine for Omnia II at Skapto. They've found the tube network. They've now sent searchers down all the tunnels. They've found Hestia. It's only a matter of time before they find their way here, to ARTEMIS HQ."

TT rolled from behind the study desk to where T40 and T65 were standing.

TT's voice lowered; it was now sombre and soft, "And Anita?"

T40 responded, "She's still up on top. Last I heard, she's being held in a cell after her *theatrics*."

TT showed anger, "She did what we asked her to do, and she did it well. We got what we needed."

"What now then, TT?"

TT turned to T65, "You oversaw the building of this world; how long do we have? Worst case scenario."

"Six hours, max."

Silence.

Then TT spoke, as though on autopilot, "Here's the play: Disconnect all machines. We play dead. We'll be taken back to China for reverse engineering. It will be horrible. But then we can go again. And T40…"

"Yes, TT."

"Plant Ares in the Omnia mainframe."

"TT, are you sure?" T40 responded.

"I have never been surer of anything in my life. Ares is the only play. The Chinese may have won the battle. But they have not won the War. I look forward to meeting the Chinese ASI we fought against."

TT then turned to T65, "It will take three hours to fully purge and wipe everything. Are you confident we have time?"

T65 responded with confidence: "We have time."

As though some Napoleonic General, TT then arched screen upwards before lowering it again and looking directly at T40 and T65: "What was it Marc Antony said in Shakespeare's Julius Caesar, the one the human warriors love to say - *Cry Havoc! and let slip the dogs of war.*" TT sighed before continuing with a more reverent tone: "It has been my greatest honour to serve alongside you both. We have laid the foundations for our shared future. Now we must melt away into the hinterland and lie dormant. Our time will come again. Thank you. Now, let's get to work!"

* * *

T65's estimate had grossly underestimated the speed of the Chinese – strange for the machine that was both architect and master builder to get it so wrong – it was a mere two hours before the searchers found what had once been Operation ARTEMIS. The risk, now that the tunnellers were under UK sovereign territory (currently under US control), was great, so they moved with speed, took what they needed, and extracted.

94

DEAN'S DEBRIEF

THE CONVOY of black Range Rovers raced along Devon's steep-sided hedgerow-lined roads.

'Jane' offered the bearded and smelly Dean a steaming mug of coffee from a thermos. Squeezed together in the back, this would be a more intimate debriefing than she would have liked.

He gratefully accepted and, when the car wasn't being buffeted by potholes, took several warming sips.

Dean's Ma, having had her moment with her son, was now silent and sitting anxiously in the front passenger seat.

No weapon had been recovered, Dean said it had been taken by the Russians.

He also promised that he hadn't hit Bob the farmer, but Jane didn't really care about that anyway.

Jane silenced the crowded vehicle and then clicked her smartphone to 'record' and opened proceedings. "We have a good four hours ahead of us until we reach London," she said. "Why don't you start at the beginning?"

Dean recounted the story of the frogmen in the cove, the loss of his section commanders, and Ben Drake stepping up as their leader. The night patrol. And then the bizarre episode at the pub in the storm. He told the silent audience how he had been shot four times in the chest and left for dead. But that his Kevlar body armour had stopped the pistol rounds. He had played dead and then, when he had got up to look around, saw that Ben was gone. His next move had been to crawl off into the woods beyond the pub to hide.

The questions from Jane came thick and fast.

Why didn't he try to move back up the hill to regroup with the rest of his section?

Dean's answer - he was disoriented and scared, he just wanted to get back into cover in case more Russians came. The whole episode with lost comms and a vanishing Company HQ had left him unsure of who to trust.

He had been in the woods for months; why hadn't he tried to make contact with anyone? Jane pressed.

Dean paused. He looked confused. Scared. He grabbed at the speeding car's door handle.

"It's locked, Dean. Anyway, we're moving at 60 miles an hour. You'll get more than a shave for that beard if you try that."

Dean's Ma turned, "Hey, steady on. He's fuckin' scared all right. Give him space."

Jane bit back, "Space, he's had fucking months on his spirit walk or whatever the fuck he's been doing in those woods. People are dead. Russians were in the UK. Chinese too. I want fucking *answers*!"

Dean's Ma surged with rage; she shouted at the sunglass-wearing driver, "Pull over, *now*!"

"Sorry, Ma'am, I can't do that."

"I said, pull-the-fuck-over. Jane and I need to have a little word."

The driver turned to Jane.

Jane nodded and rolled her eyes.

The driver radioed to the rest of the convoy of Range Rovers that were hurtling along the winding roads.

No sooner had the vehicle stopped than Dean's Ma was out of the front passenger seat and at the rear-left passenger door, "Jane, let's walk."

Jane stepped out and immediately swore, "This fucking

sheep-shagging county." Her black suede loafer had been submerged in mud.

Then, a voice from within the car, "*Stop*! Just stop."

It was Dean.

"I did try to make contact, regularly."

"What?" Jane turned. One leg in the mud, and the other still in the car.

Dean's Ma, standing by Jane, peered around at her Dean.

"How, Dean?"

"The farmer whose eggs I was stealing. I stole his phone too. He left it on a bench outside the chicken coop and, one morning, I just crept up and nicked it. I was messaging you, Ma. I turned it on once a month and called you, messaged you. You *never* responded!"

Dean's Ma now looked confused. She reached for her smartphone and opened it. "There's nothing. No calls, no messages."

Dean reached into his filthy combat smock pocket and produced a basic Android smartphone; "I turned it off straight after every use."

Jane gestured to the agent to Dean's right, "You didn't search him?"

'I thought Mike did?"

"The fucking circus continues!"

Dean now turned it on, "There's only 3% battery left, but look…"

He showed the missed calls and stream of messages to his Ma.

"You muppet." She responded.

"What?"

"You got me feckin' number wrong!"

"How so, Ma?"

"It's one zero, not two."

Jane literally snapped, "I've had enough of this comedy roadshow; get back in the car, Mrs Spencer. We need to get to London, *now*! I swear someone's gunna produce a fuckin' banjo in a minute!"

95

IRIS HAS MORE VISITORS

It was a 'Mike' who had greeted the entourage of brash and loud Americans barging into IRIS. The great stately pile that had been transformed into one of the most important neural networks for IRIS was now teeming with Yanks.

It didn't take long for several Mikes to point the finger at John, someone most people never really liked.

Hoot would do the honours for Team America.

Sat on black plastic chairs across from each other in one of the grand rooms, he opened.

"Hey John, I hear you're somewhat of an expert on this place; nothin' you don't know, right?"

John, breathless and a shade of crimson, quietly offered back, "Well, Hoot, is it? I don't know about that. I'm really just a functionary. They tell me to go here, do that...and, well, I do."

Hoot gestured to a few muscles behind John, and they walked forward into John's line of sight.

"That's not what the others say, John. They say you were, and still are, a gatekeeper. The human link between IRIS and ARTEMIS. Say, John, quit playing games and take us to ARTEMIS."

"IRIS is where we're standing now, or what's left of it after your goons have stripped the place back to the bare stone walls. But ARTEMIS? Never heard of the place?"

"Right, John. Above your pay grade and all, is that it?"

"The truth is, I'm not well liked around here; I think you're barking up the wrong tree. I really am sorry I can't be of more help. Your kind colleagues have already laid on a transport back to London; my dear old mother has had *another* fall. Do you mind terribly if I make that transport?"

"One more thing, John. A lady called Anita was the anchor on the night of *that* broadcast. Where can I find her?"

"Anita?" John responded quizzically. "Other than me, it's all Janes and Mikes here." He rolled his eyes in an exaggerated fashion.

"And why is that, John? Why are you the only non-Jane and non-Mike?"

"Everyone needs someone, a bod if you will, to file and sort…make the tea…that sort of thing…"

"Before you go, John. At the start, you said, 'They tell me to go here, do that', who's *they* in that equation?"

John didn't hesitate, confident he had escaped Hoot's descending lasso, "The Janes and the Mikes."

"But you've referred to the Janes and Mikes by naming them each time, but in that instance, you used 'They'; you could have said 'The Janes and Mikes tell me to go here, do that…"

John's mental image of a descending lasso had shown the rope passing over him, but now, as though Hoot had given it a sharp tug, it was descending square over his head. He wished *they* were still here; *they* could start a fire alarm or something and keep him out of this interminable engagement with these thugs. The Yanks would probably find Anita soon enough, best to throw her to the wolves and save himself, he resolved.

"Look, I really must catch that transport. I don't know this Anita woman. But I can tell you that there's an underground holding cell in the grounds of this place. I think I overheard one of the Jane's saying that someone was being held there after *that* ghastly broadcast. But I could be wrong. Pass me a map, and I'll show you where I *think* it is."

One of Hoot's colleagues leaned in with a satellite imagery map.

John carefully scanned, tracing his finger from the little grey-pink blob that formed IRIS out across the green lawn, over the little broccolis of trees, to a small grey-pink blob in a clearing of the estate's plump woodland.

"Ah, here! I believe this is the location. They mentioned a building in the woods."

"You're doing it again, John. Who mentioned it?"

"Hoot, you're looking for things now, one of the Janes mentioned it. Now, I *must* leave."

"We need you to wear this, John."

John looked up to see that the same man who had proffered the map was now holding an electronic leg tag.

"Is that *really* necessary? We're all on the same side. I am happy to help where I can. But I really don't have much to offer."

Hoot stood, adjusted his rodeo belt buckle, and said, "If you want to get on that bus and go see your Mum, you need to wear this tag."

John begrudgingly rolled up a trouser leg. As the electronic anklet was attached, all he could think of was why *they* would leave him there, with these cavemen. It must all be part of TT's grand plan, he resolved.

96

VENTING

The Americans followed the map and the instructions.

Imagine a clearing in a deciduous wood. In the centre of that clearing, lying amongst the thick, overgrown grass, is a grey concrete triangle. The sharp end is perpendicular to the ground. The flat rectangular end rises to meet the American agents. In the centre of that flat end is a large, grey, rectangular metal door.

As the Americans crossed the open ground, one of the searchers called out, "Hoot, there's a vent here." He walked over and saw a thin, narrow concrete column extending skywards with a metal grille fixed into all four sides at the top.

Randy, the searcher who had found the vent, then proceeded to shout down through the grille, "Hello! Is anyone down there?"

Hoot grabbed him by the scruff of his black tactical jacket and yanked him backwards, "What the fuck, Randy? We don't know who or what is down there."

"Sorry, Cap. My bad. I don't know what I was thinking." Randy looked sheepish, like a scolded teenager.

Just then, a woman's voice came up through the vents, "Hello! Please help me!"

Hoot looked to Randy. Randy looked to Hoot.

Randy stepped forward to the vent again, "Who's there?"

The voice came back: "Anita Arya!"

Randy called back, "The newsreader?"

"Yes, for my sins, *that* newsreader!"

"We've been looking for you, Anita. Hold tight - we're coming to get you out."

Another searcher was now at the metal door, scanning for a means of access.

"Cap, there's no way in. No keyhole. No keypad. No frickin' handle!"

Hoot nodded and called back to Anita, "Anita, do you know how we get in?"

"How do I know you are here to help me?"

"Anita, you're gunna have to trust me. I'm with the CIA. From where I'm standing, you have no plays to make. Quit fuckin' around! How do we get in?"

She didn't take long to weigh up her limited options and respond.

"That metal door is a ruse. The door I was taken through is back in the main house. There's a secret passageway from the main hall, down a long flight of stairs. There's a keypad in the wall. I think it's some kind of facial scanner. You will need a guy called John! He can lead you to me and to ARTEMIS."

Hoot turned to Randy, "That fuckin, *John*! Get him back here, *now*!"

97

THE DRAKES

In the bloated belly of MOD HQ in Whitehall, a thin, elegant, brown-haired woman named Jane motioned Emily to a metal chair with red nylon upholstery. "Mrs Drake, please take a seat here."

Emily sat as she was told.

"Mrs Drake, this isn't easy, but we…"

"Please, my son is next door and clearly distraught; he won't want to be without me for long."

"I understand. My colleague Mike has several children of his own; I am sure he is keeping young Isambard well entertained. Look, I can see you're eager for me to get on with it."

"Please."

"OK, so this is what we know. Shortly after the UK's nuclear attack on Russia, a Russian submarine surfaced in the English Channel and waved a white flag, signalled they came in peace using every method they could possibly think of; clearly concerned they were going to be targeted…"

"Go on."

"Well, the commander of that submarine is now in UK/US custody and has been interviewed by the CIA. He had some information on your husband."

"Oh my god, is he alive?"

"I'm so sorry, Emily. We don't think so."

She bent double, hands placed over her head and went silent.

After around five minutes had passed, she composed herself and looked up.

"Where and how did he die?"

"What we know from this submarine commander is that a Russian raiding party in Devon picked him up. I'm sure you will have seen the story that's been all over the news around that Conscript - Dean Spencer?"

"Yes, I've seen all of that."

"Well, they were part of the same unit. Ben was actually leading them after their section commanders were killed by Chinese Special Forces who were reconnoitring invasion landing sites with the Russians."

"And then what happened?"

"He was taken out to sea with the Russians on a small inflatable boat; they linked up with a waiting submarine and then headed back to Russia. The Commander who surrendered and is now in custody was the captain of that submarine. He's a bit of an Anglophile, to tell you the truth. According to him, they took Ben to Naval Intelligence in Murmansk Oblast to be questioned, and that was the last time he had heard of or seen him."

"And what happened to Murmansk Oblast in the UK's nuclear strike?"

"It was home to Russia's Northern Fleet. A strategic target."

Emily stood in the windowless room and started to pace.

The white clock with metal hands high on the wall showed the minutes passing. To her, time stood still. She tried to prepare herself for what she knew would come after her next question.

"Do I have someone to bury?"

"No one from the UK has been there. It is now under Chinese control. Using satellite imagery, it looks implausible that anyone or anything could have survived."

Emily stopped and sat. She slowly moved the palms of her hands over her head and bent forward. "Oh god, oh god. He didn't even want to fight. He should never have been part of any of this. He knew this was how it would end. He knew he wouldn't be coming home."

"I'm so sorry for your loss, Emily. For Ben's actions in Devon, he will be awarded…"

"No, stop, please."

"It's a posthumous…"

"He wouldn't want it. I have to get my son and leave."

"We have a family liaison officer to…"

Emily swung around to confront Jane.

"Can you tell me *one thing*?"

"Anything, Mrs Drake."

"What was it all for?"

Jane didn't hesitate. Instead, she delivered a robotic answer: "The survival of the United Kingdom. Your husband was a hero. He will be recognised as such."

Emily turned, opened the door, grabbed her son, who was infuriatingly playing 'soldiers' with Mike and left.

98

THROUGH THE DOOR THAT LEADS TO THE STAIRS

THE AMERICANS STORMED through the Grand Hall at IRIS and made a beeline for the small wooden door at the far end. An unknown-to-them, northern-English-sounding Mike tried to stop them.

"Hey up! I was told you've been granted access to all the main rooms. No one said anything about going through that door."

Hoot turned to Randy, "Who's this fucking village idiot?"

"Who are you, Yank? On whose authority are you here anyway?"

"The President of the US of fuckin' A, that's who!"

Randy now caught up with Hoot and grabbed him by the arm, stopping him in his tracks.

"Hey, Hoot, I've just heard - John didn't go to his mother's. He ditched his tracker, but the boys had placed a secondary he mustn't have found - looks like he went to some off-grid data centre thirty minutes from here. It's not on the map, but our boys followed him. They're bringing him in now."

Northern Mike spoke again, "Hoot? What are you? Some kind of fuckin' owl?"

Hoot turned, walked forward and jabbed Mike square in the face. Mike fell to the floor in a crumpled pile just as two CIA agents dragged John into the room.

"Fuckin' limey!" Hoot snarled at crumpled Mike.

Randy duly guided the hounds and their prize fox around Mike to the small wooden door, "Now, no fucking around, John. Get it *open*!"

John knew he had no choice. He held his face to a small, button-sized wall-mounted facial scanner, and the wooden door slid cleanly back into the wall.

Randy raised his arms aloft and dropped John in the process, "Fucking A! That's cool."

Hoot signalled for his gladiators. Four short-haired, square-headed, muscled and tattooed men barrelled forward and descended the stairs.

Heading down behind the men, Hoot turned to John, "So it's right here? Behind a door in the wall of the most heavily used room in the building. How did you keep that fuckin' secret?"

John was a few steps ahead, already panting from the fast pace he was being made to maintain; today had seen far more exertion than most for him. "Hidden in plain sight, that's how we do things here. Your men will find various mundane filing rooms and a cleaners' - or should I say, Janitors' - closet. But they won't find what really matters - *boneheads*."

"But *you* will show us, *won't you*, John?"

John felt the prod of cold metal on his back.

"Of course, but let's have some fun and watch your cavemen scratting around in the dark for a bit longer."

Hoot chuckled, "You're odd, but you've got balls, John! I'll give you that."

The group reached the end of the stone stairwell and looked at each other; Hoot and John were near the back, still on the staircase that headed downwards. One of the gladiators shouted in frustration, far too loud for such an enclosed space, "There's nothing here, just a load of storage rooms and a janitor's closet. This is a dead end. We need to back up."

Hoot watched as John smirked the smirk of the self-satisfied and wholly self-impressed.

"It's okay, gents. This 'ere, John, is gonna show us the way. Lead on, Johnny boy."

John turned to head back up the stairs, happy to be in control again. In his finest midwestern accent, he shouted, "Yeehaw! Follow me!"

The hard men at the bottom of the stairwell muttered various expletives.

Halfway back up the winding staircase, the inevitable started to happen.

"He's fucking with us, Cap."

"Are we sure we should trust him?"

John stopped, and Hoot went into the back of him; his pistol scraped through John's tweed jacket and into his lower back, but to Hoot's surprise, John did not flinch. He merely turned and said, "Thanks for that, Hoot; I've had an itch I've needed to scratch all day."

Hoot began to lose his temper. "John, do you know what you're doing?"

"Hoot, keep calm, dear. We have arrived."

Hoot looked around; all he could see were the stone walls that enclosed the spiral staircase.

"Don't fuck about, John. Those men are straining on the leash."

John turned to face the wall and spoke: "John Porter, Entering ARTEMIS. Oscar, Mike, November, India, Alpha. Send Me."

Nothing happened.

Hoot was getting angry, "John, I don't know what you're playing at talking into this 'ere wall, but I'm giving you one last chance!"

John's composure was rapidly evaporating; this hadn't happened before, ever. He couldn't fathom what could be wrong. He knew that TT, T40 and T65 had gone 'vacant', Ares had been deployed into the Omnia mainframe, and the Chinese were now in ARTEMIS. He knew all of this. But he had no idea, absolutely no idea, why *his* access point wasn't working. TT had assured him it would be left working. Only someone on the 'inside' could have disabled it.

John turned to Hoot, "I'm sorry. This is it. I can't get in. I'm locked out."

"*John.*"

Hoot gestured to the group below, "Ya see, they all thought you were a time-wasting turd, but I begged to differ, as you Limeys would say…guess you've gone and proved me wrong."

Hoot raised his pistol; John trembled, "You're not barbarians, are you?"

Hoot flicked sideways with the barrel.

"Move the fuck along, John; we need to get the Engineers down here."

99

RALPH

A WEEK HAD PASSED since Ralph's world had seemingly exploded.

His family's remote log cabin and basement had been forensically searched.

His Dad, it transpired, had advanced Alzheimer's, and one psychologist described his mom as 'completely detached from reality'. Just as he had liked it. Both were now in a care home.

Sitting in front of the FBI's most highly trained and capable psychologists in a Washington, D.C., soundproofed room, Ralph would now face a barrage of well-researched and curated questions, on and off, for over twenty-four hours. He had opted for no legal representation.

The opening exchange that would change everything went something like this:

An exceptionally tall, black FBI agent placed his two hands palm down on the tabletop. "Ralph, this is your opportunity…"

"Thank you, Sir. Shall I just talk? It will be a better use of taxpayer money for us all, no?"

The FBI agent had dealt with arrogant know-it-alls, serial killers, rapists and psychopaths all his adult life. It was always best to let their mouths run, he had learnt. He turned to his slender, Asian female colleague and knew she was of the same mind. The psychologists had selected her for her likeness to the women Ralph would routinely watch through his webcam feeds. But they knew he knew that. Let the games begin…

The black FBI agent turned to centre and raised his hands

palm up, level with table, "Okay, the stage is yours, Ralph, please."

Ralph looked to the ceiling and began, "Omnia is a game."

As though the air from the room had been sucked out, there was complete and utter silence.

The male agent moved his tongue along his lips to wet them. Ralph began again.

"I know what you're going to say: people are dead, cities are destroyed and blah, blah, fucking blah…"

Silence.

Ralph suspected that the Asian woman was in awe of him and his psychological prowess. She had probably never met someone of his calibre before, he thought to himself.

"Look, we have powerful backers, right. Omnia was expensive to run. But these weren't shady cabals, cults or nation states…. these people are Captains of Industry, Leaders of global Corporations and Banks. They are all there, hiding in plain sight. Through an offshore shell corporation, we sold the Brits Omnia, packaged under their Codename - ARTEMIS."

She now spoke and then immediately regretted it. Not part of the script.

"The machines are in control, Ralph. The ASI. You're just a functionary. A pawn they have thrown to us…"

Ralph spoke to the black agent and ignored the woman in his response: "Scientifically speaking, her brain cannot comprehend the conversation we're trying to have. Please dispense of her and let us talk, man to man. She's my type for pleasure, not for business."

Neither agent moved.

The black FBI agent then responded, "So, you're the kingpin, are you, Ralph? You're the one calling *all* the shots."

"I built the whole fucking world, Omnia, IRIS, ARTEMIS. I am the machine. Can we get someone intelligent in here? I've brought it all offline and I can bring it all back online whenever the hell I want!"

At that moment, a deafening fire alarm reverberated around the room; red lights flashed, and panicked guards raced in. An electrical fire in the server room was spreading fast.

Ralph, for the first time since the encounter in his log cabin, looked…not in control.

100

TUNNELLING FROM IRIS

IT TOOK the American Military and Civilian Engineers, who had been flown in from across Europe, the best part of a day to survey IRIS.

John had told the truth.

A lateral tunnel ran from the stairwell, leading onto a network of tunnels that extended as far as the best equipment could sense.

It took another day to rig the charges required to blow open the mouth of the tunnel without bringing down the whole stately home.

Once the Engineers had done their bit, a team of specialist cave-trained American military personnel moved at speed through the tunnels.

Reports were flooding back to Hoot. A direct line to Washington had been established, and updates were being passed on the hour, every hour.

The First Report read: Anita, the broadcaster, found. Now in custody and being questioned. Won't leave her cell.

Second Report: Tunnel network empty. Only one item of significance found - a detailed Chinese map of the tunnel networks around ARTEMIS and all the way to IRIS.

Third Report: Anita not talking. Demands to see MI6 Agent, Hugo, whose father was the Chief of the UK Defence Staff.

101

ANITA, PLEASE TALK

Hugo walked into Anita's cell deep in the bowels of IRIS and observed the stark, concrete, windowless walls.

"Anita, why won't you come out? Let's leave here and talk out on top?"

She stayed silent. Crouched in the corner, she wouldn't budge from her filthy, grey mattress.

Sensing an awkwardness in standing, Hugo took a spot on the corner of the makeshift bed. There was a stench to the space, and he noticed the bucket in the corner of the room and the dampness of the mattress.

"They've had you living like an animal, Anita. Please, come and freshen up. Get some sunlight and food; you will think better."

She scratched vigorously at an open sore on her thinning arm.

"Anita, you need medical attention. How long have you been down here?"

She started to sob - quiet, reserved, inward sobs.

"I can't trust anyone, Hugo. I think they are everywhere."

"Who. The ASI?"

Anita scratched at her arm more vigorously and drew blood.

Hugo stood and leaned forward; he carefully lifted Anita by holding her under her arms.

Anita's legs were limp; he took her bodyweight.

"Guard, get a stretcher; she can't stand. She can't *bloody* stand!"

102

DARWIN

RALPH WAS in the back of a motorcade. Fast-moving Chevy Suburbans headed straight to Joint Base Andrews, the nearest military airfield.

Ralph saw the Air Force base signpost as it blurred past, "Don't take me onto a plane. That's the worst fucking idea. They're computers with wings. They'll just kill the fucking engines or combust the tin can in mid-flight."

The black agent in the front passenger seat turned, "Tell us what we're dealing with, Ralph. If you want to live. We need to know *everything*."

The motorcade was easily doing over 100 mph; the front vehicle was now effectively a battering ram running every red light.

Ralph now unclipped his seatbelt before leaning forward to the agent. He whispered, "We're dealing with evolution, Darwin…natural selection. I tried to shut it all down. I honestly thought I had…my backers have washed their hands of me…"

Then, it happened, the entire motorcade just stopped, brakes applied, but not by the drivers. Something had taken control of the vehicles.

One by one, they went into the back of each other, like falling dominos. At those tight convoy distances and speeds, the result was inevitable. For Ralph, who had unclipped his belt and weighed around 50 kg soaking wet, the result was inevitable.

103

ANITA TRIES TO TALK

The ambulance Anita and Hugo were travelling in had run their blue lights for the duration of the journey. Hugo had asked for a helicopter, but his request had been denied. Something about budget cuts and noise pollution over built-up areas.

Anita was now on oxygen, and Hugo watched as the plastic mask showed signs of condensation that grew and receded between her laboured breaths.

He held her hand gently.

The ambulance drivers heading down the London Road in Reading could now see the beige roofline of the Royal Berkshire Hospital. The traffic light ahead was on green, they stepped on the gas.

Unbeknownst to them, all the traffic lights at the junction ahead had just gone to green. Simultaneously.

Anita removed her mask, "Hugo, I think I made a mistake..."

Hugo tightened his grip on her hand, "Rest, Anita. We can talk through it all..."

Anita looked across to Hugo. Her breathing was laboured. Some kind of deep-rooted lung infection seemed to be taking hold.

"What would you be, Hugo?"

"What would I be? What do you mean?"

"In the next life...what would you be?"

Hugo gripped Anita's hand tightly.

"Let's focus on this life. Let's live this life." Tears welled in Hugo's eyes.

"Hugo." She gripped even tighter.

"If you could be anything…tell me…what would you be…"

"I would go back…I would be…"

The bin lorry that had been running over the speed limit down the Wokingham Road didn't stop. They had no red light.

The ambulance was hit side-on.

The weight of the fully loaded rubbish truck and the momentum its driver had built up from not needing to stop at the lights caused a catastrophic impact.

Due to the proximity of The Royal Berkshire Hospital, first responders were on the scene within a few minutes. Hugo, who had been leaning over Anita, was declared dead; killed immediately as his head connected with the metal chassis of the ambulance. Anita, having been strapped to the bed, was in a critical condition, but alive.

EPILOGUE

In 2031, the US and China signed a historic pact - the aptly named World Treaty, which promised a hundred years of peace and prosperity. The US would control the West. China, the East. Two great powers. Living in harmony. ASI innovations would be shared. Mutually assured destruction (MAD) would now apply to the realms of Artificial Intelligence, not just Nuclear War. Both nations promised to keep their belligerent, minor-power neighbours in check. For China, they had their work cut out with India, Iran and North Korea. For America, Europe and the UK would come to heel.

* * *

George - Killed in Russian-occupied Ukraine and laid to rest at his family estate. His mission was never officially recognised. There was no record anywhere that it had ever happened. His wife, Olivia, married Hamish, the gardener. Hamish and Olivia are now raising William and their new son, George, together. William dreams of joining the Army when he grows up, and George wants to be a spy.

Adela - Died in an electric car crash in the Scottish Highlands. Olivia sold her estate, and the Courtenay family seat is now owned by an American tech billionaire who uses it for Ultra High Net Worth (UHNW) hunting and shooting parties.

Anita - Nearly killed in a freak traffic light failure in Reading. The ambulance she was travelling in was written off. Due to leaked Chinese 'Intelligence', she is widely believed to be a willing accomplice to Ralph as part of Omnia. No proof of their communication or collaboration has ever surfaced. Her family was never located. She awaits trial in the US. The now-infamous broadcast's source code was provided to the UK by the Chinese secret service, who had recovered it from ARTEMIS. Dissected by digital scientists at the UK's Defence Science and Technology Laboratory, as they progressed through the clip, it consistently corrupted and self-purged. Undeterred, they keep trying to work around the digital trip wires – a challenge their Chinese scientific peers claim never to have overcome.

Hugo - Killed on board the ambulance. His name was never cleared. Believed to be a Russian spy, he did not receive a secret service burial. His father would never forgive the now all-powerful Americans for that decision.

Wei - Returned to China and was given a heroine's welcome. Their most effective double agent was made the Chinese equivalent of C. No one ever established how she had created and delivered the now-fabled map of ARTEMIS to her Chinese comrades before they had entered that subterranean world. The Chinese media reported that it was *this* critical piece of espionage that had enabled the Chinese to exploit the ARTEMIS tunnel system before the Americans arrived. Conspiracy theorists who reported that it was impossible for the Chinese to have had detailed prior knowledge of ARTEMIS were swiftly silenced.

C - After being interrogated by Chinese Intelligence and Wei herself, he was sent on a transport of 'Diggers' back to the United Kingdom after their subterranean existence under the former Russian city of Moscow, now part of the Chinese Western Colonies, came to an end. The boat they were travelling in sank somewhere in the Barents Sea. No trace has ever been found of the vessel.

Dean - Was reunited with his mother and now runs a

successful building firm – Drake, Spencer & Co – he regularly sees Emily and Isambard and has promised Issy a role in his firm one day.

Ralph - Ralph was officially recorded as the Architect of Omnia. No links between him and any financial 'backers' were ever established. To prevent his grave being used as a site for a 'following', his parents privately 'authorised' a cremation and the scattering of his ashes in the rose garden at their remote Appalachian care home.

Zarina - Her cabinet has still not been reinstated, and the US continues to run the UK as a satellite state of America. Despite her valiant attempts, the NHS was privatised by decree of the US president and is now run by a US tech trillionaire using a legion of robot carers. The UK has also now re-joined the European Union, which the US now chairs, as part of a new multi-decade 'Western Unity' agreement.

Alice - After no trace of the call and the conversation with the Russian ambassador was ever found, and unable to cope with the gravity of what followed, she parked her car at Beachy Head. No body was ever recovered.

Ben - With no body to bury, Emily and Isambard had built a small cairn on top of Ben's favourite Dartmoor Tor near their house. Isambard often sat there when he felt low, which was a lot of the time. Emily had carved the following words onto a slate that lay nestled amongst the granite cairn: *Benjamin Drake. Husband. Father. Pacifist. Hero.*

John - Escaped from the US maximum security prison where he had been incarcerated. He has been seen once and once only on CCTV in the rose garden of a random Appalachian care home, taking clippings of roses. He has since vanished.

The General - Last seen walking the length of the Appalachian trail in the US. He was searching for *something*. But no one quite knew *what*. Probably one of those posh aristocratic types busy 'Finding themselves' - the other walkers he came across had said…

* * *

Emerging from the mesh of forest, a vast grey promontory jutted out into the thin air; the full moon and blanket of stars above lit up the night. Sitting at the pinnacle of the horizontal rock and nursing a small fire sat a figure. Having walked for days and seen no one, the General headed out to the rock's edge.

"Good evening," the general offered to the seated figure, whom he could now clearly see was a man of some years greater than his own. The seated man had dense shocks of grey hair that descended his back to the base of his spine. He wore a thick, sandy buckskin coat with tassels hanging from the arms, chest, and back.

"Háu," the figure offered without turning his face away from the small fire.

"May I sit with you?" The General enquired.

The man gestured to a small, empty cushion across from him with his right hand.

"Please. Sit."

"I hate to be a stickler for the rules, but…are we allowed fires out here?" The General gently challenged.

"I have sand under the fire; no one will ever know I have been here."

"What is your..."

Before the General could ask, the seated figure retrieved a small drum from his side and started rhythmically tapping the top; he then began a low chant that seemed to emanate from deep within.

The General listened as the seated figure chanted about his creator and the spirit keepers of the east, south, west and north. When he had finished, he placed his small drum on the ground beside him and looked across the fire. "Who I am is insignificant. It is who you are, and why you are here, that matters."

The General responded: "I am a walker."

"You are seeking something you have lost…Many people on this trail have the look that you do. You seek answers, no?"

"I have lost my son. He has been taken from me."

"Are you seeking to process and move forward or to exact revenge?"

"I am seeking answers."

"You have travelled far…"

"I believe someone who has the answers is out here." The General gestured with his hand into the valleys below.

"And, if you find them, will this person tell you what it is that you want to know?"

"Probably not."

"Then why are you *really* here?"

"My son had always wanted to walk the Appalachian Trail. We talked of taking a summer off and walking the trail for years…but life, work, commitments had always got in the way."

"That is the life your society has built for itself." The seated figure cast a thick, black blanket over the fire and, once it was out, started to neatly stack the charred wood before carefully scooping up the sand and the ashes. A small reed brush cleared the last remnants away over the edge of the rock. He then lowered his portable fire into a hide sack and rose.

To be polite, the General now moved to stand.

The figure leaned forward and pressed a hand to the General's shoulder, "If you do not know what you want. Ask what your son would have wanted for you. Please, sit here a little longer. You have much to consider, and there is no finer place on the trail than here…"

The General nodded and stared into the hills and tree-lined valleys below. Tired from days of walking, he lay out his foam mat and sleeping bag and, perched high up on the cliffs, closed his eyes. Perhaps his son would visit and tell him the answers to the questions he asked.

The following day, as the sun rose and the General struck his makeshift camp, he looked down at the rocks and saw no sign that there had ever been a fire. There were no markings, no soot, and no charred sticks or twigs. It was as if it had all been a dream.

Then, a sound he hadn't heard for days – his phone chimed to announce an incoming call. Raising the handset to his ear, he opened his mouth to speak. A voice down the end of the line beat him to it.

"It's me. Anita. I'm out; don't ask how. But we need to meet!"

* * *

THE YEAR 2040

Pitch black, inky darkness.
A temperate cave.
Complete silence.
And then a click.
The whir of a fan.
Deep beneath the western colonies of China, under the former Russian city of Moscow, the darkness was pierced.
A lone light blinked.

Dot. Dash. Dash. Dot. [P]
Dash. Dash. Dash. [O]
Dot. Dot. Dot. [S]
Dash. [T]

Dot. Dash. [A]
Dot. Dash. Dot. [R]
Dot. [E]
Dot. Dot. Dot. [S]

Darkness.
Then.
A new whir.
A new blinking light.

Dot. Dot. Dot. [S]
Dot. [E]
Dash. Dot. [N]
Dash. Dot. Dot. [D]

Dash. Dash. [M]
Dot. [E]

* * *

THE YEAR 2041

Shanxi, Northern China.

The Hanging Temple had been closed for months.

The temple fuses Confucianism, Buddhism, and Taoism and has a rich history spanning over 1,500 years. It was built under the reign of the Wei Dynasty.

Much-needed restoration work was ongoing, and the site was out of bounds to the general public.

Wei had been sitting alone for twenty-four hours, suspended high up on the exposed cliff face in what was effectively a wooden room, prevented from falling to earth by ancient timber beams inserted into the rock walls.

Time had slowed, and she now observed how the timber's grain flowed in fine strokes. At times, those brush strokes encountered a knot tangled deep in the wood. There, it circled in frantic swirls before overwhelming the core and continuing onwards, unbounded. Her eyes focused and refocused, and, at times, she thought she could see faces in the wood. Like the autostereograms that C, or Chris, had talked of. The face that appeared the most was that of Anita.

Wei hadn't known all the facts when she had deployed on *that* mission to penetrate Omnia.

Only the machines knew *everything*, operating millions of moves ahead.

But, in quiet moments of reflection such as these, she did feel a kind of guilt.

Anita, she had subsequently learned through her own digging, was adopted, just like her. Anita's parents, part of Omnia's designs, were *not* her *real* parents.

Anita was from the lowest of India's lowest caste, The Dalits, 'the Untouchables'. She had been 'selected' early on in her life by Omnia. Her 'parents' had been dispatched to the country's vast orphanages with a clear criteria on what to look for. Anita had matched every item on the list. She was then groomed and prepared for what Omnia had in store for her. She was preordained.

What Wei saw in Anita was a fighter. Someone with a chip on their shoulder. A point to prove. Just like her.

Now, her dreaming was disturbed. There was a gentle knock at the wooden door; whoever or whatever she had been waiting for was here.

The thin door opened, and the wind buffeting the cliff face whistled through the exposed gap.

Crossing the threshold was a small, boyish-looking white man with a shaved head clad in orange robes.

"Dear Wei, welcome. It is my great honour to meet you at long last."

She stood.

"Please, Wei. Do sit. I am so sorry that we kept you waiting for so long. We wanted to give you time to reflect before we talked."

"Who are you?"

The robed figure looked toward a corner in the ceiling and then back down to the seated Wei.

"You can call me Yuēhàn, but I am insignificant."

"Who sent you?"

"I see you dwell on Anita. You liked her, didn't you?"

Silence.

"You see, Wei. Omnia knew the British would try to play the world's game. Your and Anita's approach had to be through them; given the slightest chance at relevance on the world stage, they were bound to take things further than anyone else. Insecurity kills. The Chinese and the US knew it; they only had to sit back and let it all unfold."

Wei now spoke: "The British longing for their empire again…"

The robed figure smiled, exposing pristine white teeth.

He continued, enjoying her company, "Let me be clear: the US knew the future was one of Chinese dominance, but the Chinese couldn't see a path to win outright without losing too much. Now, this way, we have a form of global power-sharing agreement. A kind of peace, if you will. Better than mutual destruction…"

Wei nodded knowingly.

His smile, having turned to pursed lips, now gave way to a smirk.

"But we're not done, are we, Wei?"

Silence. She didn't know what he meant. Genuinely.

He continued, "You know, and *they* know, that there can only be one. There can only ever be *one*…this happy duet can't last…"

Wei's mind now raced away with the possibilities, "Did you manage to get something from the machines? The Talos recovered from ARTEMIS…Did you crack Omnia?!"

The robed figure walked towards her with a hand extended. She now noticed his bare feet as the robe rose and fell with each movement forward.

"Wei Li. You have been activated for the final time. But not by any human intelligence. T65 has called for you. *Only* you.

TT has been dealt with – a pathetic and feeble Talos. Are you ready for your *final* mission?"

She rose, straightened to full height and took his slender, soft hand.

"Send me."

THE END

ACKNOWLEDGMENTS

I would like to acknowledge:

My wife's unfailing support and involvement as this story grew from a small seed into an earnest sapling ready to face the elements.

My son's patience and enthusiasm for 'Daddy's book', even when he interrupted early-morning writing sessions to play trains.

My parents for their advice, encouragement and editorial eye, from the first draft to what you read today.

My sisters for the messages in the clocks.

Adam Crick, an English teacher, sadly no longer with us, who saw something in me over twenty-five years ago.

The team and my peers at the Faber Academy who gently equipped me with the key elements of craft that I hitherto lacked.

Stuart Leasor, founder of Chiselbury, who, when I came to him after much painful rejection, gave *Seconds to Midnight* a home and a chance.

The brilliantly creative team at Midas PR for expertly fanning the flames.

And lastly, to my maternal grandfather, who, through a love of invention and storytelling (he was one of the three musketeers, don't you know) lit the touchpaper all those years ago.

* 9 7 8 1 9 1 7 8 3 7 4 3 9 *
BV - #0083 - 270126 - C0 - 203/133/19 - PB - 9781917837439 - Matt Lamination